A Net of Dawn and Bones

C. Chancy

To the Clearview Library,
Happy reading!

Christel R. Chancy

Digital art by Mirella Santana
Photography by Cathleen Tarawhiti
Model - Georgia Stanwix
http://mirellasantana.deviantart.com/
http://cathleentarawhiti.deviantart.com/

Manufactured in the United States of America
ISBN-13: 978-1514759837
ISBN-10: 1514759837
Library of Congress Control Number: 2015910664
CreateSpace Independent Publishing Platform, North Charleston, SC

Chapter One

Darkness, illumined only by the seeping red glow of magma cracks below, the shimmer of ice falling over black cliffs to rumble and hiss into the spreading lava plain. The creak of rock and ice to steam and the wailing souls caught between them wove a net of agony that covered the world, shrouding one small cove of silence.

"...In nomine Patris, et Filii-"

"I cannot *believe* you still pray, after all these years."

"...Et Spiritūs Sancti, amen." The spirit in the form of a young woman glanced up, certain of what she would see. And therefore worried. Her friend knew well that time meant little to spirits. Much less to the Lord of Heaven. *For a thousand years in His sight are as yesterday when it is past*, she'd murmured to him, as she tended ethereal wounds. *Like a watch in the night.* "Good evening, Aidan. How fare you?"

The fiery spirit flickered on the dark river's shore; now a whirling globe of flame, now the ghost of a tall, red-headed man with amber eyes. "You don't even know if it's night or day!"

"Possibly not," Myrrh admitted. *Very worried, if he chooses to think of the mortal realm.* Aidan was a practical spirit, when all was said and done. Why dwell on Earthly sunrise when it was the murks and piercing lights of Hell that brought enemies seeking him? "Still, Hell is a place created, as all places are created; and as such a place, it has tides and rhythms of its own. Perhaps it mocks the world above. Perhaps not." She nodded toward him, half-cloaked in deeper shadows. "But from the way you flicker, I would say it is night."

One finger raised in the start of yet another taunt, the ghostly fire froze. "...Oh, I give up."

Myrrh drew a breath, and picked up a pitcher of odd steel, dipping it into the sharded ice near shore to fill with cracked white translucence. "Despair-"

"-Is a sin, heard it before; *clue*, lady! Look around you!"

Yes, I look, my friend. And I listen. Something had to be badly wrong. Though it couldn't be an immediate danger. Aidan was *fire*. He wouldn't snap and snarl, he'd *act*.

If he's that worried, he's not taking care of himself. Again.

Myrrh drew her pitcher out of the ice, and walked back to the sheltering alcove she'd found among the rocks. The shadows were fathomless here, swallowing all but the faintest glints of ice-white, but at least eddies of wind dampened the endless moans. "For I listened, as the whirlwind passed over me; but God was not in the whirlwind," she murmured to the ice. "The Lord was in the silence."

Ice shuddered, as if shifting from under a great weight, and softened into water.

Myrrh held still and breathed, gauging the pitcher's position as much by weight and touch as by sight. Now the alcove was utterly dark, save for glints of firelight and whatever stray glow might wisp from strands of white hair. Earthbound caves were dark, but that mortal darkness was as a downy coverlet, compared to the leaden weight of Hell lightless.

But she didn't need to see water. The slosh of it, the cool of the pitcher where it rested inside, the shift and whisper of air as liquid moved - all told her as much as mortal vision could. More; mortal sight would only see black water. It took an enchantress' Sight to see that liquid was *only* water, lacking the haunts and taints of Hell.

Moving deliberately as a tea ceremony, Myrrh poured two cups. "Would you have water, Aidan?"

"*Fire* spirit?"

"So you say." Myrrh shrugged, and waited. "What have you seen in your wanderings now, that leads you to seek me?"

Flames flickered into long limbs, dressed in black and gray like a patched motley of trenchcoat and hooded sweatshirt. Hidden under both, she knew, was a white cord cradling an obsidian pendant, match to the red and bronze concealed under her shadow-shift; the reason he *could* find her, with all the wilds of Hell to search. "You're never getting out of here. You know that, right? No one does."

"So you've said." Myrrh withdrew her hand as he fumbled with the rounded handle; Aidan never wished to admit it was difficult to take a fleshly form. "But as I've told you, Aidan, the Gates are shattered and thrown down. They have been cast down a very long time."

"Eh. So *you* say." He sipped, haunted amber eyes searching the darkness. "Why doesn't anything ever catch you?"

"You know things try," Myrrh nodded. "If not for me, then for those whose hopes I carry." Her hand touched the phial at her breast, silver cord twined with red; the pale glow of sleeping souls hidden by the shadows that clothed her. "Do you need shelter, Aidan?"

Amber eyes almost disappeared as he drained his cup. Even the glow of fiery hair dimmed, like embers under ash. "...Fire spirit *in Hell*."

"I believe I did notice that, yes." Myrrh tried not to chuckle too loudly. After two decades, it was almost a joke between them; like an alley-cat, her friend walked on his own. If he happened to curl up where someone else was, while various loud and dangerous things roared by, it was just a coincidence. "Even fire may need shelter from a flood. Do you need help?" Patience. Patience was the key.

That, and not yielding to the impulse to upend the entire pitcher over his head. Splashing Aidan *never* ended well.

"Damn it!" He flung up long hands, white fire flickering at his fingertips. "I've been pestering you for *twenty years*. Why the hell won't you think I'm a demon?"

"Questions like that, for one," Myrrh murmured. "Or perhaps, the simple fact that you've shared my cups for the past two decades."

"Right," Aidan grumbled. "Because only an *idiot* turns down clean water in the middle of the Wailing Plains."

Myrrh inclined her head. "One would think, yes. Oddly enough, that which harms evil is often a boon to those of good intent. If a hostile demon had drunk that water...." For a moment she let an edge creep into her smile, sharp as a wolf's. "Well. He might find it a very unfriendly drink, indeed."

Aidan froze. Amber eyes flicked toward her. Toward the cup. Toward the river.

"As kin of mine once said," Myrrh smiled, "I am not a *tame* lion." She breathed out, and spread an open hand. "Aidan, if I'd ever thought I would do you harm I would never have offered it. Fire, demon, spirit - you are a wounded soul. Not an evil one." She shrugged. "It's wiser not to be thought a human spirit in these realms. I know that more than anyone."

"Yeah, because you say you've been here a *lot-*"

"I have." Myrrh settled back against stone. Part of what seemed basalt oozed, but hot tar found no purchase on shadows. "Is that what you find hardest to believe? That there might be a way to realms brighter than this?"

"*Nobody* gets out of here alive."

"No one here is, strictly speaking, alive. In the mortal sense," Myrrh stated carefully. "So that loophole is quite open, for those with eyes to see. What troubles you?"

"Hey, I've been down here a while too, y'know. Nothing bothers me." Amber eyes bored into quiet gray. *"Nothing."*

"As you say." Myrrh inclined her head. Patience. Though oh, it was hard to sit, and wait, and listen. Something had hurt her friend, and Aidan was very hard to injure. He might not have the strength of a demon lord, but he was quick, and wily, and had the nerves of a phalanx veteran. There were few things in Hell he could not dodge or flee.

Yet he found one. Or... did one find him?

"But a little while ago, there was something...." Red flame flickered from where teeth bit his lip. "Maybe I'd better just show you."

"Hmm." Myrrh shaded her gaze with one hand, clinging to a sheer face of basalt with the other as she peered at the distant pillar of aching whiteness. From the winged specks circling near the base, it was as wide as a ziggurat of Babylon. Yet its walls had no steps, only razor-sharp straightness that pierced endlessly upward. "Well, that's not good."

"Oh, you think?" More crackles than words, from the globe of flame bobbing near her shoulder. "Freaky bright impossible *thing....*"

"Hmm." Myrrh tightened her fingers on tiny cracks in stone, making certain her grip was secure. It wouldn't do to be careless. Not with such as that loose in Hell.

And how had that foul creation grown so strong, without her notice? She could have sworn she'd wandered this part of the Wailing Plains less than a year ago. There should have been a sign. There should have been at least a foundation, and walls half-built of fear and agony. The sorcerous craft necessary to build such an edifice was neither easy nor swift. The chants alone should have taken years on Earth; few sorcerers dared stay out of human sight long enough to complete more than one a moon.

Either this was crafted in less than a year - which seems impossible! - or it was hidden from my sight.

Which also seemed impossible. If any creatures had laid a glamour strong and subtle enough to hide such awful power, why did she sense no trace of that spell now?

Then again, I am not alone. And spells meant to bar such as I from discovering this horror, may have been crafted with quite a different intent for a... wandering fire spirit. "Were you drawn to it?"

"Hell, yeah. Tell me something that isn't pulled in by that! I saw those weird spike-winged guys go whizzing by, and soul-wisps, and something that kind of wriggled, and - one light source in the middle of for-freaking-*ever* dark, dark with screams, dark with ice, and more dark-"

"But instead of venturing near it, you came to find me," Myrrh observed. Slid a glance toward bobbing fire, one pale brow raised.

"Hey, who said I had any sense?" The fire's flickers slowed, heart-fast instead of hummingbird-flutters, as the globe ducked behind her shoulder. "You're the only thing around here that's not heading for that - that *twist* in the world. I want to know why."

"I imagine you do," Myrrh mused. "As much as you wanted to know why you felt drawn to it, and yet in fear for your very existence if you followed that call?"

"...You've got no right to be that freaky." A crackling snort. "Fire spirit. What, a little light, me worry?"

"It isn't light." Myrrh clung tight to basalt. The dark stone might be hell-stuff, but at least it was honest in its will to shake climbers from it, to fall in screams and terror. Answer that honesty with her own stubborn will, and she had nothing to fear from it. Unlike that hellish creation glowing ahead of them. "That energy only appears to be light. And that is the greatest lie of all." She lowered her head and looked away; time to get somewhere a bit less exposed. "Think of it as supernatural flypaper-"

"Say *what?*"

"A spiderweb might be more accurate," she admitted. "It pulls in souls to power it, and so draws demons to glut themselves on human fear." And which fate Aidan might suffer - she doubted either of them wanted to find out. "Don't go any closer. You fought off the pull once; and that must have taken all the will you could muster. You're a strong soul-"

"Hey! Not a-"

"-It's a Demongate."

"Um." If flame could gulp, Aidan did. "That what it sounds like?"

"Yes. And no. A moment." Reach out. Find the next handhold, and the next, feeling her way across shadowed stone.

"Easier if you just dropped, you know?"

"I am a human spirit," Myrrh said between movements, feeling slick stone catch and slide across skin and clothing shadows. "I can't fly."

"Key word there being *spirit*," the fire said testily, hovering along as she climbed. "C'mon, you know there's no limits-"

"There are limits because I choose to cling to them," Myrrh stated. One more hold. And one more. "Limits can be armor stronger than any breastplate, Aidan. And burn as fierce as any fire. I am human." She almost chuckled, grim as the situation was. "I've told you. I have done this before."

"Uh-huh. Sure. Right." The fire flickered into near-human form once more as she reached a long crack that was almost a downward-sloping ledge; he clung to the shadow between them and the shining pillar. "Demongate?"

"The Hellish side of one, yes." Myrrh leaned back against stone, righteous rage stirring from its chained confines in her heart. Acting too fiercely, too impetuously, would doom far more than her soul. But it was hard to be calm. So very hard, knowing what she knew. "Someone on Earth is doing very terrible things."

"...What, we're looking at the downside of D.C.?"

She had to laugh. "Thank you, Aidan. But - no. Not likely."

Another sigh, and her lips wrinkled back from her teeth. "No. Someone is doing this with intent. Rapine. Murder. Torture. Those are what build a Demongate. Yet all the pain and suffering in the world cannot breach it from this side to Earth... unless one on Earth truly wills it open, and knows the means to snap loose energies into rigid, captured form." Gray eyes narrowed. "Usually that takes a summoner of demonic entities. And the ones who live long enough to gain that knowledge are rare."

"Huh. You lost me." Aidan fidgeted against stone, obviously trying not to peer around the ledge. "If that thing's supposed to open up some Hell on Earth, how come lots of demon summoners don't live long enough to learn it? You'd think Hell would like that."

"Hell is jealous of its powers," Myrrh shrugged, shifting her shoulders against stone. "You've seen that in your wanderings. Hell is jealousy. And hate, and envy, and all manner of darkness. To have the forethought to open a way to Earth - that takes discipline. Few are the demons who can chain their desires enough for that." She breathed in, and nodded. "Thank you, Aidan, I can deal with-"

"Don't you dare do something stupid!" The hand that gripped her arm was hot as sun-warmed asphalt. "Who the hell am I going to mock if you charge in like an idiot, huh?"

"I assure you, I have no intention of charging in," Myrrh said dryly. "Like an idiot, or otherwise."

"But you were thinking about it!"

"A soul may think many things, and then think better of them," Myrrh observed. "That, is the gift of reflection." She did not move his fingers. Not yet. "I know my limits, Aidan. I can't dismantle that edifice with one lone assault." Though she could *damage* it, yes. And if the Demongate grew closer to completion, she might consider that option in more earnest. "To be truly closed, we must find the sorcerer on Earth. And... persuade him to see the error of his ways."

"Weeks she seems so nice, then she says something like that- *wait* a minute." Amber glared at her. "What do you mean, *we?*"

"Ah. A slip of the tongue, perhaps." She met his gaze like still water; fire might burn her, but it could not destroy. "This will take some thought...."

A wailing drifted on the wind.

Shrugging off hot fingers, Myrrh leaped.

"Get it away, oh those teeth, that tearing- no, get it away-"

Thump.

Hmm. A very solid ghost. A new soul, then, Myrrh determined, letting her weight pin translucent ectoplasm to the black rock below them. "Hush, lost one," she said softly, to what had once been a young woman. "You were lost, but you are found. Tell me of the beast that slew you."

"I'm a human, she says. I can't fly." Aidan's snarl, as fiery fingers touched her shoulder. "What the heck do you think you're-*Whoof.*"

Myrrh let the trembling ghost rise a little, the ragged mess of the spirit's throat still seeping silvery fluid. "Did you see what hurt you, young one?"

"You don't look old." The ghost's whisper was ragged, doubled; human fear, and the raspy growl of the demon-wolf. Pale eyes flickered gold. "Shouldn't be here... I had Cap-Silver, it should have gone away, I shouldn't be *here-!*"

Myrrh struck as the mouth gaped wider, showing fangs. *Nose, jaw-point, ear and grab!*

Misty flesh twisted in her fingers. Face pressed to unyielding stone, the lost soul whimpered.

"What- she-!" Aidan gulped. "She's not human-"

"If she tries to bite you, burn her." Myrrh's voice was cold and unforgiving as winter. A chill that hurt her soul like frost; she wanted to comfort the lost, not terrify them further. "Do not let her fangs scratch you. Her soul is cursed."

"...Fire spirit?" Aidan said weakly.

"And the last thing I need, truly, is a *flaming* werewolf." Gray eyes caught amber. "Don't worry. That curse cannot seize on me. Even if I were wearing flesh."

"Werewolf?"

"Most likely, from the wound," Myrrh nodded, keeping the whimpering ghost pinned as stifled howls shifted to human sobs. "Though there are many forms of therianthrope in the world. Still, wolves are the most common demon-breed of that ilk."

"...Werewolves are *demons?*"

"And you said you'd seen everything." Myrrh almost smiled, body under her or no. Sometimes it was all too obvious how young Aidan really was. She'd no doubt he had seen werewolf demons roaming the nearby Hellish realms. But he apparently hadn't seen enough of them to realize they were any different from wolf demons, or any of a dozen other breeds that might rejoice in the title *hounds of Hell.*

I need to teach him more. If I can get flame to sit still and listen. "Most werewolves are demon-tainted, yes. Some few are not. But if this lost one had been attacked by a wolf-shifter under a saint's curse, she would only have died. Her soul would not be tainted... and it would not be here." Myrrh kept her voice quiet, easing her grip on an ear near-human once more. "Do you know where you are, young lady?"

"...I'm not dead." The ghost bristled. "I'm not!"

"Yes, you are," Myrrh sighed. "I'm so sorry. You're fortunate the situation is such that the locals are... distracted." She glanced at not-true-light, lips thinned. "Though if you'd kept drifting that way, you would not be lucky at all. A werewolf's victims are meant to haunt him. They'd have used your link to his soul as one more lever to pry at the barrier-"

"I'm not-!"

"Rest in peace." *Thump!*

"You just KO'd a ghost." Aidan had moved a long step back, eyes wary, weighing how the knife-blade of her flattened hand had struck a wounded throat. "Didn't think anything could do that."

And why should he? Most tormented souls were conscious of their sins. Always. "God helps those who help themselves," Myrrh observed. She moved off the still form, pulling the phial out from under her shirt, a soft blue glow in the endless dark. "And such as she is, are my job. Please step back. This might hurt you."

He didn't move, white-lipped and dripping fire. But he didn't come closer.

Good enough. Myrrh made the sign of the cross over the unconscious spirit, and uncorked her phial. "Seek peace, and healing. When I once more breathe mortal air, you will be free to step forth, and be judged among the righteous."

Slowly, the silver blood ceased to flow. Ectoplasm knit together in a building light, fangs and gilded eyes and hair-tipped ears blazing away like dross in a raging fire-

White as stars, light shot into her phial.

Stone lay before her, empty.

Behind her ashes rustled, as Aidan stumbled back. "What. The. *Hell?*"

Fear, shivering down her spine like the Wendigo's Arctic breath. Her friend, one of the few creatures here she might trust with her existence, feared her.

And I have no time to explain.

Myrrh corked the phial and hid it again, breathing hard. "I'll tell you. If I live that long."

Pushing to her feet, she ran.

In the darkness, something roared. And something answered.

Even without the bounds of flesh, a human soul could not outrun a demon. Not forever.

"I look unto the hills," Myrrh muttered as she ran, steps silent as the grave, "from whence cometh my help-"

"Little earthquake right now *would* help, sure." The fire-globe's voice was taut, untrusting. Still pacing her as she fled from bare, ashy ground into the steely thorns that cloaked these undulating hills of lava, far enough from the river that ice might grudgingly seep water to bare soil. But pacing at a distance; as if any moment flames might simply vanish in the endless night. "I can see 'em flying, you know. You really think they're going to let you steal a soul?"

Shadows snared on a reaching limb of thorns. Myrrh sighed, and took the extra second to free herself. Panic... was natural, but not helpful. "Is that what you think I have done?"

"You sucked her soul into a jar!"

"A phial. And there is a reason-" Thorns jabbed deep, and she winced. "Genesis, Exodus, Leviticus...."

A howl pierced the darkness, trailing acid down her bones.

"You hear that? That, is why I think you're not human, lady. 'Cause any sane person would be swearing his head off by now!"

"Do not take the name of the Lord in vain," Myrrh gritted out.

Ah, but that hurt. Though not all the acid taste in her mouth was fear. She could smell something beyond the rust of steely thorns; fur, and leaves, and blood. "For in his name are done mighty works; both mighty, and perilous."

"Yeah, and a hell of a lot of death and destruction-"

Thorns whipped without wind, a horde of hissing forms leaping out to rend and tear.

Barbweasels!

Neither bramble nor beast; bloodthirsty as any earthly weasel, with the cunning of Hell's own snares. The tangle swarmed her, briar-fangs and thorn-claws tearing at shadows, seeking the pulse of a spirit's heart.

Myrrh drew in a deep breath, accepting the pain. It would only last an instant more. "Wickedness has blazed forth like fire, devouring thorn and thistle! It kindles the thickets of the wood; they turn to billowing smoke!"

For a moment, it felt as if she herself were aflame; her skin was the thorns, her bones the tangled briars. And why should it not? They were all soul-stuff here.

But she knew who she was, and what she was. Smoke pulled away as the flames spread, devouring the tangle and shrouding them under impenetrable darkness.

"I thought I was supposed to be the pyro around here... hey, what gives? Running, remember?"

And if this were only a mortal night, and mortal smoke, she would. Blind, Myrrh listened, and assayed one step. Another. There had been shadows among the thorns to her right, hints of what should be a concealing gully-

Her foot stirred a shard of rock, grating against the roar of flames. She froze.

"...You can't see anything, can you?"

Now. If he truly fears me, it will be now.

It wouldn't be hard. Whatever he was, Aidan was no ordinary mortal soul. He could see in this murk like a lion; and like that king of beasts, he had the strength to match ten heroes. Did the fight come to bone and sinew, she was no more match for him than a mouse under a cat's paw.

And he knew it. They'd battled before; once or twice near

serious, before she'd made it clear she would withdraw rather than attack. As Aidan had watched and snarled at her over the years, he'd gradually come to believe that she had no interest in harming him. He'd begun to wander with her, often as not; to trust her enough to take solid form and spar, or even to seek her aid against things that hunted them both.

Now that trust was torn and bleeding. And there were so many, *many* things a wounded soul might do. Attack. Retreat, and leave her to the moaning hunt. Or simply cough, and draw them all down like the wrath of Hades.

Aidan. I'm sorry. I didn't think.

She didn't know how his spirit had come to be in Hell, but from what she suspected-

He likely has seen soul-jars.

She'd hurt him. An apology would only be salt in the wound.

He's young, but he's quick. Where there's one soul captive, there may be more. He knows *I have stolen souls from Hell.*

And she couldn't tell him *why.*

And what would I say, if I could? Myrrh wondered. *That the powers here have sought me for longer than he can imagine? That if they catch me, they will inflict all the horrors of Hell? He knows the torments a soul can endure, and yet still exist. He's survived them. That no one human would turn any soul over to the hordes? He clings to the fact that he* is not *human. And I've seen far too many humans do more horrible things than that.*

Silently, she prayed. And waited. She might fight him or the hosts, but never both of them.

If I've shattered your trust in me so horribly - let it be swift.

Strength seized her, bruising arm and side as it hoisted her from the rocks. She swallowed back nausea as the world moved around her; leaving solid ground, even Hellish ground, always threw her inner calm into a raging sea of turmoil.

Wait. Wait for the right moment, you don't know where you are-

Hot fingers released her.

Myrrh dropped to ashy ground, dampening the sound with her shadows. Curled into the gully, breathing soft and soundless as she could make it.

Silent, a globe of flame sheltered under her shadow-cloak. More shadows seemed to curl in towards them, thickening over them like smoke.

There was a thunder of wings, as if the hammered vault of the firmament above had been riven by bolts of lambent star-fire. Cackles and gibbering filled the wind that tore at her where she crouched, head down, shadows and smoke pulled over herself and her ally in a shrouding veil.

"And if one look to the land, behold darkness and distress...." Myrrh held her eyes closed as that tumult roared out above them. Their enemies were numerous as the schools of the sea, and more powerful than a pounding ocean. The two of them must be only a chip of bark on the waves; floating, damp, but never drowned.

The roaring faded.

"After this is over?" Aidan's voice was quiet as falling ashes. "You owe me a long. Long. *Long* explanation."

Myrrh blinked, noting how the wind of wings had torn at concealing smoke. "I do, indeed. For now - time we were away."

"Hey, they went past here. If you move-"

"Those were the winged host," Myrrh said dryly, as the fire-globe floated out of her shadow. "Next will come-"

A long, mournful howl, shuddering over skin like cold blood dripping down her hand. Echoed and reechoed moments later, by a score of other fell throats.

"The hounds-!" Gold eyes glinted in the flames. "But they never call the whole pack out...."

Myrrh wanted to laugh. Or cry. The utter *shock* in that voice... he truly was young. A quarter of a century, she'd managed to slip clear of most notice. Now she'd tampered with a Demongate's prey, and any hellish lord with a talon in the game could never let that pass.

More than that. The lords of Hell are old, and proud, and learned. *They know how few entities have the power to snatch away their prey.*

And one of those few, is me.

Well. Spilled milk, as old tales said. "I am, perhaps," Myrrh admitted, "a bit more infamous in certain demonic courts than I may have mentioned."

"No, really?" Aidan deadpanned.

"Really." Brushing away ash, she set off at a run again.

"...That's it?" Flames flickered; almost a haunted face. "Just keep running? Don't you even care?"

"What should I care for, my friend?" Myrrh spoke between strides, settling into the rhythm of a gait that had run down werewolves, when she had to. "What you did - or what you did not do?"

"They're going to catch you, damn it!"

"They have not," breathe in, "caught me yet." And out....

Back to the gleaming pallor of the Demongate, Myrrh ran. Distance. As much distance as she could put between them. Demons were cruel and cunning and relentless, but most of them were slaves to their desires. And the Demongate called them. Souls in Hell could always be caught for later torment. Souls on Earth....

Which would have worked, had the rolling hills of gravelly basalt and ashy thorns not suddenly sagged into wet mire. Darkness turned thick and sodden here, lit by the ghostly flickers of tiny, bloodsucking creatures of twisted chitin and fungoid wings.

"Always knew mosquitoes were evil." Red hair flickered into being in the night like a torch; Aidan swatted little monsters with a snarl, eyes snapping sparks. "No offense, but I think you're screwed. Unless you can pull a Moses and part the waters...." He trailed off, giving her a sudden wary look.

Catching her breath, Myrrh smiled. "Not quite." Oh, but she was tired....

But she was not done. Not yet. She peered at the marsh ahead, picking out a tuft of luminescent gray-green, a stump slimed with brown, and beyond a patch of higher ground thick with knife-edged grass. Yes. That would do.

She gathered her will, and her faith. Raised one hand, and held it out flat over the dark and oily pool. "The watercourses are dried up," Myrrh murmured, "and fire hath consumed the pasture of the wilderness."

Under her hand, balefire blazed. With a crackling of ice, frost forged outward like unseen hunting hounds, sucking away water and leaving a trail of frozen mud.

Face steady, Myrrh walked forward, icy clay threatening to

throw her with every step. Just a bit longer, just a bit farther....

She set foot on the slippery hillock, and stumbled. Like a hiss of steam, frost vanished.

The grass was as sharp as it looked.

"Okay, I stand corrected." Aidan's voice was oddly soft, as she pulled one foot from sucking mud. "*Now* you're screwed."

"You may be right." Myrrh dropped to her knees, and said a quick *Ave Maria*.

"Um. This isn't exactly time for praying-"

"It is precisely the time." She was getting her breath back. But not fast enough. "There is no farther I can go from here." She stared into the bleak night, watching, listening. "Still. There is always the chance I might get lucky."

Something shifted in the marsh wind. Something cold, and cruel, and terribly familiar.

"Or not," Myrrh muttered, loosening the phial in its hiding place. "Aidan. If I fall here... and that is likely, I know who walks in this wind... take these souls and go."

"Look, I don't know what you're up to, and I'm not turning you over to them, but like hell I'm going to steal souls!"

"Ah. But it is my *job* to steal souls, Aidan." Myrrh smiled, even with the promise of death moving in like the pressure of a storm front. "I am a hell-raider."

He almost flickered into form, then back to near-inscrutable flames. "A... what?" Fire waved like a hand brushing off insanity. "This is *Hell*. Nobody gets out-"

"Oh, but one did. And since then, many have. The Gates are shattered; all it takes is the courage, and the skill." She raised pale brows at him. "Even you have heard the prayer, long ago. *He suffered, was crucified, and was buried. He descended into Hell; the third day he rose again from the dead. He ascended into Heaven-*"

"...Jesus *Christ*."

"Indeed." Myrrh inclined her head, even as the ripples of that careless naming whispered out through the marsh. It wouldn't be much longer anyway. "No human soul has strength enough to *break* the Gates. But they are already broken, and utterly cast down. And as he was the Son of Man and the Son of God, so other sons and daughters of Eve have dared to follow where he has led. We die. And we descend into Hell, to rescue those cursed, and brought here not by their actions, but by others. By demonkind, and cursed bites, and unholy sacrifice, and... all manner of things you have been fortunate enough not to meet, yet."

Hmm. Had he twitched at *sacrifice?*

As I thought. I do owe you an apology, Aidan. Though I doubt I'll have time to give it.

"You die." Aidan's flames shuddered. "On purpose?"

"To die in the service of life is not a sin," Myrrh said gravely. This was not the time to get into complex theology, much less the shouting matches she'd held with many priests over the centuries. "Though usually, our deaths do come at other hands. As my last one did."

"Last- *how many times have you done this?*"

"I was born," Myrrh said, listening to the hate on the wind while she calculated the numbers, "somewhere around... hmm. The numbers *are* a bit tricky, between the Empire and your modern archaeologists. You would say, about 250 A.D.? I think."

Dead silence. Only the blurred buzz of fungoid wings. She slapped one away before it could bite.

"...There's a way out." Aidan was a fiery shadow, hunched into his trenchcoat. "Man, I so wish I could believe you."

"There is," Myrrh inclined her head. "Which is, unfortunately, why this was one rescue too close, and too many. There are... those who have met me before. And one of those comes, now." She sighed. "He knows I may escape. He will not wait patiently for me to falter."

"Hate to point this out, but if you've got a way out-!" Hands flung upwards.

"Ah. That." She almost had to laugh. "Well. That depends on... certain circumstances." Oh, the listening *hurt.*

I will not despair.

"Oh. Joy." For one who claimed to be a fire spirit, Aidan seemed to be rubbing a very human headache. "So no rescue, huh? No angels coming down from Heaven to yank *you* out of this. Souls or no souls."

"No rescue," Myrrh agreed softly. "As you might say, I knew

that when I took the job." Gray eyes sought amber flickers. "If I am taken... please. Do not leave them to be dragged back into the darkness."

"...You don't know me."

"I know what I have seen you do. And not do." Myrrh felt the pressure build; even the glowing pests skittered away. "It is enough." She straightened. "Ill met, Lord of Minor Pestilential Midges."

"...You're deliberately hacking off a demon." Fire ducked behind her, incredulous. "Never seen this woman before in my life...."

"Hell-raider." The voice was thick and choked; a muddy swamp surging over ancient fallen trees. Arms like tentacles reached out, absorbing any bloodsucker not fast enough to buzz clear. "Found you at last."

"Tch. And so long it took you!" Myrrh smirked at the walking, buzzing mire on the far shore, calculating how long it would take his will to suborn the landscape and let him surge through it like water. Not long, marsh calling to marsh. Pity. "Why, ten centuries ago, you would have known my hands at work in a day!" She clicked her tongue. "You are *slipping*. Have my comrades wreaked such harm on your schemes? Have humans forgotten how they feared you, when the *mal'aria* stalked and none knew why, and quinine was but an impossible fantasy?" She waved a languid hand, heart pounding like a drum. "Or perhaps your fellow lords seek to suck away your power, and turn you into naught but a squirming larva to be molded into cannon fodder-"

In the distance, a clarion horn rang.

Oh, sweet Jesu. "As you know they would," Myrrh went on, ringing like copper cymbals sweet in her ears. The first trumpet of dawn. Time. She needed only a little more time!

"Not distracted this time, soul-seeker. Not even by petty little fireling." Jagged stumps of chitin-teeth snarled at her. "Hmm. Munch the fire-brat, or bring him back to... heh heh heh. Fireling *knows*."

"Go jump in a lake and drown!" Aidan flickered into form beside her, one finger extended. "I am not heading anywhere near that son of a bitch again, you can rip me apart first!" He stopped, and blinked. "Oh, man. You're a horrible influence on a poor helpless fire spirit. You know that, right?"

Myrrh drew in a steadying breath, hearing that second, silvery call. Dawn. Somewhere on Earth, her anchor knew a mortal dawn. "Oh, I do indeed. Do you trust me?"

Aidan waved an arm, lighting flames that showed the boggy hosts gathering behind their enemy. "This is a heck of a time to ask!"

"Oh, but it is the best time to ask," Myrrh murmured. "The only time it seems I will have... do you trust me? Will you come with me?"

"Come-" Amber eyes jerked to meet hers, shocked. "You said-!"

"Hell-raider words are ash and sand!" The demon surged into oily water, spreading over the surface like a walking cesspool as he and his minions advanced. "See? Marsh does not burn! Hell-raider has run too long! Stolen too much! No power left. No *grace*. Prayers will not bite; words will not stop us this time-"

Myrrh smiled.

Like a slowing avalanche of filth, the demon paused. Snarled, a dripping arm lashing out-

One more breath of will. Of *belief*. "Turn our captivity, oh Lord," Myrrh declared, "as streams in a dry land."

Her vision swam. Her heart ached. But an inch from her face, muck whipped back on itself.

Now. Now! Blindly, she reached out behind her, seizing trenchcoat and flames. Hoping. Praying. At the very least, she might free a repentant soul from torment. Yet if Aidan was what she believed he might be, this would do so much more. "Aidan! Trust me. *Believe*."

"I believe you're fucking *crazy-!*"

The golden peal rang out, and there was light.

And, quite possibly, one hell-raider's hand raised in the *digitus impudicus*.

Someone had to keep up old Roman traditions, after all.

Chapter Two

"We're staking out a *graveyard*. Church, this is a new low."

Chafing her arms against October chill, Detective Church tried not to roll her eyes. "Tom? You read the report."

"Right, right; ancient who-knows-what's-in-it box, doom, gloom, destruction, end of the world... come on. It's the evening news all over again. World gets darker, ministers yell themselves hoarse, at the end of the day nobody gives a damn." Detective Tom Franklin shrugged, leaning back in the driver's seat of the old gray sedan to try and head off leg cramps. There was plenty of room for his legs most of the time, but stakeouts were a lot more aggravating than driving. Especially when Annabel Franklin had made it clear she was just a bit fed up with her husband keeping late nights with another woman. Work-related or not.

For her part, Church thought longingly of the lonely smoke-blue eye-shadow and pale lipstick on her bathroom sink. Not to mention the double-chocolate milkshake recipe she'd meant to spring on Coral the next time the pair of them went looking for cute guys at a midnight movie. If she had to walk into headquarters in the morning with raccoon eyes, she at least ought to have gotten a good time out of it. She blew out a breath, and wondered when it'd be light enough to see it fog. "You could always quit."

Tom snickered, rolling his eyes in a flash of white. "What, and miss the sparkling company?"

"The Friday night druggies...."

"A new chemical cocktail in every cell," Tom said expansively.

"The Saturday night hookers...."

"Cute, if you don't mind the tattoos."

"The *Sunday* night hookers...."

"Did you catch that one who said she was a succubus?" Tom's face smiled, but he shuddered, and scratched at dark brown sideburns as if he'd felt a spider wander over his cheek. "I dunno. Pretty, but - something *wrong* about that woman."

"How could you ever give that up?" Church deadpanned. Sipped her water, shallowly; they were pretty well hidden by an old mausoleum from most angles, but too many times opening the door might catch stray ears, even if Tom had taken the precaution of blacking out the overhead light. *Something wrong, huh? That's not what you said when I caught you and Eagleman flirting with her.*

There was pretty, and then there was *too* pretty; eyes too wide and bashful for a lady of the night, a smile that sparkled like diamonds. Church had taken one look to estimate the depth of the puddle of drool on Eagleman's desk, then passed by and flicked salt over her shoulder. She didn't know if it'd done any damage, but the resulting shriek and swears had at least gotten her fellow detectives' minds back on the job. Thankfully.

Eagleman had the excuse of being single. Tom had a ring on his finger.

The tourniquet worn to restrict circulation, you said. Sometimes I think Annabel's right. You need to spend more nights at home.

Not this one, though. If this tip didn't pan out in an hour, they were going to see the sun come up.

"But seriously," Tom shrugged, made just a little stiff by his shoulder holster. "You think the captain's not just shoving us off somewhere away from the gala?"

"The farther the likes of us are away from Herr Mayor and his silk-tuxedo philanthropist buddy Savonarola, the better, my friend," Church shrugged back. Glad, now, that she'd skimped on fancy dinners and stuck to a dozen cheap ways to make meat and rice for as long as it took to afford her own fitted holster. Bad enough to be sore, cold, and sleep-deprived without being *chafed* on top of it. "Does it matter?"

"...I think she got the tip from Halo."

Whoof. Okay, maybe it did matter. "What makes you think that?" Church asked warily. Hand gripping the armrest, so she didn't pull up the collar of her coat. It wasn't any colder than it'd been a minute ago. She just felt like she'd been dipped in ice.

"A box that holds a willful return to darkness?"

Oof. Church had talked to the so-called street seer once or twice. That definitely sounded like Halo's style. "Evidence is evidence," the younger detective said, deliberately casual. "If it takes a guy who sees angels around the sun to lead us to proof

Snake Bradley got knocked off by Switch O'Connor, I'm not going to complain."

"It's the history on that box before Snake had it that creeps me out."

"Thought you said you knew all about the end of the world?" But Church gave him a sympathetic look. Being tagged as the captain's unofficial go-tos whenever a homicide case stank of the supernatural never helped anybody's career. But somebody had to do it. Ever since the Dark Day.

Hard to imagine it's been twenty-one years since then.

Since the zombies had crawled out of the graveyards, and the monsters had oozed out from under everybody's beds. Oh, and not to mention the sorcerers who had set the whole thing off, duking it out with *fiery dragons* in Times Square.

It'd taken a week, ten recorded vampire attacks, and one werewolf transforming on the ground floor of a Shriners' convention before the mainstream media had admitted it wasn't just more Hollyweird madness. Church still remembered staring in sophomore jealousy at the sappy looks on the senior cheerleaders' faces when they'd been picked up by a pair of "lonely ones of the night". It scared her, sometimes, looking back on what a dumb sixteen-year-old who'd never gotten near dating the football team had thought was the epitome of cool.

Finding the bodies splayed out like disassembled Barbies on her high school gym floor the next morning? Not so cool.

Of course, nobody had ever proved it was vampires. Not *those* vampires. Not beyond a reasonable doubt. And after the ACLU had won a slew of cases against so-called "bitter clingers to antiquated religious interpretations" for trespassing, assaults with deadly, etc., and gotten a host of people twenty to life for hate crimes against alternative lifestyles....

Cap-Silver in your pocket was legit. Not much *good*, given you had to spray the pepper-silver nitrate mix practically up a were's nose to get it to pay attention, and by that time an angry wolf probably had its teeth in your throat. But legit. Silver and hawthorn bullets in your gun? Did you have a license for those?

Church did. Tom did. A few other cops. And all of them had to keep their noses very, very clean. Hard to do when they got handed history like this.

A human skull set with jade, that word on the street says Snake looted from the Cat House ashes, after some loony broke into Rasputin's Cat House to put it there, just before the whole place mysteriously *burned down,* Church thought. *We're going to prove that's arson someday... point is, rumor said* Snake *had it, before someone - we haven't proved it's Switch - took him out. And now Switch's guy Ginger is going to be handing Snake's little skull-art off to Rajas Feniger, and if we can just catch them at it, and there's no tags proving it's a legit artifact, hello deal or jail time, tell us what Switch* knows....

If, if, if. She'd chased down thinner leads. But damn few that might lead so high.

Savonarola. You may look clean, but I know you're scum. All I need is proof!

She'd known it even before she'd done some digging, looking at the *tragic* deaths of his father and brother. Deaths that had left Steven Savonarola heir to all the power and political connections Judge Jeremiah Savonarola had cultivated over a lifetime; not to mention leaving him a very, very wealthy young man.

And what he'd done with that wealth since.... There were reasons she'd let Xanthippe Coral paint diamond-water runes on her apartment walls. And it wasn't just for girly bonding.

Grabbing Ginger wouldn't give her Savonarola. Not *directly.* But Ginger was Switch's gofer, and Switch was a classic hitman. He didn't work for people, he *undertook projects on their behalf.* Yet people did work for Switch, and for all his lack of anything approaching a conscience, the hitman apparently considered it good business sense to show his employees the same loyalty they showed him.

So if she could get Ginger over a barrel she might - *might* - be able to put some pressure on Switch. Maybe. If what she wanted wasn't something Switch cared about.

And if she was really lucky, and the rumors on the street were right about Switch suddenly turning frosty toward Savonarola, and if the reason Switch had wasn't anything the street thought, but instead was because he shared some of the same cold suspicions she did....

When you're in the same headspace as a hitman, it's time to reevaluate your life.

Not to mention the key word there being *hitman*. If Switch were sure that Savonarola had anything to do with little Megan O'Connor's death last October, he wouldn't waste time scrambling around to find evidence. He'd have walked into the Savonarola mansion with a stolen gun, double-tapped the bastard, walked out, and dropped the gun in somebody's swimming pool. It wouldn't be the first time.

So he's not sure, Church thought. *But it takes a psycho to know one - and they know each other. I've seen it.*

One short glimpse in the courthouse, when Savonarola had been walking in and Switch had been sauntering out. She'd been over in a corner trying not to bruise the wall on her knuckles, because she'd handed a young assistant prosecutor a good case, a solid one, and he'd somehow cocked it up like a green rookie-

Savonarola had been within yards of Switch; the lawyer heading the opposite way from the hitman, gray eyes meeting cold Irish blue. Just another set of dueling glances in the ordinary walk of human life.

Until it wasn't.

Church still didn't know what had caught her eye. Maybe a sense of gazes holding too long. Maybe a slight hesitation in the echo of footfalls. But she'd looked up, and she'd known.

Predator meeting predator. Killer seeing killer. They know.

Church couldn't take *I just know* to a judge. Law didn't work that way. But if she could somehow put together enough of the circumstantial evidence around Megan O'Connor's death... maybe, just maybe, she could get a warrant for more.

All of which meant she was trying not to feel like low-lying scum right now. Tom thought they were after Switch and Rajas. And they *were*. Rajas was a bad guy. He might not be the real perpetrator of a little girl's murder, but he hadn't ended up the Detective Division's favorite suspect by accident.

And Switch always makes a deal with somebody. Why shouldn't we make it a deal for somebody who's worse than he is?

The D.A. probably wouldn't see it that way. According to the district attorney's office, the Savonarolas had been a good family of decent upstanding citizens, and their last surviving son had suffered enough tragedy already. Anyone who said otherwise was just a burned-out, frustrated cop trying to tie up hopelessly unconnected cold cases.

I wish I was. I really wish I was.

Well, if she was right, Tom would say nail the bastard. He'd forgive her.

Annabel, not so much.

"End of the world, sure," Tom said at last. "Fire dragons and ice serpents and basilisks, sure; and none of my kids are ever keeping snakes, period. But if Rajas really thinks the stuff in this box can let him call up a demon...."

"We've shot demons before." What people called demons, anyway. Ugly supernatural things, sure. But she'd always thought something that deserved the name *demon* would be more subtle.

"Yeah. Little ones." Tom shifted in his seat. "This one? May not be that little."

"Yeah, yeah; everybody says there's nastier things than the spiky guys out there, but seriously. If there was worse, don't you think they'd be up here wreaking havoc like-"

Tom's hand slapped over her mouth.

Church almost bit him. But she could see the bobbing flashlights, now; why the hell hadn't they seen them before?

That's a hell of a lot more people than just a handoff!

Automatically, her gaze flicked to the notepad in her lap. Times were scrawled in, every five minutes; a habit she'd ground into herself just before she'd made detective, after the first time she'd broken loose from a vampire's gaze. *Okay. We didn't lose time. We just didn't see them. So why do we see them now?*

Could be a host of reasons. Charms could wear out. Running water, even underground, might zap something that hadn't been spelled correctly. Or - simple, but potentially *very* nasty - there was an active magic-user in the group who'd just gotten *distracted*.

Oh, joy.

Rajas Feniger might play up the big bad sorcerer angle, but his main schtick was black-market potions and everybody knew it. If he had active magic going, either he'd teamed up with somebody new in town, or he'd gotten his grubby hands on somebody's little black book. And not the innocent kind that had call-girls in it.

This is Rajas. He probably bought a cheap charm and figured it didn't matter. What kind of idiots would be hanging around in a graveyard, anyway?

She was going to enjoy reminding Rajas how many times he'd called cops idiots.

Silent, the pair of detectives eased out into the chill before dawn, sneaking to the corner of the old family tomb. No weapons drawn, not yet; this was supposed to be a watch and arrest.

Not a mob scene. Or a... what the heck are we looking at, anyway? Painting stuff on the ground....

It was too dark to see clearly. But it smelled like blood.

"Backup," Tom breathed.

"Oh yeah," Church murmured back, heartbeat picking up speed. Rajas was a potion-brewer. Sure, they used runes and circles in their work; she'd even run into one nasty little old lady who pulled in magic by way of knitting and macramé. But no potion she'd ever heard of needed any setup circle this big - and only the worst used blood. "You?"

"Yeah. You watch them. Your eyes are better." Tom edged back around the mausoleum, cupping his cell phone so no light would give them away.

Yeah, usually they were. She could pick out Alcor and Mizar in the Dipper's handle even with the sky going pale. But this time she'd missed over a dozen strung-out crazies showing up out of nowhere. Tom knew as well as she did, that meant this was going to be bad.

Focus on Ginger. Him she could see well enough, dark or no dark. A little too well; Church rubbed at a headache that meant she'd been up way too late. Or early. Getting on toward dawn.

"Rajas." Ginger's eyes were flicking around the chanting crowd, sneering at the little brushes dabbing at grass and frosted stone. "Do you have to make such a stink?"

Long hair full of jangling bits of metal, Rajas was an island of near-stillness in the sea of frantic robes and buckets of blood. "Do you have what we bargained for, or not?"

"Rasputin's little treasure chest? Sure." Ginger hefted a small pack, eyes unsmiling. "You don't really believe this belonged to some crazy Russian monk, do you?"

"Pray it does not." Rajas smiled, sharp as a razor. "If it did, it would be the wrong Rasputin, and you'd have cheated me."

...Okay, Church was going to ignore that chill going down her spine. Minor magic. She knew a dozen people who could fling it. She hadn't known Rajas was one of them....

But it fits. He's playing with bigger, badder magic than just potions. Question is, how big?

The camera nestled snug into her hands, set without flash. She got the handover. What she wanted was an *arrest*, but two cops against about fifteen people was-

Crunch.

Plastic shattered in her hand. And then the world was grunts, and shouting, and-

Church never quite lost track of what was going on, and never quite blacked out. The fight was dirty and painful and too many people piling on her when she tried to get to Tom. And thank god she was wearing a thick coat on top of her vest. Though who knew what was on that knife scoring her ribs....

Hope we've got time to worry about that later. Tom was still breathing, tossed on the ground by her. Ginger was *gone*. And something about that really, really worried her-

He doesn't expect to have to explain.

Which meant he expected them to be dead. Because that was the only way two cops weren't going to bring the whole IPD down on his head.

"Keep them alive, for now." Rajas' eyes gleamed hungry as a wolf's, as he waved his hand; Church found her jaw locked tight, even against a scream. "Our new servant will appreciate a... welcoming gift."

Servant? Damn it, Tom's breathing didn't sound good at all, if she could just get these zip-ties off-

Rajas opened the pack.

...Blank. A blurry blank where there should have been memory, with her head ringing like she'd gone ten rounds with Ali. What... what had happened? He wasn't a vamp, not even newly turned; pretty as most people found the bloodsuckers, she'd never been able to ignore that *dead* feeling around them. And he wasn't holding an evil-eye charm. So where had the mind-whammy come from?

"One of mystic blood." Rajas was smiling down at her where she and Tom lay in the lower third of the circle, like a leopard might smile at a particularly toothsome Chihuahua. Behind him something shimmered like air over hot asphalt; Church yanked her gaze away before that blurry blankness could swallow her again. "No wonder you've been such a consistent thorn in our sides. It's almost a pity you weren't born one of us."

Mystic blood? Shyeah, right. She was about as mystic as last week's obituaries. Church strained her jaw to say that. No luck. She couldn't speak. She couldn't even whimper. But if looks could kill-

Rajas flicked his fingers, as if brushing away ill intent like a fly. "As I said. A pity. Now...." He turned toward glossy black bone in the center of the circle, the center of the shimmer, and inclined his head.

That's not the right skull!

It wasn't even a human skull. More like a bear, if a bear had ever had too many eye sockets and weird horny outgrowths that curved near its jaws like scimitars. And it looked all of a *piece*. Not some Hollywood composite of what a bear-slash-horror-alien might look like. One coherent, unique skull, glittering as if it'd been carved from dark opal.

So where's the human skull? Halo's poison but he's accurate; *if he tipped off the captain that this gig was going down, then it should be here-*

In the thin light before dawn, a faint whiteness caught her eye. There. Outside the circle of blood, where it looked like some careless hand had flung it against a gravestone. One old, dry skull, dull glints that might have been ancient jade set above each empty eye.

Great. There was her evidence. Not that it was going to do either of them much good if she couldn't get loose-

Rajas spoke something that sounded like Latin, and the world seemed to freeze. Shadows held still. The wind stopped whispering. Even Tom's breathing seemed to stop.

Yet in that impossible silence, Rajas' voice went on. Hissing.

Imploring. Demanding, with a sort of sick sideways offer of *I have what you want*, that made Church want to throw up.

Somebody stop him. Somebody. Anybody. I'd do anything if I could just never hear that again-

Blue flames blazed in the not-bear skull, spreading over opal like a wildfire.

"...Anything?"

It was compelling. It was a promise. Just one wish, just one, and all of this would go away.

But Church had looked into a vampire's eyes, and been lucky enough to live through it. *Get away from me, you sick freak of nature!*

Blue fires surged outward, rippling into ebony fur and long, dagger-edged paws and a face that looked vaguely of *bear* but would have sent an Alaskan grizzly running for its mommy. It reared up on its hind legs, now four feet tall, now eight and still growing. And it was laughing.

"Malursine." Rajas smirked. "We have brought you prey as you prefer it. Servants of Michael, failed in their duty, bound and helpless at your feet."

Servants of who? She was a sworn detective of Intrepid, North Carolina. She and Tom weren't anybody's servants. Unless you counted public servants, which she never had.... Oh good, Tom was still breathing, she could feel him shivering against her in shock. And damn, it was petty, but her tight-bound hands were almost in his groin and he was heavy-

Pants pocket. Tom always carries a pocketknife. If I can just get to it!

Right. Time to make like a mole, and gopher it.

...And if Tom were conscious, he'd throw a spitball at her for that one.

Fingers wriggled into warm cloth. Wallet, change, why did the knife have to be all the way at the bottom-

"This one is not failed, yet." The malformed snout wrinkled; the breath that blew at her was hot, and stank like a corpse not found for three weeks. *"Strip her of the prince's scales, that I may feast."*

Rajas blinked. "The... scales?"

Steel bit her fingers, one of the smaller blades unfolding as her fingernail snagged the notch meant to open it. Church yanked the knife out, fingers working it upward to close on plastic. *Come on. Come on!*

"The scales, little sorcerer. The scales that belong to That One, who you have warded out. That weigh Justice, and Mercy." A rumbling snarl. *"Take them from her. Or I will feast on those others here, who have forfeited That One long ago."*

Funny. Seeing the sick looks on some of the weird cultists' faces didn't make Church any happier.

"We shall," Rajas said grimly, stalking into the circle toward her. "In the meantime... feast on her partner."

A growling chuckle. *"With pleasure-"*

"Bastard!" It was a thin croak, but it felt like triumph as she surged up, half-sitting, and threw steel like the biggest, most unwieldy shuriken made. "Get *away* from him!"

Edged steel bounced off fur like it'd hit a brick wall. But white sparks flew, and the demon shook its head, teeth away from Tom for one more moment-

In the first glimmers of dawn, bone gleamed.

Old bones don't turn white....

Light and shadow swirled together, silvery as moonlight on snow. There was a tingling in the air, a promise of *be brave, all will be well....*

"Sorcerer!" the demon-bear howled, charging away from Tom. *"Slay it! Slay the soul-stealer before it rises!"*

Light and wind and a vibrant, living red, leaping into existence quick as a flame-

A redheaded man in a dark trenchcoat rolled away from the demon-bear's strike, hands full of fire. "Oh no you don't!"

Black nose singed, the malursine roared. Lumbering fur charged the man like an avalanche-

Silver sang.

"For behold." A woman's voice; a shape of shadowed cloak and flowing hair and a bright, sun-white blade, rising from where old bone had lain. "I bring not peace, but a *sword*."

Sizzling black smoke, one of the demon-bear's paws fell to the ground. The shudder felt like a boulder cracking.

Suddenly off-balance, the demon skidded on wet leaves.

"Could've cut it just a *little* closer, right?" Long red hair wild around his face, the strange man dodged another swipe of unnatural claws. Warmth seemed to ripple from him, like careless hands had dropped a slice of summer noon into autumn. "Man, where did you come from, ugly? Bet we could track you by the trail of broken mirrors left behind-"

"Aidan, *down!*"

Apparently all that crackling fire didn't block his ears. The redhead hit the ground, as some of Rajas' followers opened up with what were definitely illegal semi-automatics.

Aim like that, I kind of wish they were shooting at me, Church winced, trying not to burst into hysterical laughter as flattened lead slugs dropped off rank fur.

Snorting like a steam locomotive, the demon glared at the would-be gunmen. *"Worthless human scum! You thought to implore* me?" Fangs gaped impossibly wide, wider-

Pale green gas vomited forth from its jaws, hissing like water dropped in a hot frying pan. The vapor billowed out, touched flesh.

Flesh melted.

Oh god. Church scrabbled backwards on her hands as the screams hit a higher pitch, trying to figure out how to drag Tom and free her bound feet at the same time. *Oh god, no one deserves to die like that. No one-*

There was a whoosh, like a gust sweeping off the sea.

Flames exploded in a whiff of seared sugar, a billowing flow of red and green-ripple and terrible heat-

And roaring.

The redhead's smile was all teeth. "Oh, I *love* flammable bad guys."

Fingers slipping on the hard plastic ties around her ankles, Church swallowed. *It's burning from the inside!*

Fires were eating through unnatural fur, showing opalescent ribs in flame-etched hide. But somehow the malursine was still moving, turning on Aidan with fiery eyes. *"Foolish fire-cub,"* it snarled. *"When I eat you, all your blood will suffer-"*

There was a flutter of sound, like a whisper.

"Your pardon." White hair blew like cresting waves, as the

dark-clad woman went to one knee, sword still extended. Sweat streaked her face, yet gray eyes were pure steel. "But the sun has risen, and your time in this world is at an end."

How the-? Church's eyes bugged. *Nothing moves that fast! How the hell did she-?*

The malursine pivoted, flaming jaws open to roar again-

Collapsed, in a clatter of fur-covered bones, burning skull rolling away from a severed spine.

Gray eyes swept what few of Rajas' followers were still standing. Pale lips curved, in the shadow of a smile. "Next?"

Screaming, live bodies fled.

"Oh." The white-haired woman's voice seemed to wobble, just a little. "Good."

Flame-heat like a shaft of sun, and Aidan had her by the shoulders as she crumpled. "Where the heck-? You didn't have *that*," long fingers waved at the blade clutched in pale hands, "when we were... you know."

"Hmm. I'll tell you later. Oh, it is good to feel mortal sun...." She shook her head, and focused on Church.

Eep.

Not a vampire. Not a werewolf. Not even a demon; small, or anything like the alien-bear from Hell that'd just disintegrated. There was no *hunger* in those eyes.

Gray as the sea. Gray as the storm.

You didn't need hunger to be deadly.

Gray blinked, looking past her. And winced. "Your companion is failing." The woman's voice was thin, frayed with exhaustion. "Please. Let me help."

Stubborn fingers finally broke plastic. Church got up on one knee, ready to cover her gasping partner with her body, if that was what it took. The swordswoman looked exhausted... but she'd also blipped across twenty feet of space in less time than it took to blink. "I don't make deals with demons!"

The redhead flinched. Church shuddered. Figured. Why was it always the cute ones who were bad news?

"I am not, and never have been, a demon," the white-haired woman said precisely. Cloud-white hair around a young face; gray eyes old and deep as the ocean. She made all the hairs on Church's neck stand straight up. "Michael the Archangel, who cast down the dragon, whose shield you carry on your earthly rounds, gives dying souls in his charge a chance to make amends."

She's talking about archangels. *Come on, everybody knows that's crazy talk-*

"But your friend still needs healing, if he does not wish to account to the Lord with his soul in such disorder," the swordswoman went on. "I will help him." She turned that ancient gaze on Aidan; Church felt it lift away from her like lead weights. "I swear to you, it will not kill me."

Aidan muttered something under his breath that didn't sound like English, and almost didn't sound human. "Damn well better not," he grumbled, picking her up like an exhausted child. "I want answers."

Church tensed. *I shouldn't let her touch him!*

But there was so much blood. And the growing dawn let Church see a dent in Tom's skull, where bone pressed into his brain like somebody had punched it in with a fist. Even if she could find her cell phone, by the time EMS got here-

Damn it. What do I do?

"When I behold the heavens, the work of Your fingers," a pale hand released the sword, drifting out to rest on bloody hair, "the moon and the stars that You set in place... what is man, that You have been mindful of him...."

Light ghosted about her fingers like a mist at dawn, curling off a warm lake in the chill of the night. Slowly, the dent lifted, smoothed into whole skin and bone. Tom's breathing eased; grew steadier.

There was no sound. No drama. Gray eyes simply slid closed, as the woman went limp in Aidan's arms.

"Myrrh! Damn it." Aidan pressed fingers against the pulse of her throat. "Okay. Okay, just... keep breathing." He glared at Church. "So where's a guy go to get an ambulance around here?"

Tom was coughing now; Church helped him turn on his side to hack out spit and blood. "You want to take your demon friend to the hospital?"

"She's not a demon!"

"Oh yeah? Then what is she?" And where did she get off saying

Tom's soul was in disorder? Tom Franklin was the best cop Church knew. "For that matter, what the hell are you?"

"...I don't know." Aidan held Myrrh close, eyes hot as molten amber. "I just... don't know." His jaw tightened. "But I'm going to find out."

Sweet. Wonderful. All kinds of dramatic. But as Church got up and looked around, hoping to find some stray cell in working order so she could get EMS here faster-

Opal bones, crumbling in the sunlight. Acid-melted bodies, in pools that still steamed. Gravestones and brass markers etched and pitted, or shattered, or stained with unthinkable things. And who knew where the hell Rajas Feniger - or the friggin' skull, damn it! - had gone.

What the heck do I tell Captain Sherman?

Chapter Three

Beeping. Low, monotonous, and regular. A tang of disinfectants, and stiff cotton sheets against her skin. Not to mention an ache in one elbow, deep, trickling in the faintest businesslike sense of *will to be well.*

And beside her, a blaze of caged fire.

What have I risked? And what have I wrought?

Myrrh could hear breathing; not the wind-whistle of the undead drawing in air to speak, nor the heavy pant of an embodied demon-warrior. Just the quiet, certain rhythm of mortal flesh and bone, taking what they needed to survive.

And under that rhythm she could sense another. Faster, worried, trembling under the skin to stir a pendant of obsidian; echoed in the pulse of bronze over her own heart.

Mortal flesh and bone. Mortal breath. A mortal heartbeat.

Breaking into a hymn of thanks and joy would startle him. She'd have to sing one later. For now even the joy of a soul rescued was swamped by a shivery flood of *relief.*

I was right.

Nothing was what it seemed in Hell. Nothing could be. The hellish realms had been formed when pride and deception demanded punishment, and while demon lords might destroy pride in all lesser beings, deception remained part of Hell's very fabric of existence.

Myrrh's own deception was as simple as she could manage; she looked like a quiet, lost mortal soul. She wasn't, and hadn't been one for centuries. So it was a lie, and Hell accepted it, and did not try to warp her further.

Aidan's deception had been less clear. Sometimes he'd been flames. Other times a near-ghost. But the spectral form had always been ready to retreat to fire; always just a shade clumsy, as if mortal fingers and joints just weren't *right.*

It'd been possible that the ghost was the deception. That a fire spirit, even a slightly less evil fire demon, had been all that Aidan was. And yet....

What crueler lie could there be, than to force a soul still human to believe he could never hold that form again?

She'd gambled. And prayed. And *hoped*, even as dawn pulled them forth from Hell.

Let my friend be well. Let him win back the truth Hell stole from him!

And when the light faded, it'd been a man who'd fought at her side, flinging fire and insults at their enemies. Not a ghost. Not a lost elemental. A man.

Granted, most likely a not entirely human man. But who was she to throw stones?

Myrrh nodded, not yet opening her eyes. "You came to the hospital with me?"

"Doesn't even *look* and she knows. Why are you so damn freaky?" Warm fingers touched her elbow, above the sticky tape. "Don't mess with that. They said you were dehydrated."

"I have had worse-"

Something jangled.

Myrrh opened her eyes, and registered the clink of steel against her left wrist. Handcuffs. One on her, one clipped around the railing of the hospital bed.

Bemused, she gave Aidan a questioning look. "The policewoman?"

"Detective," Aidan said pointedly, straightening up from where he'd been curled in the uncomfortable-looking chair by her bed. "Detective J. Church, and I don't know what the J's for. Yet. Must be something embarrassing. They've still got her partner in surgery, an' I get the feeling she doesn't want you running off 'til she can *talk* to you." He tapped the handcuff gingerly, as if steel were unbearably warm. "Lady saw what you did to El Urso back there. Don't know why she thinks this would stop you."

"Possibly because she's seen for herself that iron is harmful to entities with a touch of demonic energy," Myrrh acknowledged, gingerly sitting up. Blinking, even though Aidan had thankfully left the lights off; the faint bits of fluorescent light leaking under the hall door stung eyes hungry for mortal starlight. "That malursine was limping even as it charged you. The most likely explanation is some kind of iron-burn." Hmm. An IV dripping fluids into her system; the plastic was sleeker, the bag more crisply labeled, but otherwise it looked close to those she'd last seen twenty-six years ago. Likewise, the quietly beeping monitors and heartbeat-trace displayed on a lighted screen where attending medics could read it; the displays might be thinner and lighter, the electronic digits lit softly from within, yet there was no equipment she could not recognize. How very odd. Medicine had advanced so swiftly in the years before she'd last died. Why had that changed?

Well, there was one thing that definitely hadn't changed. They'd left her in her simple black shift, instead of a flimsy hospital gown. Likely - as usual - the harried attendants had grown frustrated trying to cut fabric that looked like cloth, yet flowed back together like shadows.

Just as well. I hate immodesty. "Take care, my friend," Myrrh advised. "Whatever your heritage, you were in Hell a long time. Those are coated with chrome, so they should not burn you with a touch. But you will be vulnerable to iron for days, if not weeks. It will ache in your bones, and you will not be well. Avoid it, for now."

"Weeks." Aidan's face was almost blank. "You're *wearing* it."

"Very impolite of her," Myrrh agreed. "But none of us are at our best when we brush close to death. Or worse, when that great darkness mantles raven wings over those we care for. Give her some time to realize her partner will recover. Once that fear is lifted, we will see." She shifted her wrist, studying the play of light on metal. "An old-fashioned cop; none of those silly plastic bindings. And not a bad choice for one who may believe in the supernatural. Fay or demonic, iron will bind. Though the infernal is bound because iron is of star-stuff, born in the joy of galaxies; while the fay are bound because it is of human creation, the blood and bones of the earth formed by human will." She lifted a brow. "I've always wondered if that was the reason behind some folklore's confusion of the demonic and the fay; two groups that may seem equally monstrous to humans caught in their schemes, both vulnerable to the same metal, yet for vastly different reasons." Mischief glimmered in her smile. "I wonder if the detective's ever heard of the fay defending themselves from true evil using meteoric iron swords?"

For a moment, Aidan's features were sharp with open curiosity. But he shook it off, giving her a grumpy scowl. "You are *not* distracting me with a geek-fest."

Darn. "My flesh and bone are of the substance of this world again," Myrrh stated, watching amber eyes. Which was true; though the last time she'd let a physicist with a mystical bent ask her questions of how dawnlight could solidify into bone and blood, the resulting equations had made her head hurt. "Iron will not harm me, more than it will any mortal creature." She paused. There was no way to say this gently. But she could choose words that would cut cleanly, without venom. "You have suspected for some time that you are not wholly mortal."

His jaw worked, and his gaze slid aside. "...Told you what I was."

"You told me a convenient name for what you seemed to be," Myrrh corrected him. "In one sense, it was completely truthful; you were a spirit, and you are of fire." Gently. Gently. "But a simple elemental would not long have survived passage back to the mortal realm. Not without fuel to feed its burning. You were able to follow the pattern laid into my anchor, and mold light and air into living flesh and bone. I may not know what you may be, but I know you are no simple fire spirit." She paused, and gave him a quiet smile. "Yet more than that, I know you are my friend. So, since it is likely you do not know the weaknesses of a constructed body... have you eaten? Quenched your thirst? You should."

Amber widened at *constructed*; narrowed again, hurt and wary. "Had some orange juice from the caf. Ham and cheese on whole wheat, man it's been so long... constructed? What are you?"

What am I? hung between them like spun glass, too fragile to touch.

Myrrh sighed. She was a rescuer of lost souls, and a warrior against demons and the dark. The gentler work of saving the living... well, to put it mildly, that was not her best skill.

But I am here. "I have not told this story for a long time," Myrrh stated. "First - are we unwatched?"

"We're *persons of interest*." Aidan leaned back in his chair, almost looking casual. "That demon-bear-thing-"

"*Malursine* is one name for them," Myrrh noted.

"Okay, well - it kind of fell apart into ashes, and you didn't have anybody *else's* blood on you, so Church couldn't charge us with anything. Yet. But she sure as heck wants to." Amber eyes were dark. "Doesn't help that we've got no ID... we saved her neck, you maybe saved her partner's neck, and she wants to throw the book at us?"

"There are reasons they say virtue is its own reward," Myrrh said wryly, carefully pulling her phial out of the shadows. "But sometimes, there are others." She motioned toward him. "Go ahead. Open it."

He flinched away, hands balled into fists in front of his chest.

Myrrh winced. "I suppose I deserve that." She shook her head, a wisp of white straying before her eyes. "I hid what I was from you, out of caution. When first we met, all those years ago, I sensed a familiar aura lingering on yours." Free hand lifted, she traced Roman letters on air; breaking them in strategic places, so they would not invoke a Name.

Sword Aariel blazed between them, gold as dawn.

Light-letters shattered, and Aidan swallowed. "So... you know him."

The enforcer of Demon Lord Yaldabaoth's court? Oh yes. "I've escaped him," Myrrh said precisely. "But then, I have never been in a position to directly threaten his lord. And so he has never sought me with all the power that is his to command. When I encountered you, I wondered if he'd changed his tactics. So I did not tell you everything." She paused, and flicked up pale brows in deliberate humor. "Mind, I wouldn't have told you everything if you were the purest of human souls. Those such as I have always been rare, and we have limits. At full strength, yes; I can face a demon lord and hope to survive. If the fight is swift. Otherwise... I endured in Hell by stealth, not strength. Willing or not, you had some connection to a demonic court. So I remained silent."

"It wasn't *willing*." Another flinch, and a shudder. "Trust me."

"I do," Myrrh said calmly. Lowered her hand, and tilted the phial sideways so he could see the tiny hieroglyphs etched the length of silvery glass. "Do you read Egyptian?"

Amber eyes narrowed at her. "You have got to be kidding me."

Myrrh inclined her head, and turned the phial to a flowing

cursive script. "Syriac, then."

"What makes you think I know...."

Myrrh waited, as fiery eyes squinted, scanning from right to left.

He shall gather the lambs with his arm, and carry them in his bosom, and shall gently lead those that are with young.

"That court has often faced mortal warriors from the Biblical East," she stated, as his gaze focused on her once more. "I would have been more surprised if you did *not* know one of those scripts."

Aidan crossed his arms. "Thought most sorcerers went for Greek and Latin."

"Many modern ones do," Myrrh nodded. "Which makes those who know more ancient tongues much, *much* more dangerous."

His face was neutral, but shadows gathered to darken his features. "Doesn't look like anything I thought I'd see on a sorcerer's soul-jar."

"And that would be because I," Myrrh said wryly, "am not a sorcerer."

Aidan eyed her, face still shadowed. "But that is a soul-jar."

"It is a phial meant to harbor souls," Myrrh said, each word precise. "There is no way to draw power from any spirit held within."

Were he a cat, she would have seen his ears twitch. "Who makes a jar like that?"

"Someone who intends to open it." She held it out. "You may, if you wish."

He didn't move. "You said to stand back."

"Below, you were a soul unbounded by flesh. You were in danger," Myrrh agreed. "Here, you are not. It is safe."

"You're the only one." Amber searched gray. "The only thing down there that didn't lie to me. Why?"

"Because I am a thief, not a liar," Myrrh answered. "I am a thief of souls. It is my calling and my duty; to steal souls from the darkness, and let them free to seek the light. If they choose." She winced, at old memories. "Not all do. Despair, the belief that there is one sin, one taint, so dreadful that it cannot be forgiven if the soul truly repents... some cling to that illusion, and are lost." She took a deep breath. "But those are few. Most... well. You will see."

Aidan bit his lip. And thumbed the stopper off the phial, fast as ripping off a scab.

Stars poured out like a silent river; white and blue and all the colors of hope. The tiny lights flickered, small as motes of dust in a sunbeam, filling the room with a tide of silent light, a yearning for elsewhere, for home....

Wondering, Aidan reached out to a flicker of gold.

Oh no!

She was fast enough to grip his hand. Just barely.

Night and running and afraid, *Derek don't do this, Derek I love you, you're not a monster, Derek* no-!

Rending. Gurgling sounds of feeding, hearing her own flesh slip down the monster's throat, so cold....

Cold and dark. Not real. Wandering. Not real! Things *laughing in the darkness, telling her she had nowhere to go. Forsaken. Tainted. Be a monster soon, just wait.*

No. No! Run again. Help, someone help, the fiery monster was eating her from the inside, someone help-!

Hard hands. Pain. Words - but the Beast was eating her alive, she couldn't understand, had to get away from pain and fire-

"Rest in peace."

Pain... fading. Quiet. Peaceful.

...An open door?

Light. So beautiful... is it okay? I was so scared....

"It's all right." Eyes wet, Myrrh pulled both their hands away from that one light. "Thy way is in the sea, and thy path is in the great waters, and thy footsteps are not known. Go where you will. Go in peace."

For a moment there were no walls, no room, no hospital. Only the light of dawn, bright as the first morning.

Reality faded back, mundane and ordinary. Rough cotton. Beeping monitors. And a sobbing demon-blooded man on her shoulder, shaking in grief and memory.

Reaching up as much as she could with the chain, Myrrh stroked wild red hair. "It's better not to touch them. I'm sorry I didn't warn you. The pain of a soul betrayed, of love rent asunder - there are some things no spirit still in flesh is meant to bear. Aidan,

I'm sorry...."

He wiped away salt water. Some of it steamed. "She loved him."

"Yes," Myrrh said softly.

His fingers tightened on her arm. "She loved him and he *ate her*."

"Lycanthropy is a curse," Myrrh said levelly. *I wish I could be gentle. I wish the world were kinder.* "The demon-tainted bite spreads horror; and if it cannot be cured, there is only one mercy."

"You... would do that?" He drew back, amber gaze searching hers.

"I have stolen souls from Hell for almost eighteen hundred years," Myrrh stated, hand already missing the warmth of red hair. A solid, human touch. Lord, but she had missed that mortal comfort. "I have touched them, as you have touched. I have seen what evil does; human, and other." She nodded slowly. "If a werewolf will not be cured, if he will not fight the curse, and take the measures necessary to defend innocent souls from the demonic beast within - yes. I will kill him. I have before, and I will again. In Hell, I am a thief. Here - I do what I can, to prevent souls from needing rescue."

Aidan looked at her. At mundane shadows where there had been endless light. "Would you do that for me?"

Myrrh let her eyes half-close, seeing that aura of fire and guilt and power. "I do not think I will have to." She tapped pale skin; here a dusting of red hairs, there a freckle, and all as real as flesh and blood could be. And yet - not. "You followed my spirit, and I followed my anchor. When the net of dawn clothed me in mortal flesh once more, your magic did the same. As I hoped it would." She gripped his arm, firm and confident. Yes; there was the strength of dawn and sunlight. Though there was fire laced through it, and the darkness that cradled countless stars. "I have told you, limits can be the strongest armor. This body is as a raiment you have drawn over your soul. A werewolf's curse cannot pierce it to taint you, any more than it could me."

"A body's not clothes!"

"You asked what I am. I will tell you." She held his gaze, fierce as an eagle. "Long ago, before bishops gathered at Nicaea, or Arius was declared a heretic, there were many sects, and many teachers. And there was darkness, as there is today, and humans who swore to fight that darkness." Myrrh paused. "There was then, as I imagine there may well be now, much debate over the proper way to fight evil without falling to it. There were those who believed all with the talent for magic should be sought out, and welcomed into the ranks of the faithful-"

"Say *what?*"

Poor soul. This wasn't something modern folk spoke of much. If ever. "Have you heard the tales of the Apostles' battle with Simon Magus, or the prophets praying against the priests of Ba'al?"

"Um." Amber eyes were just a little wild. "No?"

"I'll have to find you a good translation." Myrrh reached behind her to shuffle around the pillow; hard enough to sit up and face him with her arm chained, and she meant to have *words* with the good detective about that. Never chain a danger with bonds that might not hold. Better, far better, to leave uncertain bonds undone, and rely on courtesy, when you met one who might not be an enemy.

Ah well. She'd teach the detective manners another day. For now, she had a poor lost demon-born to calm. "Well. To sum up many tales simply - in the early church, magic and miracles were much better known than today. And some of us were very, very good at them. So of course we wished to use our strengths in the service of others. Yet the leaders of other congregations had other opinions. Some felt that *render unto Caesar what is Caesar's* should refer to the legionnaire's steel, not only taxes, and that we should rely only on those converts skilled in arms to defend the flocks of the faithful. Others believed that, as Jesus urged his followers to sell their cloaks and buy a sword, Hunters should be trained within the Church itself. And yet others, that faith was the only shield against darkness, and the followers of Christ should simply believe, and do good works, and purify their souls."

"Oh, yeah," Aidan almost snarled. "'Cause having a pure loving soul works so *well* when there's a werewolf chasing you down to feed the full-moon munchies."

"You see one of the sides of the argument that has made it so bitter," Myrrh said wryly. "It was quite the acrimonious debate, then and now. Does evil strike only those who have already sinned, and so are not worthy of God's grace and the protection of His followers? Or are the acts of evil like a skybolt, or an ocean storm; tempests sweeping up the sinning and the innocent alike, and forces to be shielded away by any lawful means?"

He let go, putting some space between them. "I'm guessing you think it hits everybody."

"What I think," Myrrh said, very deliberately, "is that of all beings conceived and born in this world, only two are believed to have been without sin." She held up one finger. "Mary, mother of God, known to many as Virgin." A second. "And her Son, begotten of God. *Two*, Aidan. Of all those born with the blood of man - only two."

Aidan blinked. Some of the tightness in his shoulders eased.

"So in short, yes," Myrrh went on, as if she hadn't noticed. "I do not think there are any souls walking in flesh so saintly, that evil would pass them by." And now would come the tricky part. "Am I correct that you are not a specialist in theology?"

Aidan raised a red brow at her.

"I will skip the technicalities," Myrrh inclined her head. "When I still walked in my first life, the temples of Isis were yet open, and harbored priestesses with mighty magics. They spoke to other magic-workers; Christian, and not, from the Roman Empire to lands beyond, even to Hyperborea and China. And so the Christians who debated with the priestesses over what truly led to Heaven learned things, and thought things, that most churches of today would find... very odd."

Aidan looked at her. Looked at the phial. Cast a glance at the room around them; so utterly different from Hell. "No kidding."

She ducked her head, acknowledging the hit. There was such a thing as being *too* concise. "Those who followed my path - the hell-raiders' path - believed that as we were all created by God in the image of the Elohim, so we all contain a spark of the Divine, that may be nurtured within us." This was hard. It had been so long since she'd explained to one who did not *know*. "We believe that we, human beings, have the power to evoke miracles and wonders, by the grace of God. And if we have such power, and God has made us stewards over His creation, then to turn away from the monsters that threaten it is an act of willful blindness to the truth. We are called to follow in the footsteps of God - and Jesus did *not* turn away the poor, the oppressed, the demon-haunted souls who sought His shelter and rescue. He strove against evil. He cast it *out*. He healed, and warded, and drove away evil from even the most wretched among us. How can we strive to do less? *For as you have done to the least of these, so you have done unto me."*

Aidan went a little paler. "...I need to sit down."

"You are sitting down," Myrrh murmured.

"Lucky me." Aidan rubbed his forehead with the heel of his hand. "You... holy...." His jaw worked, and he shook his head. "You... your guys are trying to be *angels?*"

"There are reasons we've been called heretics," Myrrh acknowledged. "The kindest of those whose teachings form the Church as it became call us thieves, who would steal the glory of God and His angels." She smirked. "They are not often happy when we remind them that our Lord was crucified with thieves, and said one would be with him in paradise." She shrugged. "Well, then. If we were thieves, then we would *be* thieves, and follow where our Lord himself had led. We would descend into the depths, where He had shattered the Gates, and strive against the darkness for all those trapped within it. If demons and dark powers would steal innocent souls - then by our Lord and all the heavenly hosts, we would steal them *back.*"

Aidan's mouth opened and closed, like a carp nibbling at bubbles. "You're telling me you're a *thief*, on a *mission from God."*

"Yes." Myrrh had to grin. "Exactly."

"...We totally need sunglasses."

"And fedoras," Myrrh agreed. "It's been some years since I last wore a fedora." She winked at him, thinking of men in dark suits, and an orphanage, with nuns watching over children who grew to dance on the line between light and darkness. "I wonder if we can still rent that movie?"

The look on his face when he realized she knew what a movie was - much less *that* movie - could have made an archangel laugh.

And I've never been one of those. Hanging onto her bemused friend, Myrrh let her laughter bubble out like water.

Healing water. My God, we were so long down there in the dark. Where was my anchor? How did it stay unlooked-for so long by my brothers and sisters in faith? What happened?

And how can I tell Aidan how brave he was, just to dare to be a friend?

Chapter Four

Laughter. Church could hear it echoing all the way out in the hall; bright and rich, but with a wincing undertone every cop knew.

We came out of this one alive. We might not have been that lucky.

Still, it was laughter. And just because she knew half of it had to be pure, unadulterated stress, didn't mean the good Dr. McAliffe did. Which meant she could get a second opinion. "They don't sound like dangerous sorcerers to me."

Clanking with charms clipped to the inside of his white coat, the young doctor grimaced. "Detective, may I remind you that woman is wearing a *shadow-shift*. Even if you pay to have that magically charged, it's not something your average human can keep in one piece." He frowned. "Though I've never seen one designed for modesty before."

"She's locked up with *steel handcuffs*," Church said impatiently. "She's not doing anything magical until they're off."

The doctor swallowed. "Then why," he said through gritted teeth, "does every alternative healer on the grounds think something *happened* over here?"

Good question. Not that she was going to say that. People might say healing was all good, but given what she'd picked up from Coral and a few other people she'd jailed, anyone who could heal could mojo up some kind of bad-luck curse, and dealing with this mess was already going to be tough enough. *BOLOs out on Rajas and Ginger, got a phone that isn't crunched, got the paramedics' pics uploaded to my account; is there anything else I can get done here?* "Is Tom going to be okay?"

"Barring unforeseen complications, yes," Dr. McAliffe nodded. "The stabs were deep, but they appear to have missed the major organs. He lost a lot of blood, but with rest he should be fine. If it weren't for the scabs in his hair, I would never have believed he'd suffered a head wound. Give him a day, and he can probably go home. To *rest*," he emphasized. "He can enjoy shuffling paperwork for a while, and let those oh, *trifling* deep puncture wounds knit back up. As I'd suggest *you* do, Detective Church. If I had any hopes that you might listen."

Church grimaced, reminded all over again of the throbbing along her ribs that told of stitches. The local anesthetic was keeping it to a dull roar, but she was going to be sore for a good long while. Showers were going to be *irritating*. The less said about the aches and fever she was going to have from the tetanus shot, the better. And with all that she'd rather face a dozen more shots than Annabel's panicked face. When was the woman going to realize she'd married a cop? Coming home safe at the end of the day wasn't a promise any of them could make. "I don't like hospitals."

"I never would have guessed."

Okay, she needed a knife to cut the sarcasm around here. "You coming in with me or not?"

"Medical ethics say I have to," McAliffe grumped. "But if you have any common sense, Detective, you'll find a way to ensure these two are not part of your caseload. And encourage them to look for work in another city. Preferably on the West Coast. What's another earthquake or two out there?"

About to open the door, Church stopped, hand sweating on the handle. *"Earthquake?"*

"I have no idea." And the doctor looked even less happy about that than she felt, touching the outline of a miniature horseshoe showing through above his coat pocket. "But if I believe your account, Detective, approximately five hours ago your partner had a depressed brain fracture. Now... he doesn't. He doesn't even have a trace of a concussion." McAliffe shuddered. "I've worked with some... nonstandard religious folk with stronger than normal healing abilities. They could have treated him. They could, possibly, have saved his life, if they worked from the moment of injury until now. They could *not* have healed him in a moment. It's just... not *possible*."

Okay, now Church was starting to worry. "It can't be that bad, Doc. The handcuffs are holding her."

"Are they?" the doctor muttered. "Or is she just not interested in breaking them, yet?"

"Somebody needs to cheer up." She bumped a fist against his

shoulder, and tried not to snicker at his wince. "Come on. You get to be the good guy, while I jab at them. Should be a nice change, right?"

Not waiting for his answer, she yanked open the door.

"-Trenchcoats!" The redhead who'd admitted no name other than *Aidan* was gesticulating wildly as he sat in the visitor's chair, grinning at the white-haired woman sitting up in bed. "I've *always* wanted to wear a trenchcoat-"

Church did a double-take, flipping on the overhead lights. "You *are* wearing a trenchcoat."

....Oops. She hadn't meant to say that out loud. But seriously. She'd met sorcerers. They were a lot more on the ball than to forget what they were wearing.

Damn, he really is here. Almost hoped I was hearing some kind of ventriloquism charm. Who sits in the dark to talk? And didn't I tell Security to keep an eye on this guy? Evil-eye beads on your glasses-strap don't stop everything. Heck, they don't stop most things.

"Detective Church." The redhead slouched back in his seat, nonchalant as a poker player with half the aces even as he squinted like a bat out of its cave. "So when can we blow this pop stand?"

"How about after you give me some answers?" Taking out her notebook, Church kept her face cold, unsmiling. Tom looked okay *for now*. But throwing around buckets of magic always had a price, and she'd be damned if she let this woman out of nowhere take it out of her partner's hide. "For one thing, what's your real names?"

A shadow seemed to drop over amber eyes. "Aidan works for me."

...She was not going to shiver at how that gaze was like staring into a volcano. She was a cop. She made perps shiver. "That how you want to play it? Fine." Church eyed the white-haired woman. "What about you?"

"Myrrh is my name." She inclined her head, pale hair like a fall of snow. "I am pleased to meet you under better circumstances. Is your partner well?"

"That's none of your business." Pen working, Church stared at the smaller woman, trying to figure out what was just... *off*, about her. Outside of the white hair that belonged on someone at least fifty years older, and the air of general calm you didn't see outside of a nurse in the middle of a triage area.

It's her face. It's like... one of those old Roman paintings, maybe? Or something out of Byzantine mosaics. The ones with the big eyes, that just don't look like a regular person ought to look....

But Church worked homicides, and she'd seen prettier faces try and talk their way out of murder. "I need your full name," she said coldly. "I'm running your prints right now, so let's cut the bull, shall we?"

Huh. Aidan was trying to hide a flinch. Myrrh didn't turn a hair.

"If you need legal documentation, Detective, I fear I have none on me," the woman said, matter of fact. "Aidan is a refugee fleeing religious persecution, and it was a near thing to escape that place in time. He has no documents, he is not using his legal name, and I would be very cautious in alerting any authorities if you should find a match. Those who held him captive have a great deal of power, and I have not yet traced the full extent of their net. But when I do," her voice was hammered steel, "they shall be prosecuted to the full extent of the law."

Aidan looked like he'd been hit with a two-by-four.

Church didn't feel much better. "What?" she said flatly. Because seriously, what? *Religious persecution?* Who ran from that in America? Granted, there were members of some so-called religions that couldn't cross the border without a full pat-down and a face-full of Cap-Silver, but as far as Church was concerned, anyone who joined a cannibalistic African were-leopard cult was just *asking* for it.

Still, for a moment, she had to wonder. What she'd seen in the ambulance....

It'd been a tough call, but she knew what Tom would have wanted: *don't let the witnesses get away.*

Besides, the paramedics didn't need her tripping over them while they tried to keep Tom stable. So her partner had gotten an ambulance to himself. She'd ridden in with the cranky redhead and the impossible woman who'd keeled over from what the ambulance jocks had called dehydration.

Only it wasn't just the girl the paramedics had thought was in trouble, because once Benson had Myrrh hooked up to an IV he'd been thumping on Aidan's shoulder with a juice-pack of something that had sliced oranges on the front. And even though they'd been bouncing around as the guy up front ran the red lights, Church couldn't shake the image of how Aidan had... fumbled it.

Oh, he'd pried the straw off with his fingernails, and only needed three tries to poke a hole in the right spot. But the look on his face - it didn't seem real.

I used to know how to do this, that almost-masked panic had said. *Didn't I?*

Or maybe it was just orange wasn't his usual flavor, because the guy had choked on it. And coughed, and stared at the packet, like it'd morphed into a rabid hamster while he wasn't looking.

Then he'd deliberately downed the lot one slurp at a time, like a rookie popping away at his first man-shaped target.

With about the same level of the shakes, Church recalled now. *What kind of guy gets freaked out by fruit juice?*

Though maybe she was just kidding herself. She'd seen flinches like that before. In a city the size of Intrepid, there was no Homicide Division. Just detectives. They didn't just work dead bodies, they got the *nasty* stuff; from wanna-be mobsters to incest to any case that threatened to raise a political stink. And some of the nastiest stuff she'd ever had to deal with, outside of vampires, was human trafficking.

Oh yeah. I just love my fellow man.

Almost two centuries after the Civil War, and slavery was still alive and well and as hideous as ever. It wasn't legal, any more than cocaine. But for some slime that dose of power over another human being, the power to beat, to rape, to make sure your victim only saw the sun if you let them....

For some so-called human beings, that power was a more toxic high than any drug. She'd caught bastards like that. She'd put them away. And she'd never shot any of them when she could make an arrest instead.

Because I'm one of the good guys. Damn it.

Sometimes she'd tried to help the victims. There wasn't much she could do; a detective had to be professional, or risk tainting the case. But at least she could listen.

Aidan was a *guy*. And not a small guy, either, even if he was a little on the thin side. A guy who could throw fire with his *bare hands*.

And yet, the way he'd flinched, like he'd never expected to taste orange juice again - it made her gut twist into acid knots.

Somebody had him. And they had him for a long, long time.

And now they *didn't* have him. Which implied she might want to put word out on the wire to ask people if there were any suspicious arson-related deaths in the area. Anybody who'd managed to hold a fire-throwing sorcerer probably wouldn't have let him go willingly.

And if they're not dead - what kind of trouble do we have coming our way, if they find him?

Still, it was his partner she had to keep the pressure on. Church narrowed blue eyes at the woman. "Are you saying you're a *cop?*"

"Ah, no. I retrieve wanted criminals." Propped against white pillows, Myrrh looked innocent as a lamb. "You would say, a bounty hunter."

If she was a bail bondsman, she was the smallest one Church had ever seen. Though magic might go a long way toward making up for that. "You're a runner?"

Gray eyes warmed. "I find those who have eluded their proper judgment, yes. And arrange for them to be brought before a higher court."

Aidan coughed. But he was saying absolutely nothing.

She's playing me. I don't know how, but she is. And he knows it.

Nobody did that to her.

"Fine, Ms. No-ID," Church bit out, flipping to a fresh page. *Time. Date.* "If you're a bounty hunter in North Carolina, you'd damn well better have a license. What's your name?"

"My ID, if I had it, would say Myrrh Shafat," the gray-eyed woman stated, casually as if the handcuffs were just unwanted jewelry. "North Carolina? Hmm. I wasn't sure, we were in quite the hurry... what city?"

"Intrepid," Dr. McAliffe said before Church could stomp on his foot.

Aidan stiffened. Myrrh's eyes narrowed; relaxed again, curious.

Why?

"You're in Sacred Heart Hospital," the doctor went on, shifting uneasily in place. "And if you're feeling unwell, Ms. - Shafat? I'm sure Detective Church could continue this at another time. You were suffering from severe dehydration when the officers brought you in this morning. Along with possible other unknown side effects of large-scale spellcasting. You need rest."

"What I need," Myrrh rattled the handcuffs, "is to be free of such rude bondage. It is unkind to my charge, who was unlawfully restrained for many years. Aidan is a friend, and there is no need to cause him pain when we have done nothing wrong."

"You landed in the middle of a *multiple homicide*," Church ground out.

"So it seems," Myrrh nodded. "You're welcome."

Aidan stifled a snicker behind his hand.

Okay, so Church could feel the red flush lighting her face. Still didn't give him an excuse. "You think this is funny? My partner's still in surgery. He almost died. You know something about what Rajas Feniger was up to in that graveyard, and you're going to tell me. *Now*."

Aidan gave Church a cool look. "Who the heck is Rajas Feniger?"

"You're kidding, right?" Church glanced between them, giving up on trying to read anything from the runner. Her fire-throwing companion looked like a better bet. Anybody who said *fleeing persecution* when they had to mean *running like hell from the bad guys* was wrapped up in their own smug verbal cleverness; could take hours in Interrogation to crack Myrrh's story with careful notes. Aidan looked a lot more straightforward. "There is no way you're going to make me believe a pair of *sorcerers* landed on the local black-market potion dealer by accident."

McAliffe groaned. Aidan blanched.

Ha! Score!

Myrrh sat up straight, gray eyes cold as storm. "Is that what you think we are? For if so, then this," she jangled the cuffs again, harsh and clanging, "is very rude indeed, for innocent victims who have done nothing save aid you." Gray narrowed. "I have told you my friend is fleeing, and in danger of his life. He is a stranger in this land, and he needs help to remain free and safe. I intend to deliver him to that safety, and I have little time to waste. We do not know this Rajas Feniger, we have not dealt with him, we ended up on top of your difficulty by sheer fortuitous coincidence-"

Fortuitous? Church had to make an effort to keep the incredulous look off her face as she wrote that down. Where the hell was this woman from?

"-If you wish to know more of him, we cannot help you. Keys, please. Now."

Church caught her hand reaching for her pocket, and stopped it. Damn. She knew the tricks vamps used for mind-whammy; Myrrh hadn't used any of them. Just her tone, like good captains and parish priests: *this needs to be done. Now.*

I don't think so. "You're going nowhere-"

"Let's not be hasty, Detective," Dr. McAliffe jumped in, the sweat on his face a clue that he had visions of a burning hospital dancing in his head. "If Ms. Shafat and Mr... Aidan have committed no crimes, then surely, there's no reason for handcuffs." He glanced at Myrrh, and cleared his throat. "On the other hand, Ms. Shafat, you did come in as a Jane Doe. Currently we have no doctor or proof of insurance for you - is something wrong?"

"No, no," Myrrh chuckled. "I am sorry, I don't mean to offend. But the idea that *any* insurance company would come near me with a ten-foot pole...." She snickered, but shook her head. "No, Doctor, I fear you'll have to accept payment in cash, once I have access to a bank. I am quite uninsurable. Hazards of the job."

"Too many acts of God, huh?" Aidan's eyes were still wary, but there was a grin hiding in the corners of his mouth. Church didn't trust it one bit.

"Oh, indeed." Myrrh took a deep breath, face sober as stone. "You have no right to hold me. Therefore...." She shook the handcuffs, a third time.

With a tiny *clink*, steel fell open and away.

...You can't make magic work on steel.

Everyone knew that. Everyone counted on it. Steel, cold iron, call it what you want - anything ferrous stopped magic, cold.

Out of the corner of her eye, Church saw McAliffe back up and hit the wall.

"I believe the term is, *against medical advice*." Myrrh reached for the IV.

"Hey, come on, wait!" Aidan protested.

"I will not." She cast him a faint smile. "I am, truly, much tougher than I look, my friend. And you are in danger. And I have had enough." Deft fingers tugged out the needle, and applied pressure. "If you wish to find us, Detective, I suggest you call on Father O'Malley of the Church of Our Lady. I intend to call on him, soon." Gray eyes cast her a look askance. "You *do* know where to find that sanctuary, do you not? It is small, but in some ways, it is a more fierce defender of the faith than even the Basilica."

Sure she did, every cop on the force who dealt with the weird knew Father O'Malley. Same as they knew Rabbi Cohen, or Sister Penn; or Old Man Conseen over toward Pisgah National Forest, for when whatever had crawled out of the shadows seemed like it might be a spook from local nights.

But of all of them, Church trusted O'Malley the most. Father Gray O'Malley didn't try to drag her into a confession booth, point her toward eligible bachelors, or frown at her for carrying a gun. The guy knew people, and he knew what he could and couldn't do. Which was why he *wasn't* head priest at Our Lady, anymore. The guy was somewhere on the wrong side of eighty, even if he was fit as some cops half his age, and keeping up blessings on Intrepid's public servants had kind of become his full-time retired job. A job they needed him for, and Church had to keep herself from reaching for her gun. "What the heck's a sorcerer want with a good Father?"

"...You think I would harm him." Standing, Myrrh looked incredulous, then sad. "I never would. Feel free to call him, and tell him I am on my way."

"Yeah? Tell him who?" Church glanced down as Myrrh touched the floor, and had to stop herself from staring. Bare feet, hard-soled, with flecks of leaf mold still caught along her toenails. So not only did she show up out of nowhere and fight demons, she did it *barefoot*.

Maybe I shouldn't bother asking for names. Just check the asylums for who's missing.

Gray eyes were distant, with a bittersweet humor. "Why, I am his favorite heretic."

Chapter Five

She called me a sorcerer. A cop *called me a-*

Aidan shuddered, trying not to think about it as Myrrh politely bulldozed her way through grumpy nurses, would-be paper shufflers, deadpan security, and a bemused gift shop owner who'd scanned a weird red light gun across a pair of sandals and handed them over with barely a blink. And one extremely ticked off detective.

Well, fine. Church could stay ticked off for all he cared. The last time he'd trusted an Intrepid city cop, the bastard had turned out to be working for... somebody whose name he was *not going to think here*. Because that man was dead. Had to be. Or he'd never have made it out of Hell in one piece.

Wonder how long the cop lasted, after that night.

It'd only been twenty-five years. It was possible that cop was still alive.

Hope not. I really, really hope not. Aariel would want me to do something about that....

And even out of Hell he was still lost, because *doing something* sounded like an excellent idea. After so long in Yaldabaoth's court, he'd seen thousands of ways fire could be used to *deal with* an unlucky being, from the slow burn that might take weeks to kill, to a quick needle of flames that would sear through a heart while barely singeing a strip of chest hair.

Aariel... at least he always made it quick.

As he would now, if he were in this mess. The cop was an *enemy*, after all. Demon Lord Yaldabaoth might indulge in torturing captured enemies. Sword Aariel didn't have the time. There were too many enemies.

Twenty-five years, Aidan told himself. *And that cop was human, not a demon. He'd be - what, sixty-odd? At least? Not exactly major enemy material anymore.*

So no burning. Slow, quick, or otherwise. Not that Aidan planned to trust the guy as far as Myrrh could throw him, if a twenty-five-years-older crooked cop happened to show up. He'd made that mistake *once*. And that had led to-

He didn't want to think about that, either. But it was hard not to, feeling a heart beat in a solid chest again; remembering the hot pain of a black knife and the copper stink of draining blood....

He could smell it. Even through the disinfectants. He could *smell* blood.

Hands gripped his arm, pulling him onward. "You're no Leviathan; I can't pull you out with a hook. Just a little farther, I promise."

He trusted that voice. More than he trusted himself, right now. But it still made him shudder, thinking of that empty phial hidden in her shadows.

All these years, I've been trusting somebody who could have sucked me down like a whirlpool....

No. Myrrh wasn't *like* - the one he wouldn't think about. He'd seen her fight, and he'd seen her kill. If something had to die, she put it down quick and clean.

She let those souls go. *Him... I don't think he could have done it. Ever.*

It still hurt.

Doors. Sunlight; the sun still high, but creeping toward mountain ridges he hadn't seen in decades. Air swirling with scents of fir, turning leaves, and a hint of tickling smoke, like someone had stood out here with a cigarette to worry.

Normal. Earth.

Or what he remembered normal was like. He didn't *trust* his memory. Not after a quarter-century in Hell.

Nobody gets out alive.

They'd been facing down imminent death, and Myrrh had asked him to *believe*, and - Aidan still wasn't sure what had happened next.

It was... bright.

The harder he tried to remember, the more it slipped through his fingers. Hours? An instant? He didn't *know*.

Fighting a demon in a graveyard had almost been a relief. Demons he knew.

Flammable demon. Hee.

Cops and paramedics and dead bodies; *those* were strange.

Getting hauled off to where people *wanted* to patch him up, getting left alone in a room and following his nose and his gurgling stomach to the hospital cafeteria - that had been even stranger.

Walking in to where the food was had taken more nerves than running from the Hunt. There were people in there. *Scary* people. No bleeding eyes, disemboweled guts, or foreign objects of blackened metal and glass inserted in obscene ways. Just clothed, grumpy, elated, depressed, laughing people, in a bewildering variety of clothes, and ages, and... *something*, shining through the cage of flesh and bone....

"This body is as a raiment."

Souls. He was seeing souls.

Which should have been seriously creepy. Heck, it *was* creepy. Only he'd been seeing souls for decades. There wasn't anything else down in Hell *to* see.

And now there is. Aidan tried to take a calming breath. *Guess it's just as well I didn't think about that sneaking into the caf.*

All he'd known then was that he had to get in and out without showing a flicker of fear. Because there were people in there. *Lots* of people. And big groups of anything was *bad*.

Only nothing bad had happened. And that was *worse*. He kept expecting to turn the next corner and have some massive illusion fall apart on him, with demon lords laughing at how the little half-breed had fallen for it *again*.

I know illusions. I've broken them.

He willed his free hand to rise toward his throat; deliberately, swiftly, forcing every flex of muscle and bone to crash through his mind like a raging torrent. Illusions had no problems painting sense-pictures of unconscious motions, but they had a heck of a harder time fooling your head with deliberate action-

Fingers tangled in braided white.

...This is real.

Myrrh was with him; he could feel that, feel *her*, in the subtle lumps of the silvery plait. Spirit-hair was solid, in a way almost nothing in Hell had been, singing with a quiet *I am* not even the blackest night could deny.

Myrrh was an enchantress. She could reach out her hands and *demand* the truth of things. There wasn't a demon alive who could make an illusion Myrrh couldn't break.

Which meant Earth was real. Intrepid was real. Myrrh's hands on his arms - *real.*

He wanted to cry. He wanted to scream.

Myrrh half-dragged him away from the hospital exit, toward the sunniest patch of red-brick wall. "Aidan. I'm here. Your eyes see truly. Breathe."

Good thing his body seemed to remember how to do that. If it was his body. He didn't see how it could be, given... things Aariel had showed him. And maybe he didn't want to think about that too hard.

Still. Breathing. And seeing what's real.

Which was two big problems solved. Too bad there was a bigger one stomping on his heart with jackboots. "Church... she called me... called us...."

"I know. And I am sorry I could not correct her. But I do not know what she thinks a sorcerer *is*, if she did not identify whoever called that demon as one." Gray eyes were looking up to meet his, a worried wintery counterpoint to the warmth against his shoulders. "I was not expecting this."

"This, what?" Aidan waved hands at himself, the impossible black trenchcoat, the whole wide world. "Being alive again? Jumping into the middle of demons on earth? Coming *that* close to a murder charge, and if she finds out who I am I'm gonna be *worse* than locked up-"

Paper crinkled. "I think we can do without the business section," Myrrh said briskly. "Aidan? Burn this."

Say what?

But it was paper and not a person, and damn it, he was angry and *cold* and-

Paper crackled into licking flames in his hands, pages curling away like black silk.

...Oh. That felt - better. Like a cup of coffee on a cold morning, spreading warmth into his bones.

I'm eating *the fire.*

I'm not human.

Myrrh caught him before he could run. "There is no shame in having elemental power," she said steadily. "Though it can be inconvenient. Those of water weaken away from sea or rivers; those of earth will perish in a flood. You need to burn, in much the same way as your mortal form needs food. Those with your heritage are often the most persecuted by ordinary men, for fire is so very perilous. But flame alone does not make you evil. Only dangerous." She gave him a slight nod. "And I have no intention of leaving you to make your own way among strangers until you have mastered that danger. Be at peace."

"At peace? How can I be any kind of peaceful when-" He saw the rest of the paper tucked under her arm. The date. The *year*. "Oh, god."

Myrrh braced herself, and held him up as his head swam. "I know. It's been a long time. Much will have changed, and much will have been lost of the world we knew. Yet we must go on." A breath, and a sigh. "I don't think I've ever been down there that long. I only hope the bank I last used in this city is still open. It will be very inconvenient, getting to my safe-deposit box, if it is not."

"You've got a bank box?" He wasn't going to think about the date. He wasn't going to think about... twenty-five *years*. Damn. He'd been down in Hell almost longer than he'd been alive.

I've been in Hell.

I'm not, now.

This was real. This was Earth, this was *safe....*

No. Not safe, Aidan reminded himself, looking around at asphalt, buildings that didn't bleed, people walking from place to place of their own will without whips or chains or screaming. *Demongate. Sorcerer messing with evil energies. General badness.*

But still, Earth. Where you were more likely to get struck by lightning than munched by a hellhound-

Heart hammering, he flicked a glance up at the sky. October-clear and blue, sun shining down through cool air without a trace of clouds to be seen.

Not that that means anything. Not with where we're going. "You said you were heading to a church."

Though it wasn't just *a church*. Our Lady's. Father O'Malley. He was in such deep, deep... trouble.

"I did, and I will," Myrrh said frankly, brushing a hand over her dark shift. For a moment it was the shadow-cloak he'd known in Hell; then it shifted, gaining light and substance from the sunlight, until she seemed dressed in casual shadow-blue pants and shirt under a sober gray coat. "But if a police detective called me a sorcerer, in front of a doctor who did not know enough to contradict her - and yet that doctor still knows of magic - then something is amiss in the world, and I want to be better armed." She smiled. "Besides. If my box is intact, we should be able to gain documents for you, and so keep you out of Detective Church's clutches."

Aidan blinked, trying to follow all that. "You've got fake papers?"

"*Fake* is such an offensive word. Let us say, I have something that should serve," Myrrh nodded. "Until we can better clarify your situation."

"And you've got stockpiled weapons. Why'm I not surprised?" Aidan shifted his shoulders, trying to tell panic to knock it off already. "What happened to that sword? I didn't see Church grab it-" A tickle of *wait a minute* hit, as he poked that scattershot of fight-memories again. "Where'd you even get it? No way would a cultist bring something like *that* to a little summoning party!"

"That weapon only exists when I call it," Myrrh said practically. "It's very strong, but it is also very... hmm. *Bright*, might be the best word. It's good to carry mortal weapons as well, especially if you must deal with human minions, and not just creatures of darkness." She frowned. "The detective did not *feel* like a minion."

...Why did he suddenly have the vision of Church lugging a coffin and going *yes, master*?

"But she didn't know what most mortal human Hunters should have known, either," Myrrh went on. "And how can a doctor know I carry magic, and yet not see how my healing of her partner was not at all a sorcerer's work? Something is wrong."

Wrong. Like breathing air after being locked in eternal darkness. Like a date so far away from the last he'd seen, he kept expecting to wake up and be told it was all a bad dream. Like a paper that-

Oh, man.

"Wrong." Aidan took the folded paper from her, disbelieving fingers trailing over today's headlines. "Yeah. You could say that."

JAL installing Shinto streamers in Airbus carriers.

Orthodox churches take a stand; refuse to install chairs despite ADA.

Meltdowns hobble NSA Data Center; voodoo effigy discovered.

Search for missing girl enters third week; local vampire coven pleads innocence.

"Angels and ministers of grace, defend us," Myrrh breathed.

"Amen to that," Aidan muttered. "So where's that bank?" Weapons were sounding like a better idea all the time.

"...I think we'd better find a phone book," Myrrh said numbly; reaching out to touch the page, and shivering. "If it's moved, it could be a long walk."

It was anyway. Aidan didn't mind. Putting heel and toe to use, instead of floating... it was odd. But comforting.

...Kind of. The sidewalk felt wrong under his feet.

It's just sitting there. Not shaking. Not sliding. Not opening into a sinkhole and trying to eat me.

Weird.

But he trusted the prickle down his nerves to tell him when something carnivorous had decided to put fire spirit on the menu. Right now, the sidewalk was just numb, dead stone and concrete. Which meant he could take his eyes off the ground, and see what else was trying to kill him.

Like people. So. Many. People.

For all the countless souls he'd seen in Hell, that nightmare realm had always felt empty. Even when he'd been buried under a pile of screaming, bleeding forms-

Don't think about it.

Hard not to, with the noise and crowds around them. It was just too much to *see* all at once. All he could make sense of were... snapshots.

A tractor-truck grumbling through smaller traffic, diesel smoke drifting out to stain the once-white top of the trailer.

A gaggle of college students, hopping up and off of the rim of a fountain, the guys splashing each other with cold water to prove autumn had nothing on them.

An elderly pair bundled up in dark coats and leaf-patterned scarves, pointing out scenic overlooks on a tangled local map.

Midwesterners, Aidan thought, hearing the flatter tones than the surrounding crowd. *Come to see the leaves turn.*

Leaf season. October. Intrepid.

...I used to know this.

He had to stagger over to an echo of old stone. Lean against it, fingers splayed over the edge of a carved block into the roughness of mortar.

Myrrh's coat brushed against his; he heard a worried breath sucked past her teeth. "We could find a bus. Or a cab."

"No." Aidan blinked, focusing on gray stone with tiny flecks of red garnet. Local stone; it felt almost amused to be here, as if a century as a building were just an unexpected day jaunt for part of an age-old mountain. "No, I got this."

Don't focus on the crowd. Just focus on Myrrh. She's little, she looks harmless; anything looking for trouble will head for her first. Let her be the tripwire, while you... get used to people again. Because you've got *to.* Aidan snorted. *They're kind of* everywhere.

He had to, so he would. Not to mention the idea of putting another minute of his life in someone else's hands, even a cabbie, made him want to bare his teeth and snarl.

...Which he was not going to do, darn it. Maybe he wasn't human. Maybe he'd never really been human, no matter what he'd thought before he'd ended up in a candle-lit circle with an obsidian knife coming down.

But I'm not a monster. Not like that thing in the moonlight was.

Not to mention, Myrrh had already cheesed off at least two demons, one potion-seller, a detective, and a whole hospital's insurance department. Somebody had to watch her back.

Not that he'd done a real stellar job of that so far. Just thinking about... what he'd almost done in the darkness....

"Despair is one of the deadliest weapons of Hell."

Pressing the button for the walk light, Aidan blinked. "Uh...?"

"You flicker when you worry. Not that most eyes can see that." Myrrh's eyes were warm, and rueful. "And your brow furrows. Consideration of your sins should be a warning and a chastisement, not a goad to further despair. You need to focus on the brightness, not the empty dark. The world is full of wonders." She tilted her head, white hair tied back with a stray bit of gauze. "And one of those wonders is a man who was in confusion, and weary, and in darkness, but still refused to do evil."

His face heated up; Aidan closed his fingers into fists, hoping he hadn't seen sparks. Something about her acceptance just seemed too easy. "You said I wasn't a man."

"No. I said you were not wholly human, and you are not fully mortal." Myrrh sighed, as cars and one long tractor-trailer finally rumbled to a stop. "By this time, neither am I."

Like it was that easy to say that.

Then again - eighteen centuries of going after demons? *Not fully mortal* was probably a given by now.

Eighteen centuries. Aidan shook his head, and followed her into the brisk, impersonal building. No welcoming stone here; only a dull desert-red stucco over wood and concrete, with less sense of itself than mud stirred up in a pond. Inside was beige and brown, carpet and matte-painted walls, with a few rubber plants scattered around to give the bank's lobby the illusion of plant life. Bleah. The place could use a few scorch marks....

He backed up that thought, stomped on it, gave it a cross-eyed look to check if it was still breathing, and stomped it some more. Fires were *bad*. Unless maybe they were charbroiling an angry demon-bear out to munch you. Tight-suited bank bureaucrats didn't rate that high on evil.

"That vault has been condemned."

Then again.... Aidan eyed the smiling lady banker sitting behind the glossy desk: smart blue pantsuit, silk scarf, and decorous discreet diamond earrings. Lines of the style were different from twenty-five years back, but the impression of *professional upper-class, be grateful you're breathing the same air* was unmistakable. It made him want to break something. "Since when?" he demanded. "She's got the key, you're paid up, what's the problem?"

"Hmm." Gray eyes were still as clouds building up to an afternoon storm. Pale fingers lightly touched the wooden arm of her chair, like a dragonfly deciding it didn't like a perch after all. "My young friend is impetuous, but correct. What *is* the problem?"

"I'm sure you didn't know about it, Ms. Shafat, the vault was obviously obtained before you were given that key-"

And just where Myrrh had pulled that key out of, Aidan was not going to ask. Especially since he wasn't sure it was a real key. Myrrh had muttered something under her breath about Solomon, locked gardens and the gate of Bath-rabbim; and if he looked at it sideways, it was just a little shadowy. Put that together with thief of Heaven... heh.

"-But we recently discovered that vault had some kind of ward placed on it. Very powerful. We haven't been able to break it to check the contents-"

Gray turned winter-cold. "The point of a safe deposit box," Myrrh said, very precisely, "is that the contents are *sealed*. And kept inviolate. You had no right to attempt to open it. You had, in fact, no right to even test it for such wards; for they were only meant to keep the contents *untampered with*. As any reputable enchanter could have told you." She straightened in her chair, and cast a look of cool disdain over the manager's office. "If this is the level of security you customarily provide, I will have to take my business, and all my accounts, elsewhere."

From the way the manager paled under her makeup, that was a significant threat. Which made Aidan wonder all kinds of interesting thoughts. "Now, Ms. Shafat-"

"Where. Is. My. Box?"

...Getting a look at the inside of a bank vault hadn't been on Aidan's list of things to do today. But it was entertaining. Especially looking at the swathes of red tape around one big metal drawer that had been obviously pulled out and kept away from everything else.

Watching Myrrh sweep her fingers through the air around the tape, slowly getting angrier and angrier, wasn't quite so much fun. Especially since he could see the lurid red lines of... *something*... in the air that she wasn't quite touching.

And from the uncertain looks on the manager and security guard's faces, they couldn't see it at all.

"How very interesting." Myrrh stepped back, and gave the manager a level look that chilled Aidan's blood. "I am curious. When did you decide a vampire was a proper consultant for security on human belongings? The belongings of their natural prey, *personal items* your clients thought secure; items charged with the identity of their owners so only the rankest of magic-users could fail to establish a harmful link?"

The very thought made Aidan's gut knot up like fishing line. Granted, he hadn't seen much of that kind of magic in Hell. You couldn't get much more of a personal item than someone's soul. But Aariel had dropped plenty of hints, here and there; which was one reason he had his own personal dowsing pendant to find *where Myrrh was*. Just in case he ran into something that wanted him for lunch and wouldn't take fireballs for an answer. That pendant held a piece of her spirit, freely given, and if it ever fell into unfriendly hands... well, he knew she'd taken precautions that would destroy it before any magic could bite her too hard. But still. It was the strongest proof of friendship anyone could have in Hell.

A vampire's *got access to people's personal stuff. There is no way this is going to end well.*

The manager paled, then flushed. "Our security consultants are anonymous for their own safety-"

Myrrh blurred.

The guard didn't even have time to flinch.

Pale silk dangled from Myrrh's fingers. "You're paying him far too much. Any vampire that knows anything about security would know never to bite you *there*."

Aidan stared at the twin tooth marks on her throat, and felt his blood boil. "You... you... how could you?"

And then felt like a heel. After all, Mom had gotten fooled pretty badly, too.

Not the same. These people know *there are things that go bump in the night. And who hasn't watched vampire movies? If she got bit, she ought to be heading for the holy water.*

Of course, some movies said that would hurt like Hell. Pun definitely intended.

Blazing agony that'll eventually stop, versus something with fangs able to tweak your mind the moment sunset hits? Worse, able to tweak you so you want *to serve it, and bring it prey? I know what I'd pick. If I let something use me just because I was afraid of a little pain - I wouldn't be able to live with myself.*

...And damn it, sometimes having a solid form *sucked*. He'd gotten used to hiding his emotions in a fireball to survive. Most two-legged types who weren't shrimpy little hell-raiders couldn't read a face of flickering fire. It was safe to feel things, as long as whatever was watching him didn't have enough power to rip the truth out of his aura.

But that was in Hell. Here on Earth? He was solid. And by the way the manager was heading past beet-red toward purple, what he felt was written all over his face. Large print. Neon, even. "You have no right to comment on my personal life!" she sputtered.

"I have every right to remove my possessions - and my accounts - from someone who exhibits a distinct and distasteful lack of judgment." Myrrh pointed toward the door. "Out. Now."

"I'll be charging you with assault!"

"Oh, do." Myrrh smiled, and waved a hand at the video camera in the corner of the vault. Slimmer and sleeker than the ones Aidan remembered, like most electronics he'd seen so far, but he'd snuck through too many wards in Hell to not know the back-of-the-neck twitch of *being watched by an inanimate object*. "And my attorney will subpoena your security footage to enter into evidence. I suspect your superiors - and even, perhaps, the CEO of Suntrust itself - will find your personal life very. Interesting. Indeed." Her face went calm, and there was something fey and dangerous in gray eyes. "Smile."

The manager went chalky white.

"Ms. Gillingham?" The guard stepped between them, obviously worried.

A ghastly caricature of a smile forced its way onto the manager's face. "Let's leave the client with her box, Ed."

Aidan waited until the door was closed. "Hate to point this out, but don't these things need two keys?"

Myrrh clicked her tongue against her teeth. "What a limited thought." The words were still edged, but some of the tension was easing from taut shoulders. "What it needs, is two locks opened."

Aidan started to protest; wasn't that the exact same thing? Then blinked. And thought that over. "Okay...."

Myrrh sighed, and gave him a rueful smile. "And here I will give you a lesson in magic that does not draw on the elements, if you are interested. Technology works with physical realities. Magic, with the realities of the mind, heart, and spirit." She hesitated. "Do you wish to know more? I could open this alone. But it would be simpler if I did not. And...." She eyed the lines, with one subtle shake of her head.

"What are those, anyway?" Aidan asked, uneasy. "Alarms? Tripwires?" He swallowed, dire possibilities dancing in his head. "Some kind of magical mines?"

"A bit of all three," Myrrh stated. "I've half a mind to shield myself and set off the lot. This bank deserves it." She sighed, and waved away temptation. "But that would be messy. And loud. And I'd much prefer to leave the tripwires intact."

Uh-oh. "You don't want him to know you're coming," Aidan realized.

Gray eyes slid to meet his glance, amused. "Think bigger. And higher."

Higher? That didn't make any sense... wait. "He's a stupid vamp," Aidan said, startled.

"To make a blood slave of a woman whose job is to stand in public view, and leave his mark for any who suspected? Oh, yes." Myrrh gestured toward the red shimmers. "He had ample power to work with, but there are none of the shortcuts, the... specialized kinks to tighten the spell-weave, that an experienced magic-crafter would use. Given the amount of blood magic in his personal energies...." She held two fingers near the vault, as if testing its heat. "I would say he was sired no more than twenty years ago. Which means he's had no chance to learn of me by any personal encounter. And the power I use is too subtle for a fledgling vampire to detect on his own, unlooked-for."

"So somebody else found it," Aidan concluded. "And you want to get them." Whoof. But- "Um. If he's got that lady under his fang," and that was a scary thought, how could anybody ever think that was just their *personal life*, "won't they be able to get this on tape? Even if the tripwires don't go off?"

Gray eyes danced. "I certainly hope so."

Meaning El Stupid Vamp would then have to explain to his real boss why a tripwired vault meant to blow up in a demon-hunter's face... hadn't. "You're *evil*."

Myrrh raised a white brow at him.

Ack. "Sorry. Open mouth, chew shoe leather-"

"Aidan." She was chuckling, ever so softly. "It's fine. I appreciate the thought. Even the Virgin Mary does not tread *lightly* on the serpent." She held up a hand, and wiggled her fingers. "Shall we educate a soon to be dead again vampire?"

Well, when she put it that way.... "Two locks to open, huh?" He stepped up beside her to stand near the second keyhole, eyeing the shimmer of blood magic.

"Which means, two people with the right to open the locks." Myrrh held the shadowy key between her palms, and slowly pulled them apart. "And the tools to do so."

Holding back a whistle, Aidan took the second black key.

Myrrh held up her free hand; *wait*. "The problem with using magical wards as tripwires, is that spells tend to echo the form of their intent." She gave him a hopeful glance. "Do you follow?"

"Use the spell as a tripwire, it acts like a real tripwire?" Aidan guessed. "Which means if you don't touch it...."

Myrrh nodded, weaving her hand through the visible webwork of magic. "Do you wish to try?"

"Let's do this." His hands were a bit bigger than hers, but his arms were longer. Gauging his moves, he held the key ready over his lock.

With a nod, Myrrh let shadow snick home, and they both turned their keys.

Click.

Heh. He'd been expecting massive fireworks. But the red magic just lifted away with the lid, one solid piece of malevolence.

Myrrh, he noted, was standing so the camera couldn't get a good look inside. Nice.

What is all this stuff?

Myrrh held a finger to her lips, quickly abstracting blue and brown vials and bundles of ivory silk, tucking them into various belts and bags also in the vault. Her hands skimmed over what looked like a dark harness full of slim, blackened knives; she nodded, and passed it to him to tuck into an inside pocket of his coat.

How did she know?

He'd never thrown knives around her. Ever. Fire, sure. Beyond that, their careful sparring sessions had all been hand to hand, with a lot of emphasis on how to dodge power coming at you, rather than use the usual demon tactic of smacking it with your own.

...And that brought back dark memories of his *introduction* to Yaldabaoth's court, and he was just not going there.

One of the last things Myrrh got out was a pen and a piece of paper. Smiling, she set about scribing flowing symbols like reeds, birds, a loaf of bread....

Hieroglyphs?

Hiding her face and hand from the camera, Myrrh licked her fingertip, and traced the sweeping arcs of a Christian fish. Laid the paper in the bottom of the vault, and set the lid back in place.

Aidan listened to the locks click, and sucked in a breath as the blood magic snapped back into position. "Myrrh?"

"After we're clear of here." She waved at the camera, and briskly walked out.

Aidan followed, noting with amusement that the security guard was sitting by the door, looking shell-shocked, and the manager was nowhere to be seen.

And there were no cop cars in the parking lot, either. Imagine that. "Okay, give," Aidan muttered, as they walked out of the parking lot and back to the street. For a moment his eyes were caught by the flash of lights off some of the cars' odd, almost wrap-around headlights. *Not an attack. Just idiots with too much time on their hands polishing stuff.* "What'd you write?"

"If you can read this, *you're too close.*"

"...How are you still alive?"

Myrrh quirked an eyebrow at him.

"Right, silly me. You can stop pretending, you know." His mouth was dry, but he was going to say this. "That you're not scared."

"Wiser than you know," Myrrh murmured. "Yes. I am. More terrified, I think, than I have ever been." She walked on, sandals soundless on concrete, gaze watching for more than just traffic. "Thirty years ago, I would have spelled that guard to sleep, and taken that woman to a church for cleansing, to save her life and soul. Now... allowing an unholy spirit to feed on you is a *lifestyle choice?* What has *happened* to the world?"

"I guess I wouldn't know," Aidan said, throat tight. "First time I knew there were *things* out there... is when I started seeing 'em." Glimpses out of the corners of his eyes of things too horrible to be real. Hideous childlike laughter in the shadows. A creeping sense of dread, that had oozed into black life that last horrible night as a dripping, insect-eyed hound, chasing him toward what he'd thought was safety. Only....

"Hello, brother. I've been waiting for you."

Aidan shuddered, and didn't care if Myrrh saw it. *He's dead. He has to be.* "Guess down there, at least you knew everything was trying to eat you."

Myrrh flushed, cheeks bright in her pale face. "Forgive me. I've always lived in danger. That hasn't changed. But you said you were in specific danger, and - come. I think we can shield you from Detective Church's grasp. And any other's."

"What others?" Aidan said warily. The streets and shops looked different, a few decked out with signs like red and blue fireflies had set down to flicker, and he just *knew* there should have been a bookshop where that glittering furnishings store now stood, but if he remembered this route... yeah. They were heading into the little park by the Moon River. The one right across a side street from the courthouse.

That's not an accident. His heart leapt as he followed her through the arc of the World War II memorial, weaving through the green-painted steel benches. God, why hadn't anybody ever told him hope could hurt? "You said you had papers...."

"I saw you flinch when the detective mentioned fingerprints." Myrrh claimed the one picnic table with wooden benches, plucking a satchel from under her gray coat. "At first it didn't make sense. There are few crimes the police could still be seeking you for after twenty-five years, and I know you are no murderer-"

"How do you know that?" Aidan cut her off as he sat, chilled by more than the breeze off the river. The things Yaldabaoth had done; the creatures he'd had to face, or be ripped to flaming shreds.... "I've killed lots of things."

"Killed, yes. Murder leaves a stain on the soul. Even if one lives to repent." A white brow rose. "I've known you near two decades, my friend. You haven't repented of much."

Okay, she had a point there. Even if he did want to squirm about it.

"So I thought, what else could she do with fingerprints?" Myrrh went on, rifling through the satchel. "She could find your identity. Your true name." She winced. "And if she knew, others could as well. And there is a sorcerer, is there not? One who compelled you, while you were in Hell." Gray searched amber. "You accepted my nickname almost as soon as I gave it to you. At first I thought you were only being wary. Only the most powerful or the most foolish use their names for all to hear. Then... well, I thought you took it only for the pleasure of knowing you had my name, and I did not have yours." Her smile was sad. "Hell is distrust, after all. And you were acquainted with the Sword. I couldn't be sure you were as innocent as you appeared."

Aidan flushed. "Hey!"

"It took a great deal of time, and much reading of the energies about you, to be certain I was right," Myrrh went on, taking out a slim manila folder and a black pen. "You used *Aidan* to shield yourself, yes? Given names do have power; and if you hid yourself with that one, you could resist his call. For a while. And if you did so often enough, long enough - it takes a great deal of stamina for a sorcerer to sift out one soul among all Hell's hordes. He might think he had failed. That Hell had feasted, as it often does, and some demon had swallowed you up beyond recall." Gray eyes narrowed. "But if Church's search alerts him otherwise...."

Aidan shuddered. "She can't," he said flatly. "There's no way he gave up, trust me. No matter what nickname I used. If he was *breathing*, he would have dragged me to him. He... hated me...."

Why, damn it? What did I ever do?

Useless thought. "He's gone," Aidan stated, not caring if his voice shook. "But he was always *organized*. He'd make sure someone could go after me, even if he was six feet under. There's a grimoire out there with my name in it, I can feel it. Somebody just hasn't used it yet."

Myrrh spun the pen in her hands, gray eyes thoughtful. "That is possible. Given there is a sorcerer who's been crafting a Demongate, it's even likely. Power calls to power; and any magic-user willing to work with Hell is apt to come into possession of such malign creations." She inclined her head. "Then we should work quickly, before any police inquiries can rouse his attention."

"Not like there's any way you can stop the guy, whoever he is," Aidan said faintly. Solid wood under him, and clean air to breathe, and all of it could vanish in a heartbeat. It wasn't fair. "My name's my *name*, you can't change that...."

Paper. Pen. A courthouse. And so far, Myrrh didn't do anything by accident.

"...Can you?"

"You're not the first one I've had to hide from name magic," Myrrh said levelly. "Ten centuries ago, a trip to the river and a blessing would have sufficed. These days, there's a bit more mortal paperwork involved." She filled in dates, looked it over all again, and nodded. Turned the pages toward him, and offered the pen.

He read it like he would bomb-defusing instructions. You didn't sign stuff in Hell. Ever.

Looks okay, though. Petitions to change a legal name were supposed to be simple. America was where anyone could start over, so long as they 'fessed up to the law that was exactly what they were doing. "What gives?" he said, eyeing Myrrh as she watched the dark water.

"Until the paperwork is signed and sealed by the court clerk, your old name will still have some power over you." Myrrh leaned back against the table, still gazing at the river; or possibly a red-wattled duck who'd just surfaced, shaking water off its beak. "There is no reason I need to know it."

Aidan blinked, oddly comforted. "Thanks."

She nodded. "For a last name. May I suggest Lindisfarne?"

Lindisfarne. He sounded it out in his head. Weird. But it kind of rang right. "Why that one?" Aidan asked, carefully inking in the first few entries. It'd been a while since he'd held a regular ballpoint pen. Dark plastic was cold against the web of his thumb, slowly warming as he wrote.

"It is the name of a certain manuscript of the gospels," Myrrh said quietly, fingers feeling the wind. "Even a cursory spell-search, by one used to scrying with the aid of demonic powers, should go drastically wrong." She paused. "And I know you fear what you can do. That name should help you master it." She winked at him. "Aidan of Lindisfarne is the patron saint of firefighters."

"You want me to steal a name from a saint?" That was *so wrong*.

And yet, so Myrrh. He almost wanted to snicker. All this time he'd been playing up the big, bad fire spirit... and she'd been calling him after a fire extinguisher.

I have got to get her into a poker game.

"Not steal," Myrrh said firmly. Drummed fingers on wood, a quiet rumble. "It's common to give a saint's name to a sinner starting over. People pray to him for protection, Aidan; and you need it as much as anyone. I don't think he'll mind."

"Oh yeah?" he shot back. Because sure he'd seen Hell, which implied there was a Heaven. But he'd need a lot more proof before he thought *anyone* up there gave a flying pig about someone like him. "And who are you named for?"

"Not who. What."

Her voice was so *sad*.

Myrrh... that's in the old hymns, right? The solemn perfume, the incense for the dead....

Oh.

...And maybe he didn't want to pry into eighteen centuries of history. Could be hazardous to his health.

More hazardous than Steven?

Heh. No way to know that, yet. Heck, he didn't even know if Steven had managed to hand off his bad habits to anyone else before he'd taken the big dirt nap. Because Steven had to be dead. He'd never have quit for anything less.

He never shared his toys, either. Why would he let anyone else even peek at a grimoire?

Except the bits Myrrh had told him about a Demongate implied somebody on *this side* had to open it, and given the way he'd... died....

Deep breaths. Don't pass out.

He read through the paperwork one more time, breeze trying to pry the pages out from under his fingers. Hesitated, again, at the blank for his original name. He didn't want to sign it. He didn't even want to think it.

But if everything went right, he'd never have to see it again.

Christophe Savonarola.

Chapter Six

Smokeless flame, rising from a rectangular frame edged in solemn black. Fire that gnawed away decorative edges and the features they guarded, the clear plastic over the image warping before it started to melt and bubble.

"Damn."

Manicured hands gestured, calling a gust of cold and damp. The photo and frame burned even brighter.

"Damn and blast."

Long fingers caught up thick black velvet, tossing it to smother and quench the old-fashioned way. Words were spoken, hissing and crackling like steaming ice-

Shimmering black turned brown and smoldering, releasing a thick cloud of acrid smoke. But finally, the heat died away.

An exasperated sigh, and fingers yanked up seared cloth.

Not even ashes remained.

"Unexpected." Fingers flicked, trying to free themselves and starched white cuffs of specks of seared velvet. "Water should always conquer fire. And yet... Stimson!"

"Sir?"

"Bring up the flint set, and two rabbits. I need to begin some contingency measures."

"Very good, sir." A polite pause. "Before or after I scrub the secondary obsidian set, sir? I believe a certain Mr. Ginger has just illegally entered the grounds."

Stimson's master almost choked on a stray fleck of velvet. "He *left* Mr. O'Connor's protections?"

"I found it hard to believe as well, sir," Stimson said courteously. "But apparently the reward on offer for information on crystal skulls was sufficient."

"So he's willing to come for money when Switch has already warned him away from me." A *tsk*. "You just can't hire good help these days, can you?"

"It would seem not, sir." The butler paused, eyes gleaming in the shadows of his master's study. "Shall I have him escorted downstairs, sir? It would mean cancelling your meeting with the Chamber of Commerce...."

"Yes, make my excuses." Hands dusted off a few last scraps of velvet thread. "Mortal businesses won't be important for that much longer. And I feel inspired to do a bit of... carving."

Pain. Cold concrete. Metal weighing him down like lead manacles, back bent over what felt like thorn-carved wood. Ginger woke from dazed numbness to blind pain, trying to scream through jaws jammed with slippery seaweed-

"I wouldn't bother begging." The voice was cold, cultured, as fingers clicked over computer keys. Familiar. "You've already told me everything I wanted to hear."

He couldn't see anything. Why couldn't he see, his face hurt like fire but he couldn't feel a blindfold-

"If I were a more courteous man, I might thank you for bringing Stimson his snacks. He does get testy without them."

Memory was filtering through the numbness. Of a servile butler's eyes glowing sudden crimson, and... claws....

Yards away, he heard the sounds of chewing.

The gag wouldn't let him scream.

"I must admit, I rather enjoy the irony," his captor went on. "Switch O'Connor, the man with no conscience; the thorn in Intrepid's bleeding side. And yet if you'd kept your word to him, your city might stand, and you... why, you might have lived to see another night." A heartfelt sigh. "Just as well. The omens say Switch would have tried for me at Halloween, and I can't have that. I have *plans*."

Keys clacked, and the wood under him *twisted*. Thorns writhed against arms, back, thighs; creaking with hunger.

"Did you know that to truly bind another's will, you need a connection to them, freely given?" Something sharp teased over Ginger's collarbone, dragging slowly down. "In your case, cash sufficed. Among family, that bond is implicit, unless one of that shared blood truly renounces another. For officers of the law... well, they swear oaths. It protects them from a great deal, even if they never deserve it. But you... you left two detectives behind to *die*. I wonder....

"Just how much would they give, to catch you?"
Thorns stabbed deep.

Chapter Seven

At least the coffee's good. Church wrapped her fingers around brown ceramic as she sat in Father Gray O'Malley's little cubbyhole of an office, hidden down in the basement back behind the choir robing room. "You're saying Myrrh Shafat is an *actual* heretic."

"Under the strict interpretation of canon law and doctrine, indeed she is," Father O'Malley nodded, cupping his own stained white mug in large, worn hands. "Technically the sect of Christianity she adheres to broke off before there was a Catholic Church. So she might well be in better standing than, say, the good Patriarch of the Orthodox Churches. Whom our Father and the bishopric of Rome has traded excommunications with, a time or two."

Church blinked.

"But she's fond enough of the Church, as she is of any folk of true faith," the priest went on. Paused. "Most folk of faith, dear me. She still holds a grudge over the library of Alexandria."

Church blinked again. Gulped her coffee. Maybe she just needed to be a little more awake. "Something happened in Virginia?"

"Ah, no. Alexandria, Egypt." Father O'Malley stared into his steam. "It was a long time ago. And I never thought I'd be glad there was a vampire bar in Intrepid rather than a mosque."

A mosque in Intrepid? There weren't that many mosques left in the whole Southeast; not since the Dark Day. Nobody knew exactly what had happened in Murfreesboro, Tennessee when the sun had gone down, but the few surviving witnesses near the burn sites had nightmares about beings of walking fire. "You don't think she was mixed up in the Murfreesboro Fires, do you?"

"I know she was not." O'Malley's voice was as firm as his church's foundations. "One night we can both get blind drunk I'll tell you a tale of *ifrits* and *jinn*, and why calling either of them up to make a mischief among the infidels is a black mark on the soul. Not to mention a nightmare for any of us who can feel that hellish fire coming. Myrrh, deal with such as that? I'd sooner believe you bashed Tom over the head and stabbed him yourself. Have you heard anything on where that rascal Feniger got to?"

"Not him, and not Ginger," Church grumbled into her mug. "Crime Scene's still trying to figure out how many bodies we've got." Hot coffee. Now if only that was enough to take the chill out of her blood when she thought about acid, and screams, and a monster that *should not* be real. "Only good thing about that whole mess is that I never got a chance to fire a shot. God, the paperwork that would have meant."

"Amen," the priest agreed.

Church looked up. "None of which makes me feel any better about the fact that the picture in Shafat's file looks exactly like her. *Exactly*. And it's thirty years old." Her fingers tightened on ceramic. "What kind of supernatural is she?"

"Now you're asking a question that's driven far better men than I to drink," Father O'Malley said dryly. He turned, to get at one of the file cabinets crammed into the tiny space with them. "I always meant you to have these, after I was gone. I must say I'm glad to be able to introduce the two of you while I'm still among the living. Twenty-six years since she'd gone to hunt a sorcerer down; I was beginning to worry."

Notebooks. A pile of notebooks, almost spilling out of an old accordion folder. "What the heck are these?"

"You might call them case notes," the priest admitted.

Church picked up a few with yellowing pages, sorting through them to find the oldest. "Some of these go back to 1910!"

"Oh, there are older," O'Malley assured her. "I'm not the first priest to serve as a helping hand for our dear heretic, and I sincerely hope I won't be the last."

Older than 1910. That makes no sense whatsoever- what's this?

A dark-stained cedar box had slipped out of the pile; no larger than her own work notebook, and almost as thin.

Gathering up some of the notebooks, O'Malley chuckled. "I'm rather glad I get to try my speech on you first! Father Ricci... heh. It will be a terrible shock to that poor youngster."

That poor youngster had at least five years on her. "Speech?" Church said suspiciously, fiddling with the edge of polished wood.

There had to be a latch on it somewhere.

"The world is a much darker place than you know," Father O'Malley began. "Yes, even now, after the Dark Day. Vampires, werewolves, sorcerers and other workers of magic; you've seen them as they present themselves to the world, and to our adoring press. Poor, misunderstood creatures, condemned to hide from the overwhelming masses of humanity; that's what they claim." Blue eyes, still bright despite the passage of years, gave her a grave look. "In rare cases, that may be true. But under the cover of darkness, away from the spotlights and the politicians... they are something quite different."

Church grimaced, putting two and two together. "She's not just a sorcerer, she's a *Hunter*. A supernatural Hunter? Isn't that kind of-" She waved the box in her hand, trying to find more polite words than *sick and twisted*. "Hypocritical?"

"There's nothing about Myrrh that's hypocritical," the priest said gruffly. Raised a brow, and pointed at dark wood. "Be gentle with that. Syriac icons don't grow on trees. The good Lord only knows how that survived long enough for a Hunter to bring it out of the ruins of Edessa. The Turks wreaked havoc that's hard to believe; the vampires treated it as their private playground for decades... ah, but that's neither here nor there." Brushy brows waggled at her. "She's no hypocrite, and no liar. Myrrh is a thief of Heaven, and she may be the only thing that stands between you and damnation. Savonarola's noticed you, Church. Never think he hasn't." He waved his mug. "Step wrong, and it could be you on a blasphemous altar someday."

She was shocked. And then angry, remembering the coroner's reports she'd skimmed from Intrepid's cold casefiles; supposedly they'd been passed on to the FBI due to the possibility of an active serial killer in the area, but she hadn't seen anything like action on any of them. *Nothing in common*, the word from the Feds had been. *Call us when you have something solid.*

Which had every detective in Intrepid calling bullshit. Yeah, maybe it was leaf season, and yeah, maybe there were millions of potential victims - er, tourists - swarming through the Blue Ridge like locusts to view September and October's riot of fall foliage; each of whom could have brought along their own tangled nests of reasons-to-bump-off. But they *did* have something in common.

Not missed for at least three days to four months before reported. Possibly longer on the two Jane Does. Severe abrasions and bruising on the wrists of eighteen victims; five too decomposed to determine. Variable injuries, but most apparently soft-tissue damage. Probable cause of death: hypovolemic shock due to severe hemorrhaging from severed carotid artery.

Put it all together, and they had a serial psycho in Intrepid. And they *couldn't find him.*

Every detective in the IPD agreed on that. What they couldn't agree on was a suspect. A few names got tossed around - quietly, *hypothetically* - but every name that surfaced had at least a shaky alibi for some of the murders.

Except one, Church thought darkly.

Only even bringing up the possibility had people loudly hinting about breaking her back to patrol. Savonarola, a serial killer? Ridiculous. Where was her proof?

She didn't have proof. Just bodies. One a year, every year for the past twenty-three, somewhere around Halloween. Which was one reason she was so bristly, Church had to admit; she desperately wanted to put cuffs on *somebody* who deserved it. Because in about two weeks there was going to be dead body number twenty-four. She could feel it. Like a twisted *birthday present-*

Halloween. October 31st. And Steven Savonarola had been born on November first.

Put the box down, old means fragile, you're not going to break anything... except maybe a few eardrums. "You've never said you knew anything about Savonarola-"

"Because I've never known anything you could use without getting your damn fool self killed, young lady," Father O'Malley cut her off. "Go against him alone, and I'll be praying we can find enough of your body to bury. But if you have help...."

"She's a person of interest in a mass homicide," Church objected. "And we can't even get Ginger for more than standing by while Feniger's minions roughed us up, 'cause Crime Scene can't find that skull!" She almost slammed the mug down; thought better of splashing good coffee. "At least the tip was good. There was a human skull locked in with that... that *thing's*. Who puts jade on a skull, anyway? Kooky modern art types...." She trailed off, noting the priest's thoughtful look. "What?"

"So Ginger had her," Father O'Malley mused, picking up the icon and slipping it back into the folder. "I wish I'd known."

"Had her?" Church said blankly. "She showed up after he was already gone. After... that light...."

Light where the skull had been. Then fire, and a sword like a shaft of sun.

No way. Church swallowed. "That skull was her?"

"Not quite, no," the priest said judiciously. "Perhaps you've heard the tale of the visions of Ezekiel, preaching to dry bones, that the Lord covered with flesh and made live again?" He nodded. "Myrrh is a bit like that."

Church stared at him, waiting for the world to settle back on an even keel. "Sorry," she said at last, "that sounds like you think she was... dead."

"If you saw a skull set with jade?" Father O'Malley heaved a heavy sigh. "Yes. It's likely she was, poor soul. And given she's always been careful to drop messages for myself and others when a mission took her off suddenly - it's likely she's been dead these past twenty-six years."

Dead. He really believed Myrrh had been dead. Which was crazy.

Father's the sanest guy I know. So - what if it's not crazy? If she's been - heck, just in a coma *twenty-six years-*

Then she hadn't seen the Dark Day. And that was a scary thought.

O'Malley nodded to himself. "Which would explain quite a bit of these past few decades. I can't think the forces of Darkness would have dared to reveal themselves so if they thought a hell-raider still walked the earth."

"A what?" Church pounced, sure she couldn't have heard what she'd thought she heard.

"I'm certain she will tell you, once I can vouch you're an honest cop-"

"No. You tell me. Now." Church leaned in, focused on that scrap of info that didn't fit. "I know you. All I know about her is that she waves a flaming sword that disappears and has a sidekick who throws fireballs. Still haven't gotten any hits back on his prints. Aidan's probably an alias anyway-"

"Aidan?" The priest sat up straight, intrigued. "And fireballs... of course. *Little fire*. Though how in the world... did you see another skull?"

There's more like her out there? "Just one," Church shook her head. "It was there, and then both of them were there and the skull was gone. Why?"

Father O'Malley whistled. "Well, that's a fine kettle of fish."

And his face had that politely closed look that meant he wasn't likely to say anymore about Aidan without talking to the man himself. Damn it. Fine, two could play the change of subject game. "What's a hell-raider?"

"Ah; at my age, you'd think I'd be the impatient one," O'Malley mused. "*Hunter*, you said. Rather like most cops would say runner. Or junkie."

Church did her best not to flinch. Father O'Malley was a good man. That disapproval in his voice made her feel... not so good. "They're vigilantes. We have laws."

"We've had *laws* for most of recorded history, Detective," the priest said gravely. "Most of which boil down to, anyone who uses magic to do harm, or traffics with creatures inimical to soul or mortal flesh, is condemned to the quickest and most ruthless death human hands can deal out. If the Lord's own messengers and prophets don't get to them first."

Church gave him a flat look. She was a friend. She was also an officer of the law and he *knew* that. Bringing up old, bad laws people had buried centuries ago - he knew better. "There are no prophets of God."

O'Malley leaned back in his chair, and looked her up and down; from dark hair that still might have bits of dead leaves in it to the wince of her bandaged ribs. "Then you're going to find Myrrh very hard to take," he said dryly. "I'd invest in antacids, if I were you. You'll need them. Though she'd be the first to tell you she's not a prophet. She's a messenger."

Church was shaking her head. This was impossible. "You can't believe that."

"Hmm." The priest stared into the depths of his mug.

"Detective, you're here because I'm one of many humble servants caring for the lives and spirits of our fair city. I bless the ill and the injured; I give counsel to the mourning and the weary. I even put prayers of protection on various locations you may not want to ask about, safehouses for those who've found themselves involved with the supernatural and now find themselves desperate to escape. Blood-slaves, the were-bitten trying to battle their curse, dabblers in magic who may have strayed too far into deep waters and need to cleanse their souls. I deal with evil as you do; every day, great and petty. And here you are, alive, with your partner alive when Feniger meant him to be dead. And you think I can't believe in good as well?"

She was that close to slamming the mug down hard enough to shatter, and stalking out. "If there were anything up there looking out for us, vampires wouldn't even exist!"

"Ah; and here we do come to the sticking point," O'Malley said softly. "And this is a dark night of the soul for every one of us who faces evil unmasked; raw and hateful, not clothed in human skin. The right to free will allows the option to sin. And because some souls do sin, and do not repent, evil can creep into our world. Which would you rather have, Detective? A sterile world where no soul can choose how it will honor God? Or the mortal world we have, flawed and blessed, where those such as you and I must stand eternal watch against the will of evil?"

She clicked ceramic down on his mini-desk. "There's a supernatural Hunter loose in my city who can work magic on iron. How the hell do I keep her locked up?"

"You won't be able to, unless you can legitimately arrest her," O'Malley sighed. "You could always try talking to her."

"Tried that. She lied to me-"

Father O'Malley gave her a look she'd last seen from her eighth-grade math teacher after she'd turned in yet another set of half-done homework. "What did she say? Exactly?"

Grumbling, Church got out her notes. Read out the relevant bits, trying to keep the snarl out of her voice.

Setting his mug down, O'Malley leaned his forehead against his palm. "Ah, lass. You never could stand by while a friend was in pain." He looked up, a wry smile wrinkling his face. "She does exactly what she said, Detective. When she's not chastising demons on earth, she chases down lost souls, and frees them to seek a new judgment in Heaven."

Hell-raider. No way. "I'm not exactly a Bible-thumper, but the last time I checked? People in hell were supposed to be there."

O'Malley *hmph*ed. "The theological records I've read show a massive argument over just that. There's many who've said she probably only reaches one of the lowest levels of Purgatory. Though those are mostly the ones who'd never faced a hellspawn trying to kill them. As you did, last night."

Ha, ha, ha. No. "That was not a demon," Church said firmly. "There's plenty of monsters out there people call demons. But *real* demons? Evil spirits out of hell, rebels against God, the works? They don't exist."

"And the best trick the Devil ever pulled was making men think he didn't exist," O'Malley mused. "Lass, that was a demon. I can show you texts-"

"Written by some guy who called himself the Hammer of Witches and got his kicks by stripping old ladies naked and poking them with pins to find a spot where they didn't scream," Church said flatly. The basement felt close around her, scents of choir robes and old candle wax pricking at her nose. "No."

"Excesses of the Inquisition aside," O'Malley stated, "what you've described is what those in my line of work call a demon."

Okay. As long as they just called it that-

And damn it, she'd forgotten the priest was almost as good at reading people as a cop. "That's what troubles you, isn't it?" O'Malley mused. "The idea that there might be something outside mortal law, that answers only to the laws of God."

Church circled a finger near her ear. "People who think God is talking to them tend to go up in belltowers and start sniping innocent civilians."

"I don't believe Myrrh has ever claimed that God spoke to her," the priest replied. "That He has answered her prayers? Yes. That, I have seen."

And that just knotted something up in her gut. O'Malley was one of the good guys. "She's a sorcerer. All you've seen is her magic."

The priest smiled. "Ah, yes. Because ordinary magic works so well on steel handcuffs."

Damn it. There had to be a way Myrrh had pulled that off. Church just had to think of it-

Wait. *Ordinary* magic? "Hold on, you mean there is magic that works on steel?"

"Well...."

There was a flurry of frantic knocks at the door. "Father?" Querulous old Mrs. McAllister, who kept the church organ going by a sheer act of will some Sundays. "There's a bit of a disturbance...."

"Oh?" Father O'Malley opened the door for the old lady, and gestured the detective out. "Well,. then. Let's go rescue Father Ricci from an ulcer, shall we?"

Church eyed her watch. No way. It'd been hours since Shafat and her sidekick had slipped out of Sacred Heart. "I'm telling you, Father, they've skipped town-"

"Ah. And I suppose an experienced detective didn't consider that they'd be walking?" Eyes twinkling, Father O'Malley headed upstairs.

Walking? Who the heck walked anywhere?

...Except maybe someone who, oh, didn't have an ID. And if she did have one, her license would be twenty years out of date.

Which meant she was actually *considering* that O'Malley's impossible story might potentially have some truth in it, and good coffee or not, just thinking that gave her a headache.

Up and out; huh, this was one of the church's side doors. You pretty much had to be a cop or a longstanding member of the congregation to even know it was here-

"I said no way!"

One tall redhead in a black trenchcoat, flailing his hand near a bemused white-haired young sorceress. Damn. Church owed O'Malley's collection plate five bucks.

"It's not going to bite you," Myrrh stated, gently pushing him toward the door.

"Who's talking bite?" The redhead was digging in his heels, giving Father Ricci a look dark enough to peel paint. "We're talking spontaneous human combustion. El Zappo. Bolts of lightning from the clear blue yonder."

"Young man," the middle-aged priest said firmly, face a determined smile, "I assure you, whatever sins of absence you think you may have committed, the church welcomes all her children."

"And the original traditions of God's wrath were more closely associated with meteorite strikes than lightning," Myrrh stated, letting her hand rest on Aidan's arm. "Someone should have told the citizens of Gomorrah not to build on a plain full of natural gas." She clicked her tongue. "Then again, if they'd been willing to listen to that much sense, they'd never have sinned against God in the first place, so there you are."

In the sudden silence, Church caught O'Malley muffling a snicker.

"That's an... interesting interpretation of current archaeological work on scripture," Father Ricci said at last. "Who are you?"

"I can answer that, lad. Ah, you little rapscallion!" O'Malley shook a playful fist. "You never call, you never write; I'd begun to think you'd deserted our fair city for greener pastures." He stalked out of the church like a man on a mission, giving Aidan a raking up and down look. "And who've you brought to us this time, Myrrh? Another fugitive soul, fleeing into Egypt?"

Aidan swallowed. "Ah, funny you should say that...."

"Hush, you! I know a lapsed Catholic when I see one quaking." O'Malley shook his head, but his eyes were suspiciously bright.

He almost looks like he's... crying, Church thought, stunned. *Who is this guy?*

"If I know Myrrh, she's tromped you over half the town and barely stopped for a sup of water," O'Malley forged on. "Shame on you, young lady! The body is a temple, and even when God works a miracle, the altar needs fresh oil eventually. When was the last time you ate?"

Aidan coughed, not quite covering a snicker. "Somehow, I don't think he's gonna think an IV counts."

A light flush pinked Myrrh's ears. "Ah. I truly don't know how to answer you, old friend. The past day has been... interesting." Her glance touched Mrs. McAllister, then Father Ricci, and finally Church. One white brow rose.

"Ah yes; we've much to talk about, *much* to talk about." O'Malley smiled at the organ mistress. "It seems Myrrh's got a line on some dastardly cemetery vandals; can you believe it?"

"No!" Mrs. McAllister gasped. "Why, what's the world coming to?"

"The very same rascals that laid up poor Detective Franklin in the hospital," O'Malley forged on. "Scurrilous ba- ah, pardon me, Mrs. McAllister." The priest's craggy face crinkled in woeful contrition. "Why, it's just an awful thing to think on, that there are such black-hearted rascals out there as to try and put our own good officers of the law in an early grave! But our good Detective Church is on the case. They'll be brought to justice, you can be sure." He clapped a hand on Church's shoulder. "We've every confidence in you, Detective. Just let us feed these poor, footsore lost sheep, and you can all put your heads together to snare these blackguards."

I've just been railroaded, Church realized in stunned awe, as Mrs. McAllister hurried off with her precious nuggets of gossip. *Damn, Father. You're good.*

Father Ricci looked as though he'd just seen them tied to the tracks, and was wrestling his better angel as to whether or not he should risk cutting them loose. "Lost sheep, huh?" He shook his head, dark hair almost brushing his white collar. "Oh, I've got to hear this one."

"But," Aidan protested again, "you don't know-"

"We're going to the kitchen, not the altar," Myrrh said wryly. "I've been here before. Anything that might take a mystical poke at us will get its finger zapped."

"Mystical- who *are* you? No, wait, inside," Ricci sighed. "I'm sure some of this will make sense. Eventually."

Aidan groaned. "Oh, this is a bad idea...."

Whatever the redhead was worried about, nothing seemed to happen when he walked through the door-

Church blinked, and rubbed her eyes. She either needed more sleep or stronger coffee. For a moment there she would have sworn he'd flickered, like a candle in a winter gust of wind.

But they were inside, and nothing else weird seemed to happen. Unless she counted Myrrh slipping back into the nave to leave a dollar for a vigil candle. And taking the candle.

"Now, where were we?" O'Malley pondered that as he handed out more steaming mugs of coffee, and Myrrh was happily sectioning a mandarin orange to go with her ham and cheese. "Ah, yes. Father Ricci, meet Myrrh Shafat. Also known as Myrrh of Alexandria, Myrrh the Heretic, Myrrh the Demon-Slayer, *Mar* Myrrh, and Oh Lord Not Her Again *Arrrgh*."

"Am I still called that?" Myrrh swallowed a bit of pulp. "I thought they'd forgotten that back in '09."

"2009?" Church frowned.

"Try 1409," O'Malley advised. "And possibly 1709, and 1909... quite likely 909...."

Church stared at him. Then at Myrrh, who looked utterly innocent, and Aidan, who didn't look at all surprised - maybe amazed, but not *surprised-*

And then at Father Ricci. Who looked almost as croggled as she felt. "Myrrh the hell-raider," he said numbly. "Mother Mary, have mercy on us. I thought you were a *myth*."

"Not quite," Myrrh stated. "Though there were many times I was worried my luck had run out. Things were... very difficult, where I was." She paused. "But I found a friend. Father, may I introduce you to Aidan Lindisfarne?"

"Um." The redhead was cupping the candle in one hand, light shining through his fingers. "Hi."

O'Malley raised bushy white brows at him. And seemed to be trying, very hard, not to laugh out loud. "It's a fine name, that it is."

"Uh-huh. *Now* you give a name," Church grumbled, still reeling. Beside her Ricci seemed to have given up trying to play it cool, and had buried his face in his hands. She couldn't blame him. No way. There was just *no way* she was going to believe this little... sorceress, whatever she was, had been around for over a millennium. "Like it's a real one. Much less yours, Shafat. You really expect us to believe this? There are *vampires* who aren't a thousand years old!"

"I know." Myrrh's smile could have frozen fire. "I'll have to meet those who are, someday."

Oooo *damn* but that woman was cold. Church couldn't hide a

shudder. "If you're going to threaten legal citizens of the United States-"

"Threaten?" A white brow arched, elegant as a swan. "I merely said I wished to meet them. You're very suspicious, Detective."

"You gonna try and tell her she's not right?" Aidan muttered. "What is a vampire, anyway? Hollywood's got all kinds of versions, though I think they buried the good soulful detective ones from the seventies six feet deep. But you act like they're as nasty as the folks downstairs."

"They *are* the folks downstairs," Myrrh said simply. "They are corpses possessed by an evil spirit, who use stolen bodies and stolen memories to prey upon men. You've likely seen some of them disembodied. Demons who look as if someone twisted a body into a giant mosquito?"

If she'd been sipping her coffee, Church would have choked on it. *Say what?*

"Ugh. Those little twerps?" Aidan's face curled into an unmistakable *ewww*. "I thought vampires were supposed to be heavy hitters."

Say what?

Vampires *were* heavy hitters. Everybody knew that. Werewolves might be faster, and they didn't go poof in sunlight; sorcerers might be able to call storms and cure early Ebola. But if the sun was down, and you were within running distance of them? Vampires could charm people with a look, tear out throats in a single bite, and bench-press a bank safe. If they wanted you dead, you were dead.

"They're stronger once they've stolen a body," Myrrh shrugged. "A stake to the heart may not be the end, if the demonic spirit can find another corpse to use." She held up an instructing finger. "Stake, decapitate, then have someone purify the corpse so it is no longer safe harbor."

As if any vampire was going to sit still for that, Church grumped silently. That was the kind of idiotic so-called advice that got people *killed*.

At night, Church admitted to herself. *But Hunters don't go after vamps at night, do they?*

Some people said vampires slept like the dead after dawn.

Others, that they could be awake as long as they steered clear of sunlight. Church had never let herself be invited into a vampire's home near dawn to find out for sure.

...But then, Hunters weren't worried about invitations. Or due process, or laws in general. If you were aiming for a murder rap, who cared about little things like breaking and entering?

Myrrh hadn't even slowed down. "If you can't bring someone like the good Fathers to a scene-"

Or if they've got enough legal sense to steer clear of a homicide, *thank you very much.*

"-fire and sunlight are both effective at purification. The Hammer movies were right in that much, at least. Thank goodness. If they weren't, we'd have to hunt down all those who perform sky burials, and those faiths have suffered enough already."

Church blinked, her inner peanut gallery buried by an avalanche of sheer disbelief. Stared at Father Ricci, who looked just as lost. "Sky burial?" the younger priest said warily.

"*Hollywood* got vampires right?" Church added, just as dazed.

O'Malley waggled a stern finger at his fellow priest. "You, brush up on your Asian studies. Who knows but we'll have a Zoroastrian or a Tibetan Buddhist walk in wanting to convert one of these days, and you'd better have your arguments ready. You," he winked at Church. "Well, mostly. In some movies. Dracula was far from your average vampire. We're all in luck that the demonic pacts that allowed some vampires to walk by day were never widely known, and the churches seem to have hunted down all those master vampires who did know them. One of the few things Catholics and Protestants have ever agreed on," he mused. "You might read Hunter Morris' journals. There are scanned copies on many Hunter websites, and I believe his Bowie knife is in service to this day."

She was not going to shout at him, Church told herself firmly. *"Hunter websites?"*

"So the Internet has been useful." Myrrh folded her hands over each other, pleased. "I thought it might become so."

"It's different from the Web you knew," O'Malley advised her. "Ask my brother in Christ to introduce you to Web browsers. And the latest antivirus programs." He paused, taken aback. "Oh saints.

You, loose on Amazon...."

Which made sense if he was sticking to this crazy story, Church thought numbly. Twenty-five years of catching up on the Internet? Whoof. "There are *Hunter websites* still up, telling people how to kill vampires?"

"Why should there not be?" Myrrh inquired. "While I have known some rare few who have repented of their sins, and sought to serve the light of God, they are demons. Demons with memories of what it was to be human, yes; but that drives most of them to even darker evil. They are not," one lip curled, a tooth-baring snarl, "*good neighbors.*"

From the depths of her coat, she pulled out this morning's paper.

Church looked between her and the headlines, and sucked in a breath. That anger, that desperate flicker of fear in gray eyes, when she'd have sworn that woman wasn't afraid of *anything....*

She really doesn't know. She really might have missed the Dark Day.

"Father." Myrrh swallowed. "What has *happened* to our world?"

Church let out a slow breath. She didn't know what to say to that. She didn't know if there was anything she *could* say to that. If Myrrh was really some kind of thousand-year-old demon hunter - what did the world even look like to her?

"What she said, double." Aidan sipped his coffee like he didn't care if it was steaming, amber eyes haunted and angry in a way Church had only seen in survivors of a massacre. "First time I knew sorcerers were anything more than guys in pointy hats in fantasy books, there was a guy sharpening up an obsidian knife." Fingers made an abortive move toward his throat, stopped. "And now a cop throws that word around like - like it's just a used-car salesman, like I'd ever be something like that-!"

On the kitchen counter, a roll of paper towels burst into flames.

Holy-! Fumbling back in her seat, Church jerked her head to scan the kitchen. *Fire extinguisher. Where-?*

Yanking a massive pot lid out from an under the counter cabinet, O'Malley slammed it over burning paper.

"Aidan, breathe!"

Whump.

Crackling died into silence.

"I'm sorry." The redhead was ashen. "I'm... damn, I'm so sorry, I...."

"Look at me." Myrrh's voice was soft, but her grip on his shoulder would not be moved. "Aidan. Fire is emotion. You need to learn calm." Her breaths were regular, unhurried as a quiet stream. "If you can't be calm, find something safe to burn. The candle. A bit of paper in your hand. Even matches would work; we should get you some to carry." Her free hand covered his, wrapping around trembling fingers. "You're not used to magic in this world. You will make mistakes. They're not to be feared. Only understood."

The redhead shivered. "That could've been somebody!"

No kidding. And Church was seriously reevaluating her stance on paperwork, 'cause she'd rather dig out from under a ton of it than get lit on fire, thanks.

"No, it could not." Myrrh sounded certain as the sea. "You were upset with Detective Church. She's fine."

Waving away smoke, Church glowered. Clearly they had different definitions of *fine*. Seriously, what was his damage-

Oh. Damn.

Leave out the flaming towels of death, and Aidan's reaction fit that gut-wrenching impression she'd formed on the ambulance ride: the white-faced strain of a kidnap victim coming slam up against a reminder of his kidnappers. Put that together with the specific flinch at sorcerers - oof.

It'd fit. Hold magic with magic.

Yeah, *maybe*. If said sorcerer had all his special rune-circles up and running and never, *ever* made a mistake. Sorcery was so easy to screw up if you saw it coming....

Church went still, remembering roars and pain and blood. A sword of light. Fire with a wave of Aidan's hands.

That wasn't sorcery.

She should have thought of that hours ago. Sorcery took prep time. A *lot* of prep time. Even minor healers had to put in advance work on their talismans and ointments and stuff; kind of like making a battery, from the explanations she'd gotten. Without that stored power, your fanciest gadget just wasn't going to work.

She'd seen the paramedics go over Myrrh, and she'd given Aidan a pat-down herself. They didn't *have* any prepped items. Outside of Myrrh's shadow-shift; and that was weird all by itself. A human would have to be wearing a charged pendant to keep one of those in one piece. They couldn't just gather the magic to fuel it with a snap of their fingers.

But what if you could?

Church swallowed dryly, and scribbled that thought down with *need to talk with the Captain.* If some people *could* use magic fast....

Then we're in a deeper hole than I ever imagined. And sinking fast.

Only if Aidan could snap-cast, that threw yet another weight on the *not likely* side of the kidnap ledger. Sure, sorcerers probably came in flavors of sick and twisted, but fire was the ultimate wild card. Sorcerers liked things tidy. Why would anyone even try?

Why does anybody do anything? Power, sex, money, someone screwed them over at work-

That sent a cold chill down her back. Coral had said once that vamps got a kick out of drinking rare blood. What could be rarer than the red stuff from somebody who'd normally turn them into matches?

If he can. If that was *an accident - then maybe the fire isn't always there when he tries to throw it, either.*

Which put a kidnapping right back into *maybe* territory. Especially if Aidan could set fires by accident. Most people never wanted to really, seriously hurt another living person. She could think of all kinds of nasty ways you could twist up someone who didn't want to set fires... and way too many gruesome scenarios of what might have happened when someone pushed him far enough to decide to *live*, no matter who else got hurt.

And something must have. What he threw in the cemetery - that was no accident.

No. Those had been calculated, deadly blows, each meant to put something inhuman down for the count-

Inhuman.

Aidan had fried the demon. He'd *dodged* the bullets.

He didn't use fire on Rajas' crazies. Even when they shot at him. He didn't try to fry me; didn't even threaten to, when I had Myrrh handcuffed to the bed. Not that that lasted long.

Lethal toward monsters, stammering and apologizing when innocent paper towels went up in flames. Not the attitude of a trained killer.

So maybe a sorcerer could hold Aidan after all. And in her experience, vampires had plenty of money to persuade somebody to take risks. Even when they ought to know better.

Easy on the drive there, Detective. You hate Cruz and her whole damn coven. And yeah, they could pay for something like this. Doesn't mean they did. Get him talking.

Which meant she had to be patient, and not chew him out for nearly barbecuing her. Darn it.

"You are not going to burn a living soul by accident, Aidan." Myrrh eyed the window Father Ricci had just yanked open so smoke could go elsewhere. "The landscape's another matter. But people? No." Gray eyes turned on Church, chill with warning. "Because you are not a sorcerer, who works by his command of spirits willing and unwilling. You are an elemental mage; and fire is far less willing to burn the living than most would believe. All that lives has water in it. Fire would much rather feast on a bit of dry grass, or a scrap of paper. Burning the living is *work*. And fire will always take the path of least resistance."

Aidan blinked. Church felt like blinking right back.

The redhead shook himself, and seemed to focus on Myrrh again. "...Did you just call me lazy?"

"Hmm. Let me think," the demon-hunter mused. "Sloth is one of the sins."

"You did. You...." A sheepish smile fought its way onto his face. Aidan took a deep, smoke-tainted breath, and hunched his shoulders toward the priests. "Um. I'm sorry about that? I'm not used to... things were a lot less fragile where... oh man, I shouldn't even be here...."

Part of Church wanted to tell him to just go. Leave, take his crazy self and his crazy fire and his insane hell-raider along with him. The world was insane enough as it was.

But I'm a cop.

"My partner's in the hospital because you two landed on the perps that were trying to kill us," Church got out. "I want to know what they were doing. I want to know why. And I want to know how to stop them."

Aidan's chin came up. He breathed a bit deeper, even if he was gripping Myrrh's shoulder like a cliff-growing tree.

Shaky, but he's hanging in there, Church judged. *Damn. He's one tough guy.*

Not the macho bravado she'd seen in way too many pimps, or the darker version that gave her goosebumps from mafia made men. Aidan had dyed-in tough; the kind she'd seen in cops whose families had been cops for as long as anyone could remember. Bad things happened, and they were born to do something about it.

And he was still willing to step up after somebody had put a serious hurt on him. That wasn't just tough. That was *trust.*

He believes Myrrh's got his back. And so does the Father.

She didn't know Aidan well enough to trust his judgment, but she knew O'Malley. If he thought a Hunter and her rescuee were a working pair, she'd roll with it. Because Hunter or not, Myrrh was at least giving her answers.

Work with a Hunter who saved Tom's life, or let everything supernatural keep sucking Intrepid dry. Gee, decisions, decisions.

Looked at that way - well. She didn't have to like someone to work with them.

If I can get them both headed my way.... Church eyed the other half of the crazy pair. "You say sorcerers work with spirits? And Aidan's... elemental? I thought magic was magic."

Then again, she'd also thought magic was slow. And vampires always went poof in daylight. What else did she know that wasn't true?

Ricci steepled his fingers on the table, listening intently. "What?" he said at Father O'Malley's chuckle. "I know she'll have a different explanation from the seminary."

I don't want to know, I don't want to know... aw, heck. I've got to ask. "You teach this in the seminary?" Church said numbly.

"We do now, yes," O'Malley nodded. "And in the nunneries. Amazing how many new sisters we have, now that the ladies have seen true evil... ah, never mind me. Go on, lass."

White brows climbed. "The short version?"

"That'd likely be best," O'Malley agreed.

"Hmm." Myrrh sipped her coffee, obviously putting her thoughts in order. "There are many traditions of magic, Detective. But when the outer trappings are stripped away, there are four main forms that hold power in this world. Sorcery, magecraft, wizardry, and enchantment."

Aidan was listening intently, Church noticed. But she put on a casual shrug. "Magic, magic, magic, and more magic?"

"In a sense, you are not wrong," Myrrh said judiciously. "Any one of those forms may draw power from any source of magic; diabolical, terrestrial, fay, or celestial. It depends on the skill and training of the practitioner. But those forms differ in very profound ways." She held up one finger. "Sorcery is magic done by the invocation of spirits; willing, or unwilling. In and of himself, a sorcerer may not have much magic. What he must have is a will of pure steel. For even the most benevolent of sorcerers must match wills with the entities they seek to ask boons of, or such creatures may use them instead."

Crazy. But.... "That demon-bear," Church remembered. "It was pushing at Feniger. It wanted him to take some kind of scales of justice away from me before it'd do anything, or it was going to start eating his goons."

"Did it? Then we may have saved his life as well." Myrrh didn't exactly sound like she was jumping for joy over that. "Only a strong sorcerer should dare to summon a malursine. They are far from the brightest of demons, but they will not be ruled by one of lesser strength." Her teeth flashed white. "Binding a malursine is rather like holding onto a grenade with the pin pulled. You can do it, but if you slip...." She shrugged.

Boom. Right. "Can you do it?" Church demanded.

"No. I am not a sorcerer. I can banish such creatures, and I can certainly slay them. But I cannot summon them." Gray glanced at Aidan. "Simply being a sorcerer, in itself, is not evil. But there are very, very few sorcerers who work in good faith with the spirits they call, and treat them honorably, and so gain willing allies. Even fewer who gain friends."

Aidan folded his arms, clearly not convinced. "So it is like being a used-car salesman."

"In a way," Myrrh agreed. Turning back to Church, she held up a second finger. "Then there is magecraft. Magic tied to the cycles of the world, of day and night, the elements creating and destroying one another. Inborn magic, not sought-for; magecraft may be dormant, but nothing can rouse it in those who do not bear the gift. Aidan is a fire mage. He is unpracticed, and has a great deal to learn. But fire is his to call and shape; and even to quench, if he can calm himself. That's very difficult for fire. It is tied to passion, particularly anger. And when one is in the grip of righteous rage, it can be very hard to take a breath, and stop."

Which was not making Church feel any better about being across the table from the living firecracker. But she'd seen enough herb-charms and small spells to guess a few things. *If he's fire - heck, Father O'Malley's been trying to get me to carry more holy water. Might as well take him up on it. Though I haven't heard about anything burning down. Yet.*

Then again, Myrrh had all but stated she'd snatched Aidan away from whoever'd been holding him. Maybe she ought to be looking for diced bad guys instead.

...Except if O'Malley was right, up until dawn had hit in that graveyard, Myrrh had been *dead and in Hell.* How could she have snatched Aidan away from anybody?

He said she chastises demons, chases down lost souls, and frees them for judgment. Church bit her lip. *What am I missing?*

A third finger lifted. "Wizardry may be learned *or* inborn," Myrrh stated. "Many seek it, and some unfortunate souls find it seeking them. It deals with the numbers of the universe; the patterns of fate, and the great wheel of the stars some call astrology. Those who teach themselves are oft called diviners; those whose magic seizes them unwilling, seers. They can be very, very dangerous."

Seers. Church tried not to react to that. Halo? Dangerous? She wanted to laugh at the thought. Halo would have his work cut out for him fighting his way out of a paper bag.

And yet... cross Halo, and someone *always* got hurt. Usually in the most freakish ways.

Halo's not the one you're facing down right now. "And that leaves one," Church observed. "So you're an enchanter?" She tried to look casual. "What do they do?"

"We enchant," Myrrh said simply. "There are other ways to access that power; rune-carving, effigies, other crafts. But the word in English is from *incantare*, to sing or chant."

Church rolled her eyes. "If I wanted a dictionary... you sing things to death?"

Myrrh smiled.

And the world...

Fell...

Away.

Darkness. An endless, silent darkness. She couldn't hear her heartbeat. She couldn't hear her own thoughts. She couldn't hear herself *be-*

Light blazed from nothingness, shaping the dark into stars and galaxies and planets blooming blue and green with life.

"In the beginning was the Word, and the Word was with God, and the Word was God."

"John." O'Malley's voice, old but firm, gently chivvying the incandescence back, until the mortal kitchen once more formed around them. "Chapter one, verse one."

Church thumped a fist against her chest. Heart. Still beating. "What... what was that...?"

Father O'Malley was breathing deep, as if he'd held his breath a long moment. Father Ricci was pressed back against his chair, looking like he'd been smacked with a sparkly pillow. And Aidan-

The redhead looked scarily unruffled. Just a little wistful.

"An enchanter works name magic," Myrrh said quietly. "*Gnosis.* That is what Gnostic meant; one who holds knowledge of the true essence of things. I know their names, and so I may affect them." She bowed her head. "I admit I am more powerful than most. I am a child of Alexandria, and we have ever revered books; and so I came to study that Word, and take that knowledge into my heart and faith. So I can reach deeper and swifter than most, by invoking echoes of the greatest of Names. For all things came to be through the Word, and without the Word, nothing made has being."

"John, verse three," O'Malley murmured. "More or less."

Mirth sparkled in gray eyes. "Are we going to discuss translation differences again?"

"Ah, but I'm ready for you this time!" Father O'Malley waved a warning finger. "The latest works on ancient Greek, Aramaic, Syraic, Coptic, *and* Hebrew. We'll see who translates who!"

Aidan held up his hands in a time-out, and moved them past each other as if separating prizefighters. "Opposite corners and wait for the bell. Demon in the graveyard. Demongate on the other side; and if he couldn't even handle one little demon-bear? I *don't* think Rajas Feniger has what it takes to build one. *Focus.*"

Demon in the graveyard. Church shuddered, and caught Father Ricci wrapping fingers around his coffee as if he couldn't get warm enough.

But it was O'Malley's *urk* at *Demongate* that snapped the detective's attention to him. Because seriously, *Demongate?* It sounded like the kind of late-night schlocky horror movie thing sadistic little human larvae would try to draw up in their parents' basements, thinking they'd make a deal with Ominous Dark Powers to get out of homework or boink the head cheerleader. Not the sort of mess she normally ended up handling, but she had friends in uniform who'd spent a *lot* of time out at the firing range when missing pet cases ended in tears.

She collected names of kids like that. Sadistic to animals was one step away from sadistic to people; and it was damn chilling how many of those kids ended up in werewolf packs.

But O'Malley had *urk*ed, which meant campy sounding name or not, this thing was serious. "Father?"

"A Demongate." The old priest didn't look at all paternal now. The old spine was straight, and blue eyes were calculating; like an effigy Church had seen in a picture once, an old Crusader caught in eternal stone. "Where? And how close to opening?"

"How close - not very. Yet. It depends on how cautious the crafter chooses to be. It would take several more sacrifices to power it fully. *Where,* I'm not entirely sure." Myrrh's gaze went to the floor under their feet, as if she could peer through wood and stone to the Earth's core. "But we've walked enough of Intrepid to know it is anchored here."

"Ah."

A white brow went up.

"There have been suspicious deaths over these past many years," O'Malley shrugged. "I hadn't realized anything had progressed so far."

Suspicious deaths. Demongate. Church might not believe in Heaven, but she had plenty of proof bad guys might try to bargain with Hell. "Are we talking ritual sacrifices here?" *Every year around Halloween... oh boy.*

"We might be." A deep breath, and the Crusader faded back to the elderly priest. "These days I spend most of my time on holy ground. I missed it."

Myrrh glanced up at that, and frowned. "We can attend to it, old friend."

The old man was shaking his head. "You've been gone twenty-six *years*, lass. You shouldn't have to-"

"Hell-raider," Aidan quipped. "Don't think you can stop her." Amber eyes peered at Father Ricci. Who was still pale, hands not quite shaking on his cup. "You look like you need a life-preserver."

"These are definitely deeper waters than I'm used to," the younger priest admitted. "I... well. I'm a parish priest, Aidan. I have a calling and I serve my flock. But I'm about as sensitive to magic as rock." He snorted. "And that might be insulting the rock."

"We all serve in our own ways, Matthew." O'Malley rested his hands on the table, bracing himself. "You may want to make some calls to our Bible study groups. If we're invited to bless certain areas of the city - it won't destroy the foundations, but it *will* slow down the construction."

And Aidan twitched again at *bless*. Church frowned, pen poised to pounce-

"Do you think you might see a way to have a runner consult on your cold cases?" O'Malley said, almost casual. "Myrrh's slammed the door in hellish faces before."

The detective tried not to wince. Getting info from two stray might-be-Hunters was one thing. Invite a person of interest in a mass homicide to consult on other homicides? Church could almost feel the case getting tossed down the courthouse steps, and hear her badge clinking down carved stone after it.

O'Malley thinks if I do this alone, I'm dead.

Say he was right. Say poking these cases any more than she already had *would* end up with her grabbed for a demonic buffet.

They have to catch me, first.

She was a cop, and she was armed. And it looked like Myrrh could take somebody like Feniger with one hand tied behind her back.

Letting her into the files might blow the case. But if she's just with me when I poke the case? Yeah. That might work.

They had about two weeks before somebody else died. And she was a cop. She was supposed to protect people. If that meant making herself a target....

Church swallowed, and tried not to make it obvious. She knew how the victims had died.

But someone's got to stop him.

"I'll talk with the captain," Church said, almost steadily. "If we can get you on record as a consultant, might work. Though - one thing." Now she did let them see her gulp. Because damn it, Aidan might be the one tossing fire, but Myrrh was *scary*. And in Church's experience, people did not learn to be that scary without a very good reason. "If you can do... that thing with the stars... what'd you even need a sword for?"

"Ah. But I can't *do that*, as you put it, under all circumstances." Myrrh waved at the kitchen; homey and close, cabinets worn of blue paint on a few corners, mugs hanging on pegs beside the sink. "This is a very friendly environment to that incantation, Detective. This is where the good Fathers sit, and talk of the world and its creation, and counsel souls in need of more than a mere confession and light penance. To pluck a strand of the truth of the universe, and make it visible for a moment - that is easy here. Much as Aidan would find it easy to call flame to dry tinder. Or as you would, to find one nervous soul in the crowd at the crime scene tape."

Church shook her head. "I don't have magic."

"All that lives has magic. Some of us are more apt at focusing it than others." Myrrh shrugged. "But even the strongest magic-user has limits, Detective. I am a marathon runner where most only jog; that doesn't mean I can cast spells indefinitely. Demons are creatures of spirit, not flesh and blood. Parting the veil of the physical world a moment does not shake them, any more than it would startle you to take off sunglasses." A smile tugged at her lips. "For them, I need to take a direct approach. Just as you do."

Right. Like you're anything like me. "You have limits, huh?" Church gave her an arch look. "*I* can't shake off steel cuffs."

Myrrh inclined her head. "And if you had legal cause to arrest me, or even to hold me, neither could I."

"...Say what?" Because that made *no sense whatsoever.*

"Enchanters deal with the essence of things. I draw my strength from truth and law. Therefore, I am bound by them. It's much the same for any user of magic." For a moment Myrrh's gaze was distant. "You could think of it as a pattern, bound into our spirits. Force a bicyclist to run a marathon, and he will do very poorly. Drop a tank from an airplane, and... well." She shook her head. "No; some things are best done by mundane means. Which reminds me. Father, do you have ways to warn your parishioners against keeping their personal possessions in Suntrust vaults?"

"We've done what we can about that," Father Ricci sighed. "It's what we suspected, then?"

"If by suspected you mean manager's playing nummy snack for a vampire, then yeah," Aidan grumbled. "How'd you know?"

"I've access to Myrrh's vault in case of emergencies." O'Malley rubbed his hands together. "But since I'm not the demon-hunter the sigils were set to trap, it's never gone off. How big was the boom?"

"You..." Church sputtered. "Damn it, Father, I need to report explosives!" Father O'Malley was supporting a Hunter who wanted things to blow up. What else didn't she know about him?

"There hasn't been a boom. Yet." Myrrh blinked, utterly innocent. "I don't expect one until after sunset, at the very soonest. And there are no explosives to report, Detective. If feeding a vampire is a lifestyle choice, then surely the fact that such bloodsucking, demonic spirits tend to... react *violently* to the touch of blessed artifacts... is certainly no more noteworthy?"

"How violently?" Church asked, feeling something like dread shiver down her spine. You couldn't fight vampires. People got killed trying. If some hothead managed to stake a body lying in a coffin, it was some innocent Goth and they were a murderer. And even if you could fight vampires, they weren't breaking the law by being bloodsuckers.

Damn it.

"Hm." Myrrh looked positively wicked. "Well, that would depend on the vampire's age, and state of grace. If it is a truly repentant demon, they're likely to only have a warning burn."

"Worst-case scenario?" Aidan looked as numbly fascinated as Church felt.

"Thousand-year-old vampire lord, who has no care for how many fledglings he unleashes on the world?" Myrrh gave her a considering look. "There may not be a bank left in the morning."

There was a *thump*, more felt than heard, that seemed to rattle down Church's spine.

"Or now," Myrrh mused, gray eyes thoughtful. "And it's not even sunset yet. Interesting. I didn't sense any vampires in the vault already. I wonder how one got in?"

Church blinked at her, heart thudding in her ears. *She can't be serious.* "...The bank was still open."

The white head dipped. "I know."

"You... you...." She couldn't find the words. "When they find the explosives-"

"There were no explosives." Myrrh met her gaze head on. "Save those the vampires themselves might have put there. He who sets a snare has no right to complain if it seizes his own foot."

Church was going to shoot someone. Just as soon as she figured out who. "You don't set snares to kill innocent people!"

"I did not." Myrrh stood; a quiet, waiting stance that Church recognized as potentially as dangerous as running headfirst into a meat grinder. "Perhaps you could quell your anger until we know if anyone has, in fact, died."

"And while you're at it, maybe you want to take a good hard look in the mirror." Aidan's long fingers curled and uncurled, like licking flames. "Bank manager lets vampires slap magical booby-traps on a safe deposit box they don't rent, and you're blaming Myrrh when they go off?"

Church bared her teeth. "You walked away from something you knew could go boom and didn't report it?"

"And just who were they supposed to report it to, Detective?" Father O'Malley's voice was like a splash of cold water. "When the demonspawn hid in the darkness, Myrrh could have gone to any police station and reported tampering with her vault, surely. Now?" He waved a hand about the kitchen; work-worn and small and poor, compared to the resources Nuria's coven could summon with just one phone call. "What do you expect her to do, strip the entire force naked and check for bites?"

Damn. Father O'Malley *never* got that blunt.

And he thinks she could do it, too.

"Miss Shafat is a hell-raider, Detective," Father Ricci put in, glancing between them, white collar bright against his cassock. "If the myths... excuse me, the legends, are true... then the vampires want her dead. And they don't care how many humans they take out to do it."

"The vampires have to abide by the law, like everyone else," Church said flatly. "This isn't a war-"

"If you think we are not at war with evil," Myrrh cut across her words, "then you haven't been paying attention."

Church breathed in, and out, tamping down that lava-rush of anger. *I know what's happening in my city. I* know. "You two are coming with me."

Chapter Eight

"Bide a moment, lad."

Aidan hesitated, gaze flicking to the parking lot where Church was gesticulating as Myrrh listened, and nodded, and refused to set foot off the church sidewalk. "This is only going to get worse-"

"It may, yes. But if Myrrh can't stall our determined detective a bit longer, I don't know her." Father O'Malley looked up to meet his gaze, face solemn in the growing shadows of the sunset. "As I used to know you."

It felt like a punch in the gut. Aidan looked into the clear blue eyes of the man who'd once let him serve at the altar, and lied like a rug. "Sorry. You've got to be confusing me with somebody else."

"I think I am not." O'Malley's eyes were hooded, made even sadder by sunset's gold. "Though I know well why you would deny it." He hesitated, then sighed. "You should know that Detective Church suspects Steven Savonarola of many things, and they likely aren't half of what he has done."

He's alive. Oh God. The world seemed to swim around him. *My brother is....*

No. It didn't make sense. "He can't be alive," Aidan whispered. "He stopped summoning... somebody."

Because Myrrh had been *right*; he'd used *Aidan* as a shield against ties of blood and spirit. Only he hadn't done it straight off. No; he'd spent years - endless, screaming years - only invoking that nickname for the first few seconds of a summoning. Just long enough to see how well it fought the pull. Then he'd let the spell latch on, a little easier each time. Hiding his face and his fury in a globe of fire, no matter how Steven laughed at him. Biding his time, even as his nerves strained to the breaking point, until he was sure he could survive the wilds of Hell.

Aariel had taught him about name magic, though half of what Aidan had learned had been from what Aariel *didn't* say. Putting together the bits and pieces, someone who held a demon's name could compel the truth from them; and given Steven's blood, he'd had plenty of chances to get his hooks into low-level members of Yaldabaoth's court. Meaning if Aidan wanted to get clear of Steven, he'd have to get clear of the court at the same time. Given what he'd seen of the Hunt, and Yaldabaoth's sadistic dismemberment of souls who'd crossed the line... what he'd planned to pull would only work *once*.

He'd waited. And learned. And *endured*.

Then he'd bolted. Not straight to Myrrh; Yaldabaoth *had* called out a Hunt, and no way was he going to bring that down on a tiny ghost's head. Instead he'd run for one of her little sanctuaries, like that crack in the rocks on the Wailing Plains, where Myrrh had traced runes and hieroglyphs in a dozen subtle places to make it harder to find.

He'd made it to a shelter. And then he'd hunkered down and prayed, for what had turned out to be a very bad week.

For years after that, Steven had kept trying. Yanking on the blood-tie, as if it were a garrote around his brother's throat, fury boiling like a Yellowstone geyser. And he'd kept throwing *Aidan* between himself and that call like an iron wall, holding on one moment more, and one more, and... just *holding*, until the pain ebbed away. Because maybe he couldn't hold out forever, maybe this time Steven would win, maybe Yaldabaoth and his lackeys would swarm him while he was in too much pain to *see*, much less move, and tear him into screaming soul-shreds-

"May I call you Aidan?"

Myrrh had given him that name. Which meant if Steven ever got him back, his brother would have a straight line back into the only help Aidan had ever known.

I won't let him touch her. Not now, not ever.

One year, the summons had just stopped. There could only be one explanation for that. Or so he'd thought.

He's alive. Oh Hell.

"Aidan Lindisfarne." Father O'Malley had a hand against his shoulder, bracing him. "You have passed through the valley of the shadow of death, and returned. I can't imagine any soul who could understand what you've gone through." He paused. "Except for one."

Myrrh. Yeah, she's one in a... wait. "One?" Aidan said shakily.

"She said she was *a* hell-raider. That should mean...."

"There have never been many with the faith to descend into Hell and return," O'Malley said softly. "And they've always worked in secret. They're the stealth bombers of the Faith, and serve best when evil does not know where to find them. But I've searched and listened, these past decades. She is the last." He drew a breath, gauging the length of growing shadows as the Black Mountains glinted gold with sunset. "The forces of darkness can move freely these days, so long as they don't draw blood in public. They've grown used to walking our streets, while those who would oppose them - and Church tries to - must lurk in the shadows, never facing evil in an open fight. Into this darkness, you have brought two blazing lights. You will both be targets."

Aidan swallowed, throat dry. "I'm not a light," he whispered.

"You are a better soul than I think you yet know," O'Malley said firmly. "Like your mother, God rest her soul. Steady, now...."

Steady? How could he be steady? "What... how did she...?"

"Grief, I'd say." O'Malley sighed. "She'd lost one son, and her husband, and she suspected her last son was worse than lost." Blue eyes searched his. "She left this world in peace, Aidan. And I know she loved you, no matter what she discovered your true sire had been."

Erk.

"The Church has sheltered those with demonic blood before," O'Malley said quietly. "The sins of the father do not descend upon the son. You are responsible for your own salvation; by your deeds, and your heart." He glanced toward the impatient detective. "Your name will protect you from much, but Savonarola is a canny opponent. He will strike at you, and off these grounds, we can do little to aid you." He lowered his voice. "Myrrh knows you're in danger, even if she does not know how much. She would never fault you for taking shelter with us."

"She wouldn't." Aidan closed his eyes, remembering white hair and safety, in the midst of Hell. "I would. She needs help, Father. And," he let out a breathless laugh. "What's that thing you say, about not hiding your light under a bushel? Way things are going, I'd probably burn the whole barn down."

"You might at that," the priest said wryly. "Well, then. Give an old man a hug? For luck."

Aidan tried not to gulp. Outside of some sneaky sparring with Myrrh, touching anybody for the past few decades....

It's Father.

Swallowing hard, he wrapped his arms around the bony old priest. And felt - warm. Not fire-hot. Not frozen. Just warm. "You take care of yourself, 'kay? I need to hear the rest of it. I don't want to... but I have to."

"Godspeed, my son." O'Malley held him at arm's length a moment, as if memorizing his face. "Remember, lad. There's nothing wrong with being a bit of a rascal. Love the Lord, and love your neighbor, and give Evil a good smack in the kisser."

Aidan eyed him. "I don't remember that bit in the New Testament."

"Read up on the lives of the saints." O'Malley grinned at him. "Your namesake was a corker."

"Yeah, yeah, the fire extinguisher-"

"Hah!" The priest laughed, loud and long. "I'll have to dig you up his history. The man didn't put out fires, Aidan."

Huh? "He didn't?" Aidan asked warily. "He's supposed to be the saint of firefighters...."

"Oh, indeed he is. And the saint of *backfires*." O'Malley's grin was almost as fierce as Myrrh's. "When the Vikings set his city ablaze, he put himself in the fire's path and prayed. And the flames halted, and crept away, and roared back toward the raiders and pillagers to set them scrambling to flee. The Vikings feared him, Aidan." The priest folded his hands, as if in prayer. "Myrrh's an enchantress, lad. She'd never give a lamb's name to a lion."

A lion. He got into the passenger seat of Church's car, trying not to remember. *He knows.*

Yaldabaoth's appearance had changed from day to day and hour to hour, apparently depending on what the demon lord felt would be most intimidating at the time. But there were three things that were always part of him, no matter what he looked like. The fire, and the lion, and darkness.

Aidan ran fingers through his mane of red hair, and tried not to weep.

Christophe had had black hair. Normal hair. But after he'd

starting losing track of the days - after Yaldabaoth's armsmen had gotten *inventive,* and he'd reached desperately for anything that would make them *stop-*

"A trueborn son of our lord." Like a great sphinx made of lava, Sword Aariel had stalked around the flaming corpses of two insectile demons. Reared up onto two legs, drawing the black sword at his side, eyes amber lamps of calculation. *"Good. There is something in you worth training."*

Fire had been the first thing Hell had changed in him. It hadn't been the last.

I wonder... if there's any way to know if Aariel's okay....

And that was a scary thought, right there. Human beings didn't miss Hell, or lava-milk gliding down their throats like fire. And they definitely didn't miss demons.

But if Myrrh had been his shield, his friendly ear, and his sparring partner whenever he could remember being human well enough to take that form-

Aariel had been his sword. The lava-lion had taught him fire, whether he wanted to learn or not. How to burn. How to fight. *When* to fight - and when to bluff and run like crazy, 'cause something was too much for him. How to slip into the shadows, silent as a great cat....

Aariel had taught him to escape Yaldabaoth. His father. Aariel's own demon lord.

And he still didn't know *why.*

"Oough...."

Church snorted as she backed out of the parking lot. "Come on. Don't tell me the itty-bitty demon hunter is carsick?"

"Live two decades without a mortal stomach, and see how you like it." Myrrh fumbled at the door, pale fingers scrabbling at gray plastic. "I see the window, where is the crank...."

"Crank? Sheesh." Church pressed a button on her armrest; glass whined down behind him. "Ever hear of power windows?"

"Ever hear of water demons?" Myrrh had her face pressed against the gap, breathing in great gulps of wind. "I've landed in one. I hope you've a way to break out the windows, if you do."

"Landed *in* one?"

"Eyes on the *road,*" Aidan yelped, as Church slipped between a black-leathered motorcyclist and a cranky red tractor-trailer. When had the big rigs gotten *that* big? "Cop. Cop! You're supposed to use turn signals!"

"You really have been out of this world for years." Smirking, Church stamped down on the gas.

Dear God, Aidan prayed. *Will You forgive me if I want to strangle a cop? I'm pretty sure this counts as mitigating circumstances.*

Church wove them through traffic up to the flashing lights, parking a safe distance back from the firetruck. There were still a few drifts of steam rising from the peak of the bank roof, but the building looked almost intact. If you didn't count the shattered windows, glass blown out like razor-sharp snow.

With a thump of metal and plastic, Myrrh hit the sidewalk outside.

Aidan fumbled off his seatbelt, scrambling out to join her. The glass hadn't reached this far. Fortunately. "You okay?"

"They say one of the marks of sainthood is levitating in ecstatic visions." Myrrh's voice was almost normal as she knelt there, if ragged at the edges. But her face was dead white. "Dear God, let me never be a saint... I'll be all right. In a few minutes." She wiped her mouth with the back of her hand. "I think."

Yeah, sure she would, stubborn idiot-

His hand brushed the car door; the metal, not the plastic handle this time. And Aidan had to bite back a scream.

That. Hurt.

He shook out tingling fingers, almost not believing his eyes. They looked fine, if a little red and blistered across the knuckles. But they ached like he'd stuck them in freezing sea water.

Detroit steel. I'm guessing paint's not as good at insulating it as chrome. And Myrrh's been in Hell a lot more than I have.

Church circled the car to join them, her face all cold cop again. "Carsick, my foot. Magic and steel. No wonder you walked." She jerked a thumb back over her shoulder, to the windows like gaping teeth. "So how much did that take out of you?"

With another breath, Myrrh rose to her feet. "The only spell I laid, was to ensure it was a vampire touching the vault. Not a bloodslave. Not an entranced human. Only one of the undead." A shuddering sigh. "Which is far more mercy than they would have granted. If Father O'Malley visited my vault, he must have taken extreme care when he opened it. Or he would have been at ground zero, and then who would you blame?"

Church's lips thinned. "You two? Stay right here."

Turning on her heel, she stalked toward the uniformed cop controlling the scene.

"Lady needs to see a proctologist," Aidan grumbled. "For the stick up her-"

"She's worried for her people, and her city." Myrrh rubbed her knuckles across her forehead, taking measured breaths. "We've met darkness face to face, and cast it down. She's seen it creep across her world like oncoming night, cloaked in law and custom. She is a watchman against the darkness, and the man she relied on to guard her back lies wounded and helpless. I can't blame her for being angry." Myrrh sighed, gaze flicking over smoke, firetrucks, and the gaggle of morbidly curious bystanders. "I only hope she can turn that fury against the true enemy, instead of those who wish to aid her."

"Yeah, like I really want to... okay, yeah, I do," Aidan admitted at her mild look. Keeping his voice down; he was pretty sure all the reporters were making themselves obnoxious over at the yellow tape, but there was no need to tempt Murphy. "But what can we do? We're not cops. We can't mess with an open investigation. Not if we want her to make a clean case." And thief of heaven or not, Myrrh had already made it clear she paid attention to some laws. He'd have to pin her down on which.

"We can keep our eyes open. Like any other concerned citizens. And we can keep her alive." Pale lips pressed together. "I've nothing else pressing at the moment. Do you?"

A brother who's a sorcerer. Who's somebody Church is after. Who Father O'Malley thinks she should be after. "Demongate," Aidan reminded her.

"And the detective has already been a target of demons. I think we may yet find what we seek." Something sparked in gray eyes, like flint striking steel. "I'm of a mind to start kicking over rocks and see what crawls out."

"Good way to get bit by something," Aidan noted.

"I would be attacked if I became a hermit at the tops of the highest mountains, or sank into the depths of the changeless sea." Myrrh cupped her hands around each other, palm pressed against palm to brace will with flesh and bone. "It is what I am." She huffed a laugh, and winked at him. "If we attack first, we have the advantage of initiative. Believe me, sometimes that's more powerful than any blade."

Which made her sound like Aariel, and wasn't that a kick?

I have escaped him, she'd said. Given what he'd had to do, to learn, to escape demons... maybe that wasn't an accident.

He'd never figured out how much Aariel knew about Myrrh. The two of them had never crossed paths where Aidan could see. He didn't know how much of that was intentional on Myrrh's part, but he knew Aariel had been careful not to know anything he didn't have to about how Aidan was hiding. Or where. Or who he might be hiding with.

Aariel wanted me out of Yaldabaoth's court. Aidan looked through the deepening twilight, fall-touched leaves already lost in shadow, wondering when the monsters were going to come out. *Well, I can't get any farther out of it than here....*

Something fluttered on the wind. Aidan snatched it before he could think.

A ribbon?

Red silk, that somehow felt more real than the gray fabric covering the seats of Church's car. It was embroidered in black... but even in night's shadows, he had no trouble reading it. He hadn't had trouble seeing in the dark for years. Not since the night he'd looked through what should have been an immovable steel grate into a hellhound's eyes. "Isaiah 7?"

"Your country is desolate, your cities burned with fire. Strangers devour your land in your presence, and it is desolate, as overthrown by strangers." A short, ragged lump of dulled colors shuffled down the sidewalk, stray onlookers moving aside as if from a cold blast of wind. "Thank you for catching my bookmark."

I know you. The face was older, grayer. The body was stooped; the spine possibly twisted, unless that was a trick of off-center olive and dun patches on two layers of his coats. But he knew the man, even as faded blue eyes ducked away from his. "Harry?

Harry Lowe?"

"He is a brother to dragons, a companion to owls... a voice crying in the wilderness." Half-gloved fingers fumbled at the silk in Aidan's hand, obviously trying not to touch his skin.

Aidan tried not to shudder. *Oh, Harry. Damn. I thought you got away*.... He lifted his hand, holding the ribbon between two fingers, so Harry could take it without touching him. "Are you okay?"

"The dead walk, and the living tremble." Harry cocked his head, looking past Aidan. "She is as a silken glass, filled with light for all to see. You really should have sunglasses."

"I suppose we should." Myrrh studied Harry like she had the vault, looking at the faint light around him-

There's magic around him. Aidan swallowed, chilled. Because out of the corner of his eyes, when he wasn't thinking, sometimes it looked like Myrrh *was* light. Only her light was the clear, quiet glow of a halo around the moon, or the river of stars he'd almost forgotten in Hell. A patient light, that might not be all you wanted, but was enough for what you needed. And... a kinder light, to eyes too used to the dark.

The light around Harry was a hammer-blow of desert noon. Hot. Pitiless. Stark as bone laid bare by a flensing knife. He hated it on sight.

And that scared him.

Is that all I am? Something out of the dark, that can't take a little sun? "Harry." Oh man, he had no clue what was going on here, but it couldn't be good. "Can we help?"

"You tried, didn't you? A long time ago, before the angels danced around the sun." Harry shook his head, hair ruffling under his knitted gray and blue cap. "You shouldn't have. The jaws would have been bloody and fierce, but the spirit would have fluttered free."

Something in Aidan wanted to shrivel up and die. He'd tried to save Harry. Tried to lead that nightmare horror off, because even if he didn't know why, somehow he'd known the hellhound had come for him. Anything else it got to tear apart was just gravy.

"Unfair, stranger." Myrrh stepped half between them, gray eyes flashing. "It is not for any of us to choose the hour of our deaths. If you seek the water of life for a soul in peril, you do not ask, are my hands too dirty to bear it. You *help*. And worry on the state of your soul later." Her hand touched Aidan's arm, warm and familiar. "What descended on you was not Aidan's doing. What it drives you to, is not our doing. You cannot demand what is not owed." Her eyes narrowed. "But if you truly need help... then ask."

"He's pretty much beyond help."

Church. Aidan had thought he'd recognized that faint prickle of exasperation.

"Halo." The detective's voice was tired as she jammed hands in her coat pockets, but not half as acid as he'd expected. "You know it's not good for you to hang around crime scenes. The rookies keep bringing you in, and then they get embarrassed." She glanced at them, then shook her hands out of her pockets and crossed her arms. "These two bothering you?"

"They draw the darkness." Harry seemed to focus on Church now, an oddly gleeful smile twitching on his face. "So will you, now. I should say I'm sorry-"

"But you're not." Myrrh kept her gaze on him. "What twisted you so, that you delight to see those who would fight evil besieged by darkness?"

"Hey now." Church pushed at air in a *stay calm*, voice level and no-nonsense. "Halo's never been any trouble. Sure he's weird, but he passes on tips we can use."

"And you've never asked him how he comes by these tips?" Myrrh didn't look away from the man rocking from foot to booted foot in front of her. "Or why he's so willing to pass them to you, when you have nothing he truly wants?"

"I've asked." But Church's voice was thoughtful, not threatening as Aidan had expected. "Sometimes it seems like I'm the only one who asks. A cop gets shot saving a family from a home invader; how lucky they were he was there, shame he got put in the hospital. A fireman goes to check on some wiring, and the apartment building burns down; but everybody says it's a miracle, he's the only fatality. We stake out a graveyard to find a skull, and Tom nearly ends up demon-chow. Sure, Halo's tips save people. But the good guys always, *always*, get hurt." Her hand wasn't near her gun. Yet. "Nice to know it's not my imagination."

"You know I wasn't near any of those tragedies, Detective."

Harry's jaw worked; not quite a smile. "After all, I warned people."

"Funny thing about that," Church observed. "You always warn people who *weren't* going to be there."

Aidan took a half-step back, placing himself squarely behind Myrrh. If she thought she could take Harry maybe he'd better let her. He could always toss fire over her head.

What the hell happened to you, Harry? I thought I knew you.

Then again, did anybody know their college buddies? Really? Especially the ones who wanted to be shrinks. Harry had meant to be the doctor, not a patient. Though given the way he fidgeted and shifted, Aidan was willing to bet he wasn't anybody's patient.

Or if he is - I didn't crack when the hellhound ran me down. But... maybe I'm not human enough to crack....

No, that was *stupid*. Myrrh faced demons and laughed about it later. And maybe that was just Myrrh, but here was Church, shaken but standing, after a taxidermist's nightmare had tried to turn her into kibble. Humans could take on demons and keep going. Harry just... hadn't.

"You." Harry tilted his head, eyeing Myrrh like a praying mantis waiting to rip the wings off a butterfly. "Always you. Why couldn't they just eat you?"

"Because I'm not that easy to kill." Myrrh didn't flinch. Just stilled, the way Aidan knew so well from Hell, as if the hush of dawn was in her very bones.

Here is one who would be my enemy. Shall I allow him in range to strike?

"Did you have a message for me?" Myrrh's eyes barely flickered Church's way. "Or one you should be giving to others, if you had the courage to face your visions rather than deny them?"

"I saw you in my dreams." Harry was twisting the ribbon around his fingers, over and over, swift streaks of crimson. "But you never even looked at me. It wasn't fair. You were in *my* dreams, the least you could do was take your clothes off... what was I supposed to do? Go in and tell the cops I saw a demon kill people, only it hasn't happened yet? No. No way." The ribbon wound tighter, turning fingertips pale. "I'm not crazy!"

"That's not what Captain Sherman says." Church looked at the man like she was seriously considering the quickest option to take him down. "I thought the captain didn't know everything. But maybe she was right for the wrong reasons. I found your skull."

"Of course you did," Harry said raggedly. "I can always find what I see. So I can stay away from it. Except *you*." He shuddered, looking at Myrrh as if she'd crawled out from under a rock. "You were dead. He told me that if you were dead the dreams would stop. And they *did*. Until...." His gaze flicked to Aidan. "It's not right. The dead shouldn't come back. So I had to come, this time. I had to see this one didn't come back." Hunted eyes roved to Church. "She didn't, did she? All the red blood dripped away; all the screams stopped."

"Who's he, Halo?" Church was focused; Aidan could feel it, searing like a laser. "Who told you anyone had to die?"

"I may be crazy, but I'm not stupid." Harry snorted, standing up almost straight. "I wasn't here. I didn't do it. And you already know who did." He almost giggled, stifling it with half-gloved knuckles. "How are you going to explain to Esmeralda's coven what happened tonight?"

"I don't know," Church said dryly. "Want to come along and find out?"

Harry stopped laughing.

"I didn't think so," the detective muttered. "If you decide to come clean and tell us something that'll help, you know where the station is. Otherwise-" Her hand slashed an arc through the air; Aidan could feel *forbiddance* press against his skin, "-get *gone*."

Watching her like a mouse might a mountain lion, Harry shuffled off into the crowd. And started laughing. "You're going to lose it all, you know. *Aidan*. You're going to lose *everything!*"

The redhead swallowed hard. *Not going to set him on fire.* Not *going to.*

"The men of Israel, they say, give praise to God that they were not born a woman," Myrrh mused, color slowly returning to pale cheeks. "When pride might see me thinking myself better than that, I find myself praying to thank God I was not born a Seer. What horrors I have seen are past and done. The horrors they see are yet to pass, or may never be." She shook her hands, as if flinging away tainted mud. "And those would be the gentle ones. That man - do not trust him. *Ever*."

"I don't." Church's voice was tight. "But he's never lied to us."

"Just because he's always told the truth, does not mean he has never lied." Myrrh took a breath, and tapped Aidan's arm. "Try to ignore it. Prophecy is always dark, a maze of what might be and what never will. And never more so than when trying to see the fate of one with your heritage. There is a light that clings, even in the darkest pit. And any who look into that light are blinded."

"He... looked like he had light around him," Aidan said hesitantly. *Just say it. Get it over with.* "I didn't like it."

"Light?" Church looked between them, face torn between exasperation and worry. "Come on-"

Her coat pocket rang.

Church yanked out a black cell phone that still had a sticker on the back. Opened it, and grimaced even as she hit a button. "Church."

Curious, Aidan concentrated and *listened*.

"What did you drag Tom into this time?"

"Annabel, you know we can't discuss an active investigation."

"Investigation? My husband is upstairs in our bed with stitches, and you want to talk about making a case?"

"Exactly. I don't want to talk about it," Church said firmly. "What's Tom doing home? The docs said they were keeping him for observation."

"Maybe you can afford to blow a few thousand on a hospital bed, but my husband has responsibilities. Dr. McAliffe said he just needs someone to watch him. His family can do that. Since his partner won't."

Church sucked a breath past her teeth. Aidan could see her counting to ten. "I'm on the job, Annabel. Trying to track down who was behind this so they don't do it to anyone else."

"Well, you'll have to do it without Tom."

Church snatched the phone away and stared at it. Put it back by her ear. "Say what?"

"This is enough! Tom could have died. I don't care what he thinks you found, or who this Ginger is to anyone. He's going into Administration as soon as he's fit to man a desk."

Angry color surged in Church's cheeks, but her voice was

almost level. "Have you talked to Tom about this?"

"How dare you!"

"I'm serious. We've got nine detectives, including the captain, and Halloween's right around the corner," Church stated. "Tom wouldn't leave us in the lurch. You said something about Ginger? We need to find him, Annabel. He's a material witness to some pretty serious stuff. If you want to put Tom on-"

"He's sleeping!" A choked breath. *"He doesn't need to make any more phone calls today!"*

Apparently Church caught that sob just as well as Aidan had. "Annabel, the important thing is he's going to be okay. Right? Besides," the detective chuckled, "if Tom went into Admin, he'd have to pass that test on how to do all the paperwork without strangling anyone. And you know he's never wanted to bother-"

"Oh right, the test.*"* Annabel's huff came over the line. *"You never did know the right people. Stay away from my husband!"*

Click.

Aidan whistled. "What'd you do to that lady? Step on her prize roses? Catch her kids keying the principal's car? Burn down her white picket fence?"

Snapping the phone closed with a reflexive flex of fingers, Church glared at him.

Myrrh coughed into a fist. "Most people's hearing is not quite so acute, Aidan."

...Oops.

"Not that it's any of your business," Church ground out, "but she's usually a decent person. She's just worried about her husband and her family. And yes, one of their boys has been in trouble. Whose hasn't?" She grimaced at the phone, and stuffed it back into her coat, lifting a hand to rub a knuckle against her head. "So. Okay. Case. Maybe I don't believe in *demon* demons. But you guys seem to know monsters, and magic, and I can't help if I don't know what's going on. Light? Around Halo? What the heck does that mean?"

Oh, now *you want to help,* Aidan almost said. But kept the words behind his teeth. If that was what Church was dealing with just to get her job done, she didn't need any more grief. Not to mention Myrrh was looking at him, worried. And the hell-raider definitely had enough to worry about. "I... go ahead and tell her. I don't want to believe it either. But if we're here, and the Demongate's here, and I don't know what's up with Harry but it's bad - yeah. Tell her."

"If you do not believe that demons come from Hell, then I doubt you'd believe that other gifts may come from Heaven," Myrrh said bluntly. "But whatever Power bestowed foresight on the man you call Halo, he chose to bury his gifts instead of follow where his visions led." She paused, obviously picking her words. "Power reacts *very badly* to being ignored, Detective. It's as if you decided to get rid of raccoons in your cornfield by chaining a dog in the midst of it."

Church winced. Caught Aidan's confused look, and elaborated. "Everything inside the chain gets flattened. Everything outside the chain-"

"They get anyway," Aidan nodded. And shuddered. "Is that what happened to him? Why he's...?"

"I don't know," Myrrh admitted. "But if he's passing on his visions to see pain - whatever is wrong with him, I doubt we can fix." She rubbed her arms, as if chilled. "You know where this Esmeralda's coven can be found?"

"That's... kind of why I want your help," Church admitted. "I've done some crazy things. But there's no way I'm walking into a vampire bar alone."

Chapter Nine

"Okay, two questions. Maybe three." Aidan squirmed a bit in the back seat as he finished buckling on her knife harness. "One, how'd you know I use these? Two - no offense, Detective, but people in your line of work tend to get touchy about hidden sharp objects."

"Gee." Church drummed her fingers on the steering wheel, driving with slightly more care now that the fire was deemed truly out. Possibly she was even using her turn signals, though Myrrh couldn't take her eyes off the road long enough to be sure. "Fireballs, or sharp knives. Which would I rather explain to the captain? Oh, let me think...."

"As for knowing you had skill in knives," Myrrh said between breaths; a quarter-century had changed nothing, cars were still awful when she couldn't drive herself. "Those with an affinity for fire often favor the blade. The striking styles, the intent, are very similar. Strike with knives, you must be prepared to be cut; play with fire, be ready to get burned. But there is another reason." Measured breathing. It was the only way to survive with a shred of dignity intact. "There are some few demons - not many, but some - who believe their proper role is the punishment of sinners, no more. Whether that is a shred of morality, or only a desire to avoid a return visit of He Who Shattered the Gates, only their own hearts can say. Still, among those few are some who know what I am, and what I do, and do not strenuously object."

Church, Myrrh noted, was listening rather intently, even as she navigated Intrepid's maze of hilly streets.

"I could not mention this while we were not on Earth. It might have had repercussions. But demons are loathe to trust words spoken on this plane. They well know, humans lie so very easily." Myrrh lifted one shoulder against the restraining strap, grateful for the rushing breeze. "In short - yes, I have met Sword Aariel. He likes to use my presence to weed out those he thinks are stupidly cruel."

A sharp intake of breath behind her. "You said you *escaped* him."

"And I have. We've tried to kill each other quite a few times." Myrrh considered her next words very carefully. Knowing Aariel as she did, it was not only possible Aidan didn't know his true relationship with the demon, it was likely. "Yet if I were dangling over a fiery pit, with no other help, I believe he would pull me out. Of course," she chuckled, "he'd then toss me at the next enemy of his lord in sight. But I think he would pull me out."

Silence. Well; it was a hard thing to think about.

"Should I be worried about this guy?" Church put in.

"No."

Yes, that was a hint of smoke from behind her. Myrrh cleared her throat. "Not likely, Detective. Believe it or not, there are certain demons who don't *like* Earth. If Sword Aariel were ever summoned here... heh. His first order of business would be to find a loophole to kill his summoner, so he could get back to doing his job. He'd probably kill quite a few people in the process," she admitted. "He *is* a demon, after all. But he'd much rather be terrorizing other demons into what he thinks of as useful behavior."

Though she wasn't entirely sure that would be Aariel's first priority, anymore. Not with Aidan returned to the mortal world. The Sword was one of those few demons to whom family actually *mattered.* Yaldabaoth would never have been able to trust him so deeply, otherwise.

"So I have seen him training weaker spirits before," Myrrh went on. "He'd know well enough that you'd never be able to trade blows like a true demon in a fight. He would have taught you the sword; it is a noble weapon, and he would have you use it for foes of your own strength. But those are rare among the greater demons. For them, he would have taught you to strike from a distance, to strike quickly, and to get clear as swiftly as possible. So." Another half-shrug. "It was not hard to guess the weapon you might know."

Church was eyeing both of them in the rearview mirror. "You were trained by a *demon?*"

Aidan tensed. "You wanna make something of it?"

"I... just... how? *Why?*"

"For that, you'd have to ask Aariel," Myrrh said evenly. "Though if you've ever the chance for that, I suggest you *run*. But you wouldn't have to dig too far for a reason, Detective. He tends to train any soul with power who falls into his clutches. There's always the chance they might be useful, later."

"And that's... kind of three." Aidan's voice was barely louder than the rumble of the engine. "How come I'm not crazy?"

Ah. She should have considered this might come up. "There is a difference between power denied, and power dormant," Myrrh said practically. "It's possible - not likely, but possible - for those with even the strongest mystical heritage to live and die as ordinary souls. Before the circumstances that led to our meeting, you'd simply never been stressed in a way that would wake your inner fire. At least," she added, more softly, "not with enough time to learn what power it was you had to use."

Silence behind her. Eyes beside her, darting between the mirror and the road. Myrrh could feel the detective marshalling questions in her head.

No. Not yet. He needs more time. "Given what I've heard of current laws, I can understand why your department might want a coven to learn of the death of one of their own officially, rather than from the news," Myrrh stated. "But why you, Detective? If you're investigating the whereabouts of this Ginger, and Rajas Feniger-"

"Feniger's been known to drop into the *Nightsong* once in a while. It's a place to start looking." Church's glance said she knew Myrrh was changing the subject, and wasn't going to push it. Yet. "Even if it wasn't, Captain Sherman's a law officer, not a bleeding-heart politician. I'm licensed to carry rounds that'll make even a thirsting vamp think twice. Not everybody is." Her jaw worked. "Halo shows up connected to all sides of this mess. And on top of that...."

Silence. Myrrh's neck prickled; to an enchantress, even silence had a meaning. And this was a very *thoughtful* silence.

Behind her she heard Aidan shift, obviously feeling the weight of words unspoken. "What?"

"Never mind. We're almost there." Church's fingers scrunched on the wheel. "Halo said that was Esmeralda seared all over the bank, when even the bloodslave who was in with her couldn't make a positive ID on what was left. Which either implies Halo saw her going in - and we don't have video that says he was anywhere near here before now - or he has a really good reason to keep track of the vamp who was second in line for leader of Nuria's coven. Now, I can go one of two ways with this. I can think he really is some kind of seer, and he's just pulling tips out of thin air to mess with us for giggles. Or, I can be a detective, and do my *job*, and think that maybe he's got something beyond dreams and visions cluing him in." She rolled her shoulders, and switched on the turn signal. "Here we are. And make sure that coat covers everything, Lindisfarne. They don't like me here."

"No, really?" grumped from the back.

"They don't?" Myrrh smiled, slow and deliberate. "Well, Detective. I think we may just get along after all."

"...Why do I have this *bad* feeling when you say that?"

They pulled into a near-empty parking lot, which was odd compared to most clubs Myrrh had had occasion to visit. She looked about as they got out and slammed doors, eyeing the shadows for potential ambush. Though seeing one with mortal eyes alone would be a bit tricky; cars were shorter, rounder, casting different shadows than those she'd been accustomed to years ago.

And it's unlikely an ambush will come from outside, for the moment, she thought, feeling the last bits of sunset fading. *A vampire club. The main attraction doesn't come out until after dark.*

It tied knots between her shoulderblades. The very idea was repellent. She knew what manner of beings vampires were.

Aidan ghosted up beside her, almost bouncing on his toes with the urge to be running somewhere else. Anywhere else. "If we walk in there, are we going to walk out?"

"We should." Church didn't look any happier about the idea than they were. "Like I said, Esmeralda was one of Nuria Cruz's coven. They try to stay on the up and up. So far as I *know*."

"Huh." Aidan shoved his hands into his pockets, breath easing. "Sounds like court."

Myrrh nodded. "It likely will be. All demons share certain... habits, of power and thrall." Very unsavory habits; demon lord entertainment tended to run along lines of artistic disembowelments and sculptures of blood and bone. But both of them would survive.

Church swept a few stray black hairs back behind her ear. "You sound relieved."

"Yeah, I am." Aidan sounded a little surprised. "I've seen worse."

Most likely he had. And they were venturing into Nightsong with a cop. Anything illegal in plain view would be license to unleash smitation as needed.

"Worse, huh?" Church's voice sounded a little taut, like someone watching a truck slide inexorably down black ice to impact a hapless bridge. "Like what?"

"Law classes," Aidan shuddered. "I was so glad when my family finally gave up-" He cut himself off, pale.

Myrrh grimaced, remembering the bits and pieces her friend had let slip over the long years; tiny shreds that had let her finally conclude that whatever he might be in Hell, he had been a human soul on Earth. *Ethical hopscotch* had been one of Aidan's tamer descriptions of law class.

And then they'd encountered a water-leviathan, and survived. He'd trusted her enough then, to take her pendant as a gift and trade for his own. And light was akin to fire, she didn't know if Aidan realized how much. She prayed she'd kept her nightmares from him. She hoped he didn't know how she'd walked one of his own; a man venturing further and further onto invisible ice made of Latin and law, every step the threatening crack that would herald freezing, drowning death....

Myrrh cleared her throat, stretching her arms up and rising on tiptoes, before dropping back down to shrug tension from her shoulders. "Nuria Cruz," she said thoughtfully, letting the name echo in her memory. "I knew of a Nuria Juanita Montenegro de la Cruz, once. It would take some time to determine if she were the same vampire. If, indeed, enough records still exist to give a definitive answer."

Church's smile was wry. "What, you can't just look at her in a lineup?"

"Detective," Myrrh said, very carefully, "I don't think you fully understand who I am, and what I have done. If I knew this vampire by sight, the odds would be very high that she would no longer exist."

Church blinked at her. Took a deep breath, and glanced toward the blood-red neon lights around the corner, marking the club entrance. "Okay. I have to know this before we go any farther. What's going to happen when we walk in there?"

"That will depend on how old these vampires are, and how willing they are to follow the laws they claim shelter under," Myrrh stated. "I don't *like* the world as you have described it, Detective. I will never believe that those who prey on humankind deserve the law's protection." She clenched her jaw, and tried very hard not to snarl. "But so long as they do not threaten us, and do not break the law, I will not start a fight."

"Well, good," Church said sourly. "Because you realize, if we start a fight with thirty-odd vamps, werewolves, and who knows what else is in there, none of us would walk out alive."

"You underestimate yourself." Myrrh smiled, and glanced at Aidan. "Between us, we would."

He nodded, and raised a red brow at Church. "Anything we should know about before we go in there?"

"Stay alert. Don't look anybody in the eyes. And never let them see you're scared." Church squared her shoulders, and headed around the building.

"Yep, sounds just like court," Aidan grumbled, so quiet most humans wouldn't have heard it. "I hated court." He cast a suspicious look Myrrh's way. "You're up to something."

"Me?" She blinked, all innocence. "It merely occurred to me that Detective Church mentioned there were werewolves within. And that I might wish to ask one or two if they knew a Derek."

"Not going to start a fight, huh?"

"I said I wouldn't." Myrrh kept her voice as low as his as they rounded the corner in the detective's wake. "I never made any promises for you."

"I'm not going to start anything either...." Aidan caught sight of the bouncer; a dark man with a polished shaven head, a dark gray suit, and a subtle gold stud in one ear. "Hold that thought."

Myrrh almost nodded to herself. *You were born to a family that held power, and lusted for more.* Not that she'd ever thought any of Yaldabaoth's line would sire a child to be raised by anyone who didn't thirst to rule. But Aidan's bristling at casual arrogance was as familiar as the scarab amulets of her childhood.

When we're away from here, we need to talk.

For now she watched Church pull on a ruthlessly professional face, holding up her badge and ID in plain view. "Detective Church. Mr. Lindisfarne and Ms. Shafat. We have official business with Countess Cruz."

...Myrrh was not going to laugh, as the bouncer curled his lip in a sneer and let them pass. But if she had a penny for every vampire sire who'd claimed noble blood to keep their fledglings in line....

Then again, it might be true. Which would be *interesting.*

"You keep smiling like that, you're gonna scare somebody," Aidan muttered under his breath as they passed through the wood-paneled annex the vampires evidently thought would suffice for a kill zone against most mortal raids.

Ah, true. Myrrh dampened her smile, if not her mirth. "When was the last time you read the Constitution?"

Amber eyes gave her a sidelong glance. "It's been a while."

Not surprising; the last thing Hell wanted was that document loose below. It'd give too many souls ideas. "There is a very interesting clause within it, which might explain some difficulties you suffered," Myrrh informed him. "Specifically, on American citizenship, and the revocation of all titles of nobility."

"Great, so now I know why I ticked off... so... many...." He gave her a dazed look, as the penny dropped. *"Oh."*

Myrrh smiled.

"If she's telling the truth - not a citizen, Church can deport her undead butt if she sneezes wrong." Aidan's grin was white fire. "If she's not, and her coven finds out? Ooo, popcorn...."

It was so nice to work with someone who got the joke. She needed that humor as an anchor. Because walking into the Nightsong proper was like poling down a Venetian canal. Oh, so very elegant... yet you couldn't ever stop thinking of what was floating in the water with you.

It would seem we're underdressed for the occasion.

Suits. Dazzling evening gowns. The glitter of diamonds and

pearls, echoed in bright candlelit chandeliers and velvet drapery. Nightsong's clientele looked like a night at the opera mingling with an eighteenth-century noble masquerade, and Myrrh could feel the silence and whispers move across the dance floor as their trio hove into view.

A most unwelcome touch of outside reality, the hell-raider thought. *That should get the Countess moving faster than anything. Vampires so hate to have their illusions spoiled.*

Though Myrrh was quite glad for one element of Nuria's stage-setting. Candlelight softened human senses, blurred the clear perceptions of evil that lurked in supernatural shadows. But each candle was a living flame; and fire whispered to Aidan the way the winds and birdsong of the wilderness spoke to mortal scouts. No creature would move through the candlelight without his knowing.

We're safer than you know, Detective. I wish I could tell you that.

But with this many supernatural creatures in one place, it simply wouldn't be wise. Besides, Church had nerves of pure steel. She walked through the disdainful crowd as if she truly didn't give a damn. Her face was set, and her aura focused keen as a knife.

"Ah, the rock of penitence." The ancient Greek words were slurred and weary. *"The night just got interesting."*

Church seemed to relax a little, heading for that voice despite the veiled glance of a passing waiter bringing glasses of honey-wine to a nearby table. "Xanthippe Coral. Didn't expect you in here."

"Detective." The woman was veiled all in black mourning, hat cloaking most of her features. Only a few golden bangles, set with coral in a scarlet rainbow of reds and pinks, stood out against her formal black gloves. "Somehow I don't think you've come to dance." A bitter chuckle. *"Though it'd be fun to watch you fools try to keep up."*

From the quizzical look on Aidan's face, he was catching a few words of that. Which didn't surprise Myrrh in the least. If Aariel truly had meant to arm one of his kin for battle, he wouldn't have neglected the tongues of the enemy. And so many sorcerers used Greek and Latin to compel spirits.

Well. Here was a chance to keep the locals off-balance, and so give Church a bit more leverage when the Countess deigned to appear. *"I don't hear many tongues of Sparta these days,"* Myrrh mused. *"Has another of the Age of Iron passed? Or - forgive - is the veil for only practical reasons, oh she who bears the gorgon's blood?"*

Which any listening ears might take for mere poetry, if they wished. The legend of coral should be well known, even in these later days.

The slight susurrus under that wide-brimmed hat and shroud of black lace told Myrrh she'd read the signs correctly. *"What know such as you of Sparta?"* the ancient said bitterly. *"Slave holders, you moderns call them - as if there were any blood under the sun who did not keep their enemies as trophies! At least the ancients knew how to fight for their own!"*

Church glanced between them, then at the near-empty glass at the ancient's right hand. "Coral? How many of those have you had?"

Myrrh inclined her head to the woman in black. *"Alas, Sparta was only a tale of glory when I first heard of it. But I am a child of the West, and I will never forget the tale of Thermopylae, and the terrible cost of freedom."*

Coral blinked at them all. Focused on Church. "You are not a ghost."

"Not last time I checked, no," the detective shrugged. "Why? Did someone say I was?"

"There are always rumors." Coral looked them over again, bleary eyes a bit more alert and interested. "Unless something drastic has happened, neither of you are Detective Franklin."

"Not last I checked," Aidan said, matching Church's shrug. "Ma'am."

"Polite," Coral murmured speculatively.

"My mother told me to always be polite to my elders," Aidan said cheekily, hands stuffed in trenchcoat pockets in the best unkempt detective fashion. "Sometimes I even pull it off."

That startled a huff of laughter from her. "Definitely not Franklin."

"He's on sick leave," Church said evasively. "He'll be back."

"I'm glad to hear it." Coral tapped a gloved finger against her glass, veiled face speculative. "Rumors had you both dead." She paused. "And Rajas, as well."

"Oh really," Church mused, calm as a cat watching a mousehole. "Seen him lately?"

"If I had," Coral gestured to her glass, "I'd have something better to do."

"Yeah?" The detective arched a brow, taking a notebook out of her pocket. "Anything I should know about?"

A cold wind seemed to blow through Myrrh's soul, bringing with it the scent of old blood. "Heads up," she said quietly. "The undead deign to walk among us."

"So they do." There was a tension in Coral's shoulders as she took something slim and black out of her coat pocket. It beeped, low and quiet.

Aidan glanced toward the stir in the crowd, and flinched. "Holy...."

Church poked him in the side. "They don't like that kind of talk," she muttered. "Not polite."

"Not polite?" Aidan kept his voice down, even as the color fled his face. "Can't you see them?"

Church frowned, glancing from him to the oncoming vampiress in elegant emerald silk, attended by a swarm of at least a dozen adoring fledglings and bloodslaves. "See what?"

"She probably can't," Myrrh said quietly, as the host of skeletal corpses with burning eyes advanced on them. "Most see as through a glass darkly. But we have passed through darkness and returned, and we see face to face."

She did not meet the gaze of her enemies. Not yet. The detective had questions to ask.

All streams flow into the sea, yet the sea does not overflow. I will wait.

"Detective Church." The coven mistress' words rattled like a wind in dry reeds; though Myrrh had no doubt Church heard only a normal, human voice. "I don't believe I offered you an invitation to visit."

"Police business, Countess," Church said steadily, gaze fixed slightly aside from Nuria's eyes.

"Homicide." The skin-covered skull nodded. "Do you have a

suspect in the murder of my poor Esmeralda?"

"First, we could use some way to confirm that it is Esmeralda Martine," Church countered. "Her... companion, isn't making much sense at the moment."

"It is she." The desiccated nose lifted, aristocratic to the bone. "I know when one of my own perishes." A withered hand waved, wrist leading. "Of course, we shall offer all due assistance to see that this horrid crime is punished."

"I'm sure that will be appreciated." Church didn't turn a hair. "Funny thing is, at the moment we're trying to establish exactly what horrid crimes we've got here. We seem to have a smorgasbord."

The countess clicked her fangs in disdain. "I do not know this word. A murder has occurred-"

"Well, the coroner will have to make a ruling on that," Church shrugged. "I'm actually here as a courtesy, Countess Cruz. Right now it's starting to look like death by misadventure."

Nuria went still, in the way only one not prone to the mortal flaw of breathing could. "You will explain this - this *flippancy*."

Beside her, Myrrh could feel Aidan trying not to laugh.

"Just giving you the facts, Countess," Church said easily. "From the bank records, they had one vault set aside because of dangerous wards on it. Who knows how Esmeralda got into the vault room before sunset...."

Myrrh could think of a half-dozen ways, none of which used magic. It was possible to teleport a body from one spot to another, and vampires survived that better than most, but why spend valuable magic carrying along a bloodslave when a tunnel would do?

"But it looks like for some reason, she decided to open that box," Church went on. Paused, one brow raised. "Funny thing is, the fire department had to call in a specialist to package what was left of the vault for transport. They say there are still active wards on it. Which implies Esmeralda avoided the wards, opened the lid - and poof. I've never seen anything like it."

"And you call this death by misadventure?" Dry nostrils flared. "Who does this vault belong to?"

"We'll probably have to subpoena the bank for that." Church

didn't budge. But then, Church was probably avoiding an image of eyes a human brown, not flaming coals in a dead face. "If we can get a judge to sign off on it, with no sign of physical or magical foul play involved. Might be tricky." The detective paused, deliberately. "Funny thing is, Countess, I've talked to a few people. And we have reason to believe you already know who rented that vault. Want to give me a name?"

Dead black strands of hair seemed to rise in an unfelt wind. "How can you say there is no sign of foul play, when one of my beloved childer is dead?"

"Foul play, but not physical, or magical...." Behind them, Coral chuckled. "Of course."

"Hold your tongue, snakeskin." Nuria's tone held all the more venom for being utterly empty of emotion. "You enter these premises only on our sufferance."

"I can always drink at home," Coral mused. "Though then, I would miss the tragedy about to play out before me. Worthy of Choerilus, it seems."

One of Nuria's undead courtiers stirred. "Lift that veil," he bit out, "and we will end you."

"You leave the nice lady alone," Aidan said levelly. "She's got a lot more manners than you."

"Gentlemen, play nice." Church jotted a few notes, the picture of unconcern. "Countess. We know someone in your coven wanted to get into that vault. If you could tell me who and why, we'd have a lot more leads to follow."

Nuria sniffed. "I know of no reason one of my get would think to break the law."

"Really?" Church blinked, almost innocent. "Even if one of them found out that vault belonged to a vampire hunter?"

Oh, nicely played, Myrrh thought, as every vampire suddenly gave Church their undivided attention. *All their focus on you, and none on us... young, and careless. This should be interesting.*

Church shrugged, closing her notebook. "Well, I'm sure you want to discuss this with your coven. In case someone got... overenthusiastic, and just forgot to mention it to you." She turned away-

Deliberate, Myrrh knew, in that heartbeat as she moved. *You trust in the law. And you seek justice for your partner.*

With a street gang, it would have been a calculated risk. With vampires, demons bearing all the pride and envy of Hell, who established their rule over one another with fang, claw, and plots, who considered humans their natural prey-

Fangs gleamed. But Myrrh was already *there*, a living barrier between mortal flesh and immortal hunger.

Claws caught in her sleeve. In less than the flicker of an eye, they'd be gouging through flesh and bones.

Let there be light!

Claws disintegrated.

Light stabbed into the vampire from the brush of her skin, racing through dried flesh like lava through ice. Bones and skin cracked and convulsed, trapped in a sliver of the dawn that had given her breath and life....

Blazing incarnadine, the vampire crumbled to ashes.

Silence. For a heartbeat - an eternity, for vampire reflexes - the coven hesitated.

Myrrh held a ready stance, unmoving. *I said I would not start a fight.*

But she knew what the detective did not; she didn't have to. These were fledglings. Young, stupid fledglings, too immersed in their demonic instincts and expectations of eternity to realize human cunning might have any value. The demon within was a predator, and the predator saw immobility as *fear.*

One of their coven was dead. And the killer was *easy prey.*

Screaming, they swarmed her.

Adino the Eznite killed eight hundred men with his sword-

Sunlight was a blade in her hands, and she moved in the heart of the whirlwind. Hell-raiders weren't as strong as a vampire. They weren't as enduring. But they *were* as fast.

Two heartbeats, and the first crush died.

Four, and the slower vampires were crumbling to dust. Some of them on fire.

Five, and the bloodslaves had just begun to realize something was wrong, recoiling-

Six. And a breath, as she stood in front of the gaping coven mistress, sword of light raised in a guard Viking berserkers had fled from. "Yield. Or die."

Somewhere in the far corner of the room, speakers spat sparks, and music died.

"I'd do what the lady says." Silver gleamed between Aidan's fingers; a pulse shimmered through the air, like a heartbeat of fire. "Your wards almost got a good guy killed. If she doesn't get you - *I will*."

"You...." Nuria swayed. The psychic shock of a dozen fledglings gone would have put lesser vampires on their knees. "What are you?"

Myrrh bared her teeth, and knew the blood-demon would take it for the threat it was. "Why, haven't you guessed? You booby-trapped my vault."

"You - n-no...." Nuria stumbled backward, eyefires guttering in shock. "You can't be! You're *dead!*"

"Oh grave, where is thy victory?" Myrrh almost laughed. "They call me Myrrh Shafat." She swept her gaze across the dance floor, where even the werewolves stood frozen in stunned fear. "Myrrh the Heretic. Myrrh the Demon-Slayer."

"Or for any of you guys who came in late," Aidan lifted his voice to fill the room, smile as vicious as her own, "Oh Lord Not Her Again *Arrrggh*."

"Let go of me, dammit!" Church hissed, safely behind her.

"Not a chance, Detective," Coral murmured back. "The *vrykolakas* would kill you. And then who would I watch bad movies with? Watch. And *wait*."

"Most of you have every chance to live through this night." Myrrh pitched her voice low to carry; even demons needed time to recover from events they thought impossible. Werewolves were flesh and blood, no matter how much magic suffused them, and their impulse in the face of sudden violence aimed at something *not* their pack was to hesitate. "I come in company with an officer of the law, after all. As a concerned citizen." Gray eyes swept the room, noting a few surviving vampires, bloodslaves, therianthropes, and the random human taking out a small object with a black casing to yammer panic into it. "And you've crawled out of the shadows to declare yourselves citizens, with all the rights and responsibilities the law entails. I'd so very much like to meet whoever persuaded you to that act. It's so diabolically clever." She smiled, just a little. "And so very much your death sentence."

"Oh, this I gotta hear." Aidan didn't bother trying to keep the glee out of his voice. "You saying somebody conned them?"

"Oh, yes," Myrrh agreed. She shook her head, very slightly. "And they're all so convinced how much better they are than humankind, how much stronger, how much *smarter* - they let themselves be played for fools. All of them."

"You are the fool, Hunter!" Nuria hissed, fangs gleaming like old ivory. "I will *destroy* you!"

"If you know my name, you know how many have tried that before," Myrrh observed. "Yet here I am." She drew a deliberate breath, flicking her gaze over the crowd. "And here you see how they were fooled, my friends. You claim the shelter of the law, Nuria - and then threaten to kill me, in front of a cop? I believe any actions I would take would now fall under the category of *self defense*." Myrrh bared her teeth right back. "There isn't a jury in the country who would say a vampire attacking isn't *imminent danger*."

"I can't believe I'm hearing this," Church was muttering behind her. "This is crazy...."

"You can't kill us all!" A growl from the crowd. "We have rights!"

"Yeah." Aidan's voice was suddenly cold, as amber eyes locked on to the grizzled werewolf's. "So did a nice young lady who got eaten a few months back. Any of you guys know a Derek?"

The hairier members of the advancing mob halted. Various lycanthropes tried to fade into the crowd, sparking the first twitches of movement toward the door.

"Perhaps now you finally see the real trap," Myrrh mused. "But in case you do not," she casually flipped light from hand to hand, "let me spell it out for you. As a *concerned citizen*.

"You see, while you lurked in the shadows, you were safe. Safer, at least, than any human who did not know you walked among us. And certainly there were hunters, and some of you died - but that is the law of the shadows. The weak die, and are prey. The strong and canny survive.

"But you wanted more. You wanted to live... no, not as equals to humankind. You wanted to be *better*. You planned to use our own laws as the hammer to crush us. He suspects me of murder? Why, my pack will give me an alibi. She says I enspelled her, and raped her? Prove it in a court of law. We are the victims, not the humans, we poor benighted monsters...." Myrrh had to take a breath, to master her fury. "But I have hunted monsters longer than you can imagine, and I know what the good detective does not. Every one of you is a lawbreaker. *Every. Last. One.*"

The quiet struggle behind her suddenly ceased. "You want to clarify that?" Church said into the shocked murmur of the crowd.

"So I will." Myrrh inclined her head to the cop. "You see, I know what such as you have hidden from the cameras. You may act the tormented soul. You may even believe it. But every one of you hungers, and must feed. Possibly you fight the curse. Possibly - rarely - one or two among you are truly repentant, and ever strive to master the darkness within. But most of you just don't *care*." She would not strike. Not yet. Not without *cause*. "You get *hungry*. And there are just so *many* humans around. Petty little lives, petty little people; their bodies barely last a century. It's not as if they're important. Who's going to miss one?"

Ah. That had made even one or two of the bloodslaves blink, and start to edge away from the crowd. Good.

"I will give the Devil his due. In Europe this plan might work." Myrrh scythed her gaze across the crowd. "In Africa, in Asia; in any number of benighted hellholes across the planet. But this is America. You have names. You have IDs. You have fingerprints. The cops know to look for marks of the inhuman, now. *And there is no statute of limitations on murder*."

Church sucked in a shocked breath.

Aidan chuckled beside her, like a crackling of flames. "I love this country."

Myrrh felt the crowd *break* with that laughter, like heated ice. Human and monster, they stampeded for the exits, screams and howls rising in their wake as bodies jammed in doorways and were trampled through.

Nuria hadn't moved.

Proud? Or wiser than she looks? Myrrh wondered. Gauged the depths of hatred flickering in balefire eyes, and hid a sigh. *Proud, then. Ah well.* "The wicked flee where no man pursues... I suggest you cooperate with Detective Church's inquiries."

"Or what?" Nuria stood, even if she wavered on her heels. "You'll kill me?"

"I won't have to," Myrrh said levelly. "Somewhere in this city is a sorcerer with the strength and malice to build a Demongate." She tilted her head; polite inquiry. "What do you think he'll do, once he hears you spoke with Myrrh the Demon-Slayer and walked away alive?"

Balefire flickered in a blink. "A Demongate?"

Myrrh stared. She couldn't possibly be serious.

She is. Oh Lord in Heaven. "You... you... how young *are* you?" Myrrh sputtered. "Your sire should be incinerated for *sheer negligence-*"

"Less than three hundred," Coral stated, as Nuria bristled. "Possibly a bit older, if she missed the Great Fire of London and the 1692 Jamaican earthquake. That one was *messy.*"

"We were short of options," Myrrh admitted. "Have you ever tried to stop a sorcerer and his undead pirate minions while you're seasick?" Letting sunlight fade from her hands, she glared at the coven leader. "A Demongate is nothing less than the opening of Hell on Earth. Your sire did tell you what happens to vampiric spirits in Hell, did he not? How you're looked on as the tainted spawn of once-human souls? Weak? Helpless? *Prey?*" Her lip curled; deliberate, to shake awake the predator instincts of the demonspawn before her. "Every weakness you see in human lives, every degradation you wish to inflict on living souls, every lust for pain and terror and *shame* you would carve into human bodies, before you drink them dry and tear out their beating hearts - that, is what a demon will do *to you.*" She let her voice drop, to the hiss that would prick a vampire's ears and pride. "Your fledglings couldn't even scratch me. How do you think they'll fare, when you throw them against a demon?"

Nuria hissed at her, wordless.

Church swallowed. "Hell on Earth. The Demongate opens, it's all over?"

"No. There is hope. There is *always* hope," Myrrh said firmly.

"This is the world God gave into our hands as stewards of His creation, and as we are human we shall always have the right to fight to take it back. But the last time a Demongate opened unopposed...." She grimaced, reflecting on old, bad memories. "Spring, 1257 A.D. Mount Rinjani; today the isle is called Lombok, in Indonesia. Very much out of the way, which is how that sorcerer managed to open it in the first place. Mundane records know it as the day Mount Rinjani erupted." She shook her head. "In the end, brave warriors and priests fought the demons back, and sealed the Demongate, at the cost of their lives. Yet their power was not enough to halt all the Hellish curses unleashed, and the demon lords' last act took a lingering, deadly revenge." She stared into balefire eyes, unflinching. "Even you have read the histories of those hideous centuries. Famine. War. Whole towns, crushed by the glaciers. And, above all - the Black Death."

"...We're going to headquarters," Church said into the silence. *"Now."*

Chapter Ten

"Demongate." Tapping her scribbled notes, Captain Margaret Sherman let out a long, slow breath. "And Father O'Malley thinks she's legit?"

"He was challenging her to a Biblical translation match. So, yeah." Seated in front of the captain's desk, Church tried not to fidget. "And Xanthippe Coral says yes, Demongates are real, really scary sorcerers make them, and they do exactly what Shafat says they do." She didn't know what Coral was; she wasn't sure anyone in Intrepid really did. But ever since she'd met the monument carver while hunting down exactly what rumors had spread at an internment that had then led to gunfire and three new funerals, Coral had been a good source for detectives working homicides.

Captain Sherman caught her twitch. "Relax." She squinted through the clouded glass of her office door. "Shafat's still got your pyro burning screwed-up forms while she pokes the map with body dump sites."

"As long as that's all he burns," Church grumbled, twisting a pen in her fingers.

"If he gets pushy, we'll turn on the sprinklers," Sherman said wryly. "From what you've said, though, I think we're safe turning our backs on him." Hazel eyes narrowed. "A lot safer than we'd be with a vampire."

"I screwed up," Church admitted, gut churning. "Cruz has always kept her nose clean before. I didn't expect... that."

"Just a law-abiding gentleman's club owner," Sherman agreed. "Whose lawyer is probably going to argue she was scared out of her wits by seeing a notorious Hunter take out a dozen of her fledglings." The captain paused, and shook her head. "A flaming sword? Seriously?"

"Not flaming. More like...." Church shivered, remembering that impossible shaft of sun in the darkness. "Like she was hanging onto a sunbeam hammered into a sword. I've never seen magic like that."

"So we've got a bona fide thousand-year-old demon-slayer on

our hands, who thinks someone wants to literally set loose Hell on Earth," Sherman summed up. "Who tells you we can stave things off a little by blessing some of the secondary crime scenes - the dump sites - but says if we want to *stop* it, we have to stop the sorcerer. And she's pretty convinced stopping him, her, or them is going to take a lot more than just cuffs and a warrant." Sherman rolled her eyes toward the ceiling. "If we could *get* a warrant, given we don't have a name, we don't have a description, and we don't have a shred of evidence. And the vampire we think might know who he is, isn't talking."

Church tried not to wince. "Pretty much."

"A Hunter who hasn't even mentioned using torture," Sherman mused. "Kind of goes against all the night crowd's stories, doesn't it?"

"Captain, you know O'Malley wouldn't-"

"I know he wouldn't." Sherman tapped her notes again. "But the good Father's human, and if Shafat's supernatural, she could be pulling the wool over his eyes too. I don't think it's likely. But then, I never would have thought one person could take out a dozen vamps. Even with help. At *night*." She took a deep breath, and sighed. "Jez. What do you really think?"

"I think if I fell in a pit, she'd pull me out," Church admitted. "And that kind of scares me. Captain. You know we let the nightlife look after itself a lot. We don't have much choice. Serve a warrant on a vampire or a werewolf and they don't want to go...." She spread empty hands.

Sherman leaned back in her chair, considering that. "And now you think we've got a choice."

"Yeah," Church said softly. "I think we do." She looked down, worrying over the last few hours in her head. "Thing is, she's a Hunter. Maybe we didn't know how they do it, but we know what they do. The one who worries me is Lindisfarne."

"The pyro?" The captain chuckled. "For a guy who lights vamps on fire, he seems like a nice kid."

"A nice kid O'Malley almost broke down crying over," Church said bleakly. "A nice kid who wasn't there one minute, and was the next, and *came back* with Myrrh." She swallowed hard. "Captain, I know it sounds crazy... but I think Aidan was *dead*."

The captain gave her a patient look. "We've got a vampire in Interrogation - by the way, Mitchell and Roger said thank you *so* much for that - and charges wired over the head end of every morgue drawer in case some would-be *voudoun* gets cute. If he was dead, he's not now. And eating fire is a heck of a lot more family-friendly than blood and brains. Your point?"

"Captain." Church took out her new cell, and brought up one of the pictures she'd snapped with a paramedic's phone while Aidan was fussing over an unconscious demon-slayer being loaded into an ambulance. "Have you looked at him? Really looked at him?"

Frowning, Sherman picked up the cell. Eyed the picture - red hair, black trenchcoat, the line of nose and chin-

Huffed out a breath, as if she'd been punched in the gut.

Raising her eyebrows, Church waited. She knew what she'd seen in the car on the way to the Nightsong. For one moment copper-bright hair and burning eyes had been hidden in shadows. And with that darkness, with face and attitude and fire pared down to a simple silhouette, a detective's trained memory had perked up and tapped her on the shoulder.

Look. Look again. You know this face.

Shaking her head, the captain turned to the summary files of cold cases behind her desk. Dragged her finger down to the second drawer; thumbed open the lock to yank it open in a rattle of unoiled rollers. Paged through neatly typed labels, nodded, and dragged one inch-thick blue folder out, to open it to a *Missing* poster.

Gritting her teeth with patience, Church waited.

"Different hair."

"I know, Captain," Church acknowledged.

"Different eyes."

"Oh, definitely," Church agreed, shuddering. "Scary, scary eyes...."

"Not to mention, the cops back then found a body," Sherman pointed out dryly. "And if they didn't find the *right* body...." She paused. "I'd say he should look a lot older, but given what I've seen of some magic-users, maybe not."

"I think they did find the body." Church almost wanted to laugh at the morbid humor of the situation. If she was wrong, she'd look like an idiot. If she was right....

I get everything I want on a silver platter. Just have to prove it. Oh, and head off the end of the world.

She shook herself, and looked up. "Captain. Isn't that file supposed to be in the closed cases?" She'd hoped it wouldn't be. But....

"Technically it is," Sherman acknowledged. "But Captain Flint was never happy with it, and neither am I." She gave her detective a considering look. "Flint always wondered if this was our Halloween Slasher's first kill."

Icy claws tiptoed down her spine. "He went missing over winter break," Church pointed out.

"First murders often don't fit the pattern, profilers say. Because the killer hasn't figured out what he wants his pattern to be, yet."

Point. She'd poked that idea herself, in the car; in that blinding moment of *he can't be*. If the captain was considering it too - oh boy.

"One photo's not enough to start prying into something this cold," the captain stated. "Not when it's *officially* solved."

Church nodded, prepared to make her case. "What I've got is circumstantial. But put it all together.... Captain, before we walked into the Nightsong-"

Yep, there was the twitch of the captain's lips that meant they were going to be *talking* about that later.

"-Aidan asked if we'd walk back out," Church plowed on, never mind that the captain's lips were twitching *more*, Aidan's question had been entirely too *calm* for a civilian about to face imminent death, "and Myrrh said all demons shared 'certain habits of power and thrall'-"

"Demons?"

...Right. She hadn't laid out all of O'Malley's gut-punches yet. "Myrrh said, and both the good Fathers backed her up, that vampires aren't people. They're demons. *Low-level* demons, possessing human corpses." Church had to pause, and wince. "Just like the old legends out of Eastern Europe and China and who knows where else."

Sherman's fingers found a heavy paperclip on her desk, started flipping it over her knuckles like an unwieldy coin. "She's going to get her butt jailed for hate speech."

"Pity the lawyer that tries that one," Church snorted. "She'd push them until they filed slander instead. Then she'd prove it's true. Probably by exorcizing the demon in open court. The press would have a field day."

Sherman tapped the clip on polished laminate. "Exorcism's supposed to be a last resort."

"Check with the shrinks, check with the specialty doctors, only then go to the priest," Church agreed. "Coral says levering a spirit out of a host body can take a hell of a lot of oomph." She spread empty hands. "Myrrh's got the oomph. In spades."

"You skipped the part where demonic possession isn't real," Sherman said dryly.

"Say the *vampires*." Church smiled bitterly. "I'd bet you my next paycheck Myrrh would prove them wrong. In a court of law. Who knows? Aidan might just help with the defense. One of the only things he's let slip about his life before Myrrh found him, is he used to be in law classes. Before his family gave up and *let him quit*."

They both knew what was in that cold file. Every scrap of info they could dig up on the victim, in case it might lead them to the killer.

Architectural grad student. Previously pre-law. Witness testimony indicates a family fight over the change of career path.

"Aidan knows Father O'Malley," Church went on. "You should have seen him twitch when Myrrh dropped that name. And O'Malley knows Aidan. He doesn't hug just *anybody*. But O'Malley didn't know what name Aidan was using, until Shafat introduced him at the church."

Sherman started. Waved her hand in a *go on*.

"When I tried to get anything out of our pyro, he stuck to 'call me Aidan'. Then Shafat wakes up, and says he's not using his legal name because someone's after him. Guess what kind of magic she uses? Turns out she's an enchantress. She does *name magic*." Church grimaced. "And only after she's been up and moving for a while does the name *Lindisfarne* ever come up."

Sherman frowned. "Not following."

"She went into the hospital without ID," Church clarified.

"Somewhere between there and giving her statement here, she got ID. It's old, but it's hers; and definitely legit, as of twenty-six years ago. And guess what? *So does he*." The detective paused. "Only his looks new. And it's a really, really good fake."

Sherman whistled. She knew Church had a knack for spotting fakes no one else could. Even magically altered fakes. "You think she's giving him a new identity?"

"It would fit with what's in her records," Church nodded. "I got a chance to look some of those up. She's got a long list of contacts. Including some of our friends in the U.S. Marshals. Now, why would a bounty hunter want to keep them on her list of people to talk to?"

"To find her targets," Sherman concluded. "Or else, to make sure somebody in over their head *can't* be found."

"And that's what it looks like she's trying to do for Aidan," Church stated. "Almost the first thing she said when she woke up was, he's on the run from *religious persecution*."

Sherman tapped the file, touching some of the incident reports on suspected hate crimes. "Interesting bit of circumstantial."

"Gets more interesting," Church told her. "Want to know two other things the Father said? First, that he knows something about our generous philanthropist, but he hasn't told me, because he thinks if he did you wouldn't find enough pieces of me to bury. Second? Myrrh's a bounty hunter, all right. Who just happens to do most of her hunting *in Hell*."

Sherman's eyes widened.

"Or maybe Purgatory," Church admitted. "But he thinks Hell."

Sherman cleared her throat. "Hell. As in, not a metaphor...."

"As in, other side of the Demongate, spirits and devils, the works." Church shuddered. "I don't like to think about it either, Captain. But he *believes*."

"Kind of his job," Sherman said gently.

"I wish it was just his job, Captain," Church said reluctantly. "But... I saw how hurt Tom was, before Myrrh got to him. I saw her come back from a skull and light. And...." No. She wasn't going to get into that memory of stars and darkness. "Never mind. Let's just say, listening to those two try to figure out what the hell happened since the Dark Day, I've heard some interesting tidbits.

Myrrh's done everything but come out and say she and Aidan were both in Hell. Aidan flat-out admits he got training from a *demon*. A specific demon, with a name, who Myrrh says *hasn't been summoned to Earth*. And," she double-checked her notes, "Aidan says the first time he knew anything about sorcerers, one was *sharpening up an obsidian knife*."

And she knew, and Sherman knew, exactly what was in that trace evidence file.

Obsidian shards in the wound. He struggled when it cut him....

"My God." Sherman looked ill, as she glanced as bubbled glass. "You're saying we've got a murder victim in the squadroom."

"And he says it's a sorcerer who had the knife," Church said quietly. "*Not* a Hunter."

"Which means the bloody shirt our good citizen hero of the nightlife has been waving for decades is a flat-out lie." The captain let out a slow, deliberate breath. "We've got to get Aidan talking. After this mess with the Demongate is over-"

"No. We've got to get him talking *now*," Church cut her off. "Murder and rape, Captain. That's what it takes to set the scene for a sorcerer to open one of these things. And Coral says unless someone can pull off a huge mass murder complete with demon-worshiping cult, it's got to go on for years. Maybe decades."

"You think it's the same sorcerer." Sherman gave her a sidelong glance. "Hell of a coincidence."

"Is it?" Church tapped her notes. "Father O'Malley says Myrrh went after a sorcerer in this area about twenty-six years ago, and it killed her. Her skull's been bouncing around in a box in Intrepid's nightlife underworld ever since. Halo pretty much admitted he set her up - and then he set *Aidan* up. And we know Rajas-"

"We suspect," Sherman said sternly.

"We have compelling circumstantial evidence that ties Rajas Feniger to the anonymous sorcerer known to be employed by certain pillars of the community," Church rolled on, undaunted. "Purely for the most legitimate reasons, of course." She didn't try to keep the sarcasm from bleeding through. "From a practical point of view, Captain - where Myrrh goes, Aidan goes. And Myrrh just smacked down Nuria Cruz hard. Countess Cruz, the oh so up and up businesswoman? There's not a vamp bled who won't use political pull. Cruz moves in all the right circles, and if she can't take Myrrh down with her bare hands, she's going to call out the lawyers. And her *good friends*. What are the odds that our pyro *isn't* going to smack headfirst into Savonarola? And if this isn't a coincidence, if we're right-"

"Things get real ugly, really fast." Sherman grimaced. "Hope your partner gets released from the hospital soon, he might open up to another guy."

Gets released? Church wondered. *Tom's already home. Why wouldn't he call the captain-?*

"Who let *that* in here?"

Church spun out of her chair, already reaching for her gun. She'd had more than enough surprises for one night and the last time she'd heard a tone like that, zombies had been rising in the ER intake at Sacred Heart-

No shooting from out in the squadroom. So probably not a zombie. You couldn't make out much in the way of details through the bubbled glass, but Church could see enough. Sharp suit. Polished brass glinting from his suitcase. Discreet gray and red silk tie that probably cost more than her car payments.

Nope. Not a zombie. Much, much worse.

Lawyer!

For what felt like the hundredth time since they'd scampered out of the Nightsong, Aidan had to put his head down and just breathe. There was a rushing in his ears, the room wanted to fade out a little, and his hands were shaking so bad he could probably thread a sewing machine while it was running. "Damn it, got fire, got food...."

"It's called adrenaline." Myrrh was giving him a look over her borrowed files that managed to be sympathetic and amused all at the same time. "It's always a shock, to go to flesh from pure spirit. Give yourself some time."

And that glint in her eyes was just not *fair* to a poor guy trying to get used to breathing all over again. Because just looking at it he could see her cutting down vampires like explosions of fiery ash. And there was something seriously skewed about him after twenty-five years in hell, because instead of having the normal, human reaction of screaming and hiding under a bed, or at least running like hell, he'd been charging in right with her, setting on fire anything that looked like she wouldn't hit it fast enough. He'd had her back, and it had fit like a key in a lock. He'd *wanted* to be there.

And he was more than glad to back her. You couldn't have pried him away with a crowbar. Gray eyes had been ice, and her sword had been death to damned souls, and part of him that was some kind of flaming idiot had been all but drooling at the sight.

That was so hot.

Bad fire spirit. No charcoal. He was on Earth, he was supposed to be learning to be human again. Not wishing the werewolves had been just a little less smart, so he could have fried them, too.

They know who Derek is.

He'd wanted to go after them. So much. Wanted it the way a man dying in the desert wanted water, or a guttering flame reached for tinder. They were cursed, they associated with a murderer, and even if they weren't killers themselves he'd wanted to sear them out of existence rather than let them endanger another innocent soul.

And that's wrong, Aidan told himself fiercely. *I can't kill somebody for something they might do.*

...Well. *Can't* might be too strong a word. *Shouldn't.*

Damn it, why doesn't that bother me? I'm thinking about killing people - werewolves or not, they were people - and all I feel *is, too bad I didn't get the chance.*

Which would have been stupid. Sad as that poor ghost's death had been, she'd moved on. If the Demongate opened the whole city might go down in flames. And then the world. Evil as he was, Derek could wait.

Myrrh never lost sight of that.

Which was one of the things that made him believe the whole *eighteen centuries* of demon-slaying story. Myrrh had patience. The kind of patience that wore mountains down, one drip at a time.

Patience, and nerves of pure steel. "You're not shaking like the DTs," Aidan grumbled, as Myrrh stuck yet another sticky-note on her map to mark a suspicious body.

"I've had a bit of practice." Another yellow swatch of paper peeled off, with a barely-there *shrrrip.* "There was one particularly nasty stretch, in the Taklamakan Desert, I managed to bounce in and out of Hell three times in as many days."

Aidan had to do a double-take at that one. Yeah, he was getting the idea that Myrrh and Death were kind of on speaking terms, but still.... "In three days?"

Myrrh held up fingers to tick them off. "Dehydration. Man-eating *ghuls* in the form of *olgoi-khorkhoi* - they're called Mongolian death worms, these days. And one particularly unwashed camel thief." She frowned at the memory. "Since he was also the reason I had to deal with the other two, I wasn't particularly kind when I caught him on the fourth day."

Eep. "You killed him?" Aidan asked warily.

"Oh, much worse than that." She winked. "I healed his ailing brother. Who was very, very interested in what had been happening in the tribe while he was incapacitated."

She healed his brother. He had to look away.

"Aidan?" Myrrh put her notes down on top of the city map, sealing the sticky bits from disturbance by any passing wind. "What's wrong?"

Everything. He could have killed a man - killed a whole pack of them - because Myrrh trusted him. Because she had control hard as Arctic ice, and he... didn't. And he didn't know if he could fix that. When he let himself think about the past decades - God. He was so *angry.* "Look. There's... something you should know...."

Suit. Suit with a short dark styled haircut, a manicure, and a briefcase. Heading for their borrowed corner of two rickety chairs and an upended paper box serving as a makeshift table, his lip curling at the smidge of space Captain Sherman had been able to spare them in her cramped squadroom.

"Hold that thought," Myrrh murmured, face carefully neutral.

No kidding. Maybe the suit would still turn around and bother some other hapless cop; the rest of the Detective Division looked just as disgruntled as Aidan felt, but nobody was actively drawing a weapon on the guy, so....

The suit arrived in front of them. Aidan almost expected him to click his heels. "Mr. Aidan Lindisfarne?"

He really, really hoped the hackles weren't rising on his neck the way they felt like they were. "Who's asking?"

A twitch of a well-groomed mustache. "Taber Howe, of Dewey, Cheatham, and Howe," he began stuffily.

"Ah, truth in advertising," Myrrh said blithely. "It's so hard to find that these days." Without seeming to move, she was suddenly between him and the suitcase. "Where did you get that cologne, Mr. Howe? I think I know its kin, from an... old acquaintance. Aidan, don't you find that scent familiar?"

Huh? Cologne was cologne, all overpriced and smelly-

Wet ashes.

Steven.

Lucky Myrrh had a good grip on him, because the urge to wrap his fingers around a pampered neck and *squeeze* was almost overwhelming.

I don't kill people. Damn it, I don't want to kill people!

And the guy now babbling behind an aggravated detective's desk wasn't Steven. Steven had more guts. "-Charge you with *assault-!*"

"Post-traumatic stress." Myrrh pulled him a little farther back, gray eyes fixed on the lawyer. "He didn't touch you. I suggest you state your business and leave. Your choice of client does not speak well of your intentions."

"And association with a known imposter doesn't speak well of yours!"

Fire seemed to turn to ice in Aidan's veins. He almost sagged against Myrrh's grasp; she had to do a slight step sideways to center herself under his weight.

He took a breath, and lifted himself so she could move if things went bad. Or more like worse. It didn't make *sense*. He wasn't pretending to be anybody. Maybe pretending to be human....

"What's going on here?" Captain Sherman swept her gaze over the squadroom, ending on the luckless lawyer. "Mr. Howe. I thought you'd be with your client, Ms. Cruz."

"Our firm represents multiple clients, as you well know. This just happens to be convenient." Howe brushed himself off, retrieving his briefcase to snick it open. Reached in with two fingers, and abstracted a plain manila folder, his college ring gleaming in the overhead lights. "This is a legal affidavit testifying to the physical and mystical disturbance of the sanctified grave, and an injunction against John Doe, alias Aidan, for illicitly and fraudulently making use of the identity of said deceased, Christophe Savonarola."

He couldn't think. He couldn't breathe.

Myrrh gripped his arm, warm through his coat. Lifted one white brow, in a way he'd last seen her use on a soon-to-be-frozen swamp. "What proof have you of any such use?"

Which just put the hairs back up on his neck all over again. Myrrh wasn't actually going to lie, was she?

Except... she hadn't lied. She'd never said there was no proof he'd used the name.

But it's way after bankers' hours. The courthouse has to be closed. How could a lawyer get in there to know?

Church was right behind her captain, looking between them like she'd just had someone drop the last piece of a jigsaw puzzle into her hands. Only the piece was red-hot.

Yeah, I'm trouble all over the place... wait. Why was she looking at me? Steven got away clean for... for that night, why...?

"I have to admit to some curiosity on that matter myself, Mr. Howe." Captain Sherman folded her arms, like she had all night. "Currently Mr. Lindisfarne has been a very well-behaved, even heroic, private citizen, stepping in to aid my officers when they were in need of prompt medical assistance." Her tone turned wry. "On top of which, he has a very good alibi for his whereabouts for quite some time. I don't think he was digging up any graves. Do you have reason to file such a complaint?"

"Your own department knows I do." The lawyer straightened. "Or do you not check on your own detectives' fingerprint requests, Captain?"

Aidan had to look away. *Damn it. Damn it, I never should have let her take them, this is all going down the drain, Steven arranged this, he always does-*

"Stay calm." Myrrh's voice, level as it'd been fleeing a demonic hunt. "Toying with an innocent man is unbecoming of a man of the law. If you are one."

"If I- who *are* you?"

"Does it matter?" Myrrh's words were ice. "If you've taken

measures against magic, you know fingerprints aren't infallible."

"But they are highly suggestive evidence." Howe smirked. "In this case - they either suggest Mr. Lindisfarne was wearing fingerprint gloves, and Detective Church never noticed... or they prove that the suspect in question is resorting to mystical means to gain the prints of a dead man. A very dead man, under such horrific circumstances; I do believe Mr. Savonarola will be suing for emotional distress-"

"Shut up."

Aidan had to look up. That wasn't Myrrh.

"Church," Sherman murmured.

"No. Enough's enough." The detective's glare made Howe pale. "You know and I know your *client* is in it up to his neck. He's had a great run for twenty-five years. Now? The wheels of justice grind on, and karma *bites*. If I were you, I'd start looking for the exit."

Howe started. "I assure you, this is a legitimate-"

"You may indeed think so. For now." Myrrh's voice hardened. "Devote yourself to the cause of justice, and aid the wronged. *Drop that file.*"

Manicured fingers opened, and the folder slid to the floor.

"Don't touch it." Myrrh held her hand up to stop Aidan before he could move. "If any of that paperwork comes from a sorcerer's hand, it may have snares for you."

"You - you-" Howe was backing up fast, face an unhealthy shade of gray. "Calling any of my clientele sorcerers is *slander*-"

"Only if it isn't true." Myrrh shook her head. "Are you willing to bet your life that it isn't?"

A dark chuckle echoed out of the shadows, before Coral tapped Howe on the shoulder. "Oh, Mr. Howe often bets what he can't afford to lose. That reminds me, how is your wife? I should send her a card. I think she may have business with me soon."

Howe stared at her veil, and went even paler. Grabbed his briefcase, and bolted for the elevator.

Aidan waited for the snickers to die down, feeling like he'd just dodged a bullet. "Um. What kind of business?"

"Oh, didn't you know?" Breathy laughter rustled Coral's veil. "I carve tombstones."

"Met her at a funeral," Church added cheerfully. "You'd be

amazed how many murder suspects talk at funerals." She pointed toward the fallen papers. "Any way to make sure that's not going to blow up in someone's face?"

"You never mentioned the hell-raider was so tenaciously annoying."

"I told you to strike her down from a distance."

Shuluth feasted on the scraps from the sacrifice, trying not to crack the bones too loudly. The sorcerer had ordered the shadow-souls and the rest of his barbweasel tangle out and about on various cruel and petty errands; and he longed to be with them, as they might well find chances to take a human, slay, and feast. But one always had to remain with Sword Aariel. That was Lord Yaldabaoth's order, and none of them would dare disobey.

Besides. Others out on orders *might* find prey. The last to stay always got the scraps.

"I did." The sorcerer's hand was wreathed in inky water, molding it like clay. "And lost a half-decent patsy in the process. Do you know how tricky it was to arrange matters so Rasputin would hold his rituals near the train tracks long enough for her to catch him there? Not to mention setting up the shipping and then the derailment at just the right moment. Chlorine tanks don't usually break open fast enough to kill by themselves, you know."

"Neatly done," Sword Aariel rumbled, claws tapping by the hilt of his sword. "But not permanent. You neglected to scour the site for objects of ritual significance-"

"There wasn't anything left." A snap, as of water hitting cold ice. "I made certain of it."

"*Almost* certain." Aariel's eyes gleamed. "While you made yourself visible elsewhere, some other entered the wreckage, and sought for what they could pillage and carry away. And they found something, which changed hands, the way creations of the mystic often do, and now can be linked to you. You know this, or you would not have ordered a minion after Rajas."

"Really." The sorcerer hissed it, low and thoughtful. "Choking to death on chlorine is usually very permanent. Even for a demon. Why isn't she still dead?"

"She is," the Sword's snarl was almost a laugh, "in the service of That Which Shattered The Gates. I have found it is very hard to convince a saint to stay dead."

Shuluth cringed at the hateful word. Not one of those!

The sorcerer's foot tapped the polished stone floor. "There are no saints in this world."

"You have done your best to ensure none think so." Aariel's thick mane dipped; not quite a bow. "Then think not of a saint, but an enchantress of lost Alexandria. There are reasons Hypatia the Mathematician was flensed with shell knives. The magic of Egypt that was knew names as the essence of the world, in a way few have ever known it. To know the truth of a name, was to be able to command gods. To best one with such power you must be more cunning than a serpent." The great demon paused. "And you must be swift. The time draws near."

"More answers that don't answer anything." Flint scraped over steel, casting sparks that were quenched in dark water.

Sword Aariel hissed, stung by the triumph of water over fire. Shuluth couldn't stifle a whimper.

The flint waved threateningly through air. "How do I kill her?"

The great lion-demon's breath rasped; but he straightened, never quite brushing the edge of glowing runes. "She can be killed as any mortal woman. If not so easily." Aariel's canines gleamed in the flames from the great brazier to the south. "If you wish to know how she can be *destroyed....* That, I cannot tell you."

Water snapped like a whip, curling back on itself like a cobra ready to spit once more. "Can't, or won't?"

"Cannot." Aariel's word dropped into the dancing shadows like lead; on the brazier, embers hissed, and the scent of burnt blood swirled through the room. "She is one of Those Who Part The Gates. Her soul is light, and darkness has no claim on it."

Ink rippled, like mercury in its shine, and its venom. "Do you mean to say you're mystically barred from imparting information on how to destroy her?"

"If you are optimistic, you might pursue that quarry." Leonine eyes narrowed into slits. "Or it could be that such as I, a mere Sword, do not know."

The sorcerer laughed, quiet but long. "By which you mean to imply that Yaldabaoth might give a different answer. If I summoned him to Earth."

Cracking bone to get at sweet marrow, Shuluth went still. The sorcerer's laugh echoed of deep water, the hungry sea that would swallow a fire demon whole, and snuff it out forever.

"Oh, no. I know better than to summon my dread sire without a *win*." Water gurgled, surging in a slow arc around the circle of wards that held Sword Aariel fixed and powerless on this plane. "Though I rather wonder if he wouldn't mind, just this once. After all, how often does one of his most powerful vassals attempt to commit treachery?"

Sword Aariel's growl was low, like earth trembling in the wake of thunder. "I have always been loyal to my lord."

"Really?" A rich laugh, that yet sounded hollow. "Then why didn't you tell me my *dear* brother had another name?"

Shuluth flattened himself in the scraps, thorns drinking up the comforting stickiness of blood. Lords' names were always dangerous. The names of lords' kin, scarcely less so.

"Because he did not have one." White fangs gleamed. "A nickname, however apt, is not a name. Though even a nickname, given by One Who Passes The Gates, has power."

Water dripped, steady as the heartbeat of a living cave. "I *summoned* him. And he did not come!"

"You gave him no reason to heed your call, and every reason to fight it." Aariel's voice crackled, bone snapping in a blaze. "Yaldabaoth's blood grants its bearers strong will. Even those of human birth. Were you not up to the challenge?"

Shuluth slithered back farther into the shadows. Sword Aariel knew better than to deny the lord's own son! That way lay *pain*.

"Oh, I will be." The sorcerer took a deep, deliberate breath. "You see, I did think this through, my treacherous Sword. If my brother didn't have another *name* before, but he has one now... then some power on Earth was involved. And there really are a limited number of those in this city." A quiet chuckle. "I've always wanted to burn down my *dear* departed father's favorite courthouse, anyway."

"The... courthouse?" Aariel's eyes narrowed.

"My brother is a slave to his humanity. If he changed his name, he did it through human means. Besides," the sorcerer's shrug splashed water in an icy arc, "the number of cases pending that will have to be put off, called off, retried... our gallant defenders of the city will be forced to follow up old cases all over again, rather than pursue new ones. Which will leave the way quite clear for the rest of my work."

"An interesting tactic." Sword Aariel leaned back on his haunches. "But surely none of my concern."

"Oh, but it is." The sorcerer rubbed his hands together. "I'm not entirely convinced you have my best interests at heart-"

Sword Aariel laughed. The sound rattled the brazier against the floor. Trembled stones. Even water jittered back and away.

"I am a demon of Yaldabaoth's court," the Sword chuckled. "While you live and breathe on Earth, I will never have your *best interests* at heart." He snorted. "Especially not those of a sorcerer so wasteful as to sacrifice a half-demon as a martyr to further a cause, when a mortal sorcerer would have sufficed."

"But the point was sacrifice," the sorcerer shrugged. Water coiled and looped between his hands, glinting golden in the firelight. "As my pets' influence will whisper into Mayor Green's attentive ears. After all, everyone knows how heartbroken I was by Christophe's death. How tirelessly I worked to find the killers. Surely, I'd go to any lengths to uncover the *truth* of my brother's murder. Acting against an obvious imposter... well, he may not be able to officially intervene, but there are ways. And we're such good friends...." The sorcerer nodded. "Aside from that - even if Rajas doesn't want to be a good boy, he has plenty of associates who know not to cross my interests. It won't take much to set a few of them on a lone fire mage. If... Aidan... is just recently on Earth, he won't have any idea how much he needs to moderate his power. Play with fire, and things get burned." He *tch*ed. "Such a tragedy."

"Again, none of my concern," Sword Aariel declared. "Unless one of your minions perishes. In which case I imagine their souls would be tasty, indeed."

"Oh, but it is," the sorcerer smiled. "You see - I don't think you have my sire's best interests at heart, either."

Shuluth's ears shot straight up, shivering.

"I am Yaldabaoth's sworn armsman." Sword Aariel's growl

made the very air tighten against fur, snapped sparks against the tender leaf-skin of a barbweasel's black nose. "I come to your call because he bids me, sorcerer. Beyond that I owe you *nothing*, and him everything. *Never* forget that."

"I think you're lying," the sorcerer sing-songed. "Of course, you're a demon. What else should I expect? But Aidan has *fire*." Water sloshed from hand to hand, circled around a silken sleeve. "I think you liked training him. After all the time he wasted here on Earth, ignoring every hint of demonic magic dropped in front of him... you had him where he couldn't get away. Where he couldn't charm Father and blink his eyes at Mother and get what he wanted, just because *he* was the heir. He finally had to *work* for what he got. Well - at least a little. Fire magery. He probably couldn't summon a scrag without passing out." The sorcerer shook himself, and settled his suit over his shoulders again. "I think you favor him, just as my sire favors him, because he's fire. But he's here on Earth now. Where he can interfere with my magics, and possibly block the Demongate. Which will make my father, your lord, *very, very upset*."

Sword Aariel shrugged, mane giving off sparks. "If Aidan chooses to interfere with the Demongate."

"He will. Of course he will! He's my brother. And he always thought he was *my hero*." Firelight glinted in the sorcerer's eyes. "He'll interfere. And I'll end him, once and for all."

"That might be difficult," Sword Aariel mused. "He is of Yaldabaoth's blood. If the Demongate opens, he will be buoyed by Hell's power as well."

"No." A thoughtful sigh. "No, actually, he won't. And I owe that to our *dear* mother's ancient heritage. I never thought I'd be thanking her for that."

Sword Aariel's ears twitched. "Your mother had the blood of magic in her veins. Yaldabaoth would never choose a lesser creature for his children's dam."

"Oh, but it was very *specific* blood. You wouldn't believe how long it took me to track it down; and how simple the answer was, once I knew where to look. Mother's people were from the Orkney Isles, originally. And they have a very interesting variation of the mermaid legend there." Water turned to icy bracers, flexed back into a running stream. "We have the blood of the Finfolk in our veins. It makes sorcery easy for me, even if I can't tap the fire that should be mine by right. But my brother, my dear brother... he clings to being human, even with a demon powering his flames. To being his *mother's son*. Only that mother should have been a Finwife, and they flee the touch of the cross as leeches flee salt." A deep, dark chuckle. "And you say he has a *saint* with him."

"He does," Sword Aariel said neutrally. "And you spent enough time with your church to know the mark of a saint is compassion. She will not slay him for you, heir of my lord."

"She won't have to. She is what she is - and she will call divine power to stop my work. And fail. Perhaps my other measures will succeed; at least in driving him from that semblance of a body, we are of tough stock. But one way or another, when the Demongate opens, my dear brother's power will split right down that crack in his soul." The sorcerer took a deep, delighted breath. "I'm going to kill your little student, *loyal* armsman. And you *are not going to get in my way*."

"How could I?" Sword Aariel mused. "I can only come to this world when summoned, or if the Demongate truly opens-"

"Clever Aariel. But I've learned a bit more about hell-raiders than you ever weaseled your way out of telling me." The sorcerer smirked. "One Who Passes The Gates, indeed. She visits Hell, doesn't she? She visits *you*. And you don't have to interfere with Aidan if you can tell *her*."

Sorcerer thought Sword Aariel was talking to a soul-stealer? Shuluth couldn't believe his furred ears. That was... that was *betrayal!* Siding with the Gate-Shatterer! The Sword would never do that!

Would he?

A long, happy sigh. "So you won't. You're going to stay right here." The sorcerer inclined his head in mock respect. "Enjoy the reinforced wards. And starvation. And your student's impending death."

Footsteps faded into the darkness.

Stay? Shuluth thought, stunned. Stay up on Earth and *starve?* Sword Aariel could last for weeks without sustenance, but a weaker demon-!

"I think you've heard entirely too much, little demon," Sword Aariel mused. "And you are a sinner, as are we all."

Shuluth squeaked, as swift claws struck and pulled. Surely, Sword Aariel would not-!

Darkness.

Chapter Eleven

Manila lay shrouded in blue silk and a steel chain, both of which wrapped papers Myrrh thought were mostly harmless. As long as he didn't touch them. Because if Howe hadn't *directly* given him the various legal messes, then technically he hadn't been served, and any little magical mines they couldn't find with a quick skim of the contents could just stay there.

Funny thing, silk insulating magic. Sure, he knew the basics, what materials were best to block or amplify the four main sources of power, but he really ought to ask Myrrh for more details. When he could actually think about it, not try not to run screaming out the door at the thought of opening up old wounds. Magic had odd things in common with electricity, and things that insulated or amplified one might do the same to the other, if the magic-user doing the wiring knew what they were doing....

Focus.

"Okay, you want to know what happened," Aidan started, trying not to feel the eyes of Captain Sherman's detectives and one curious woman in a black veil. "Great. Would love to tell you guys... eh, no, not really. Worst night of my life. But according to the legal eagle out there, it wasn't me, so this is all a hypothetical. Got that?"

He looked around at Captain Sherman's people; all of Intrepid's tiny Detective Division, outside of Franklin. They'd swarmed around as Howe beat feet out of the building, curious to see what could force one of Intrepid's more infamous lawyers into a tactical retreat. But the curious and knowing looks had turned to disbelief, and then hard, calculated anger, as their captain waved an old file folder for all to see.

"We've had a break in the case."

Church had named off her coworkers in a quiet murmur, glancing at Myrrh as the enchantress committed each to memory. Mitchell and Roger, a salt-and-pepper-haired pair currently checking each other's necks for bites after turning a sulky Nuria loose with a list of charges and a warning to show up in court.

Rinaldi, who had laugh lines around his mouth and what might be a small bald spot under carefully-combed hair. Eagleman, one of the younger detectives, with a proper suit and Cherokee-dark hair cut neat and short, but wafting a faint scent of leather and herbs from under his shirt that Aidan tagged as *medicine pouch*. Heath, tall and gangly and gray from shoes to hair, lines of pain creasing his eyes any time he shifted his right shoulder a little too high; who'd out and out stared at Myrrh, muttering something about one bad night on patrol almost thirty years back. Kirsten Carlyle, the only other woman in the division, a short redhead with curls and maybe a few too many curves. And Church, staring him like her eyes were sapphire lasers boring to the truth.

Just your average everyday cops, Aidan thought. *Good people. And I'm going to wreck their day. Maybe forever.*

If anyone knew what he was about to tell them, Steven would never let it rest. They'd end up looking over their shoulders for magic they couldn't hope to fight, for the rest of their lives. Or longer. What right did he have to do that to innocent people?

What right do you have to not?

Half a whisper. Half a ripple of dawn, harbinger of the biggest fire in the world.

Gray eyes met his, sober and solemn as Father O'Malley kitted up for Good Friday mass. *They are cops, Aidan. Officers of the law, sworn to investigate wrongdoing and bring the guilty to face mortal justice.*

Light and fire and the *sense* of words, ringing through the air as if she'd chanted them aloud.

That is their duty. That is their choice.

He swallowed, and managed a bare shake of his head. *I was in Hell.*

Do you truly think that matters? This is America. A pale brow lifted. *One nation, under God, indivisible; with liberty and justice for all. For* all, *Aidan. Not just the innocent.*

Aidan shivered. And braced himself. He wasn't *worth* this... but Church had already put her life on the line.

Here goes everything.

"Let's start from the beginning," Aidan got out. "Maybe not the *very* beginning, light moving on the face of the waters, all that.

Though there's water in this story. Turns out to be pretty important. But let's start with a kid who was afraid of water."

Burbling in his ears. Deep and dark and cold, sucking him down forever....

I am here.

Dawn on the water. He could breathe again.

"...Yeah, a lot of kids are," Aidan managed. "But his little brother had no trouble heading for the deep end of the pool. And his mom swam like a fish. Turns out that's important, too. See, Mom... wasn't all the way human. Mostly. Almost. But not quite. Somewhere way back one of her relatives was something called a Finwife. That means... heh. It means a lot of things, but two of them are the ones that matter." Aidan lifted one finger. "She knew water like nobody's business." A second. "She couldn't leave her husband. Not, didn't want to. Not, couldn't afford to. *Couldn't.* If she ever did, she would have dried up and died.

"Not that her kids knew that. Not then.

"Anyway, this kid - oh, let's call him Paul - hated the pool, and hated parties. 'Cause he got shown off by his Dad there; everybody likes a judge with a good loving family, right? Only there was always something not a lot right about it. Whispers. And let's not get into the time little bro got him into the deep end, because the whispers were too much, a kid knows his own dad, right?

"Heh. Not so much."

Almost. Almost, he got it out. But he couldn't. Because thinking about his mom, what had to have happened to her not once but twice; thinking about what Yaldabaoth would have done, he knew that sadistic son of the darker side of creation....

Myrrh's fingers brushed his. *I am here.*

Like the moon. Like the stars. Myrrh made him believe she was real, even when he couldn't see her.

She was real, and she believed.

I wish... I wish I could believe....

Aidan swallowed his grief, and cleared his throat. "Anyway. Life goes on, even if people whisper that hey, the older these kids get, the less they look like the good judge. At least the firstborn son is going to do something important, like design skyscrapers, even if he's got no talent for law, period. Younger son, call him

Peter - eh, he thinks he likes law, he's not all the way sure - but pre-law keeps Dad happy, so why not? Or so he says.

"So there you have it. Paul knows the family's not happy, knows something's just *wrong*, but what can you do when you can't put a finger on it? He's out of the house, working like a dog - heh, I should say an intern, dogs get more sleep - and one day he comes home for break and there's this weird *thing* in the corner of his bedroom. Oh, it doesn't look that weird, not to your eyes; just a little black leather-bound book, with gilt edge on the pages. Could be a Bible, only there's no title on the outside. And it feels... *wrong*. The kind of wrong that's all knotted up in his family, and Paul's had more than enough of *that*, thanks. So he grabs up a stray grocery bag, never touches the friggin' cover, and dumps it out in the trash like a dead rat."

Almost as one, the detectives looked at silk and steel.

"Yeah. Something like that," Aidan admitted. "Wish I'd known more about blocking stuff back then. But if I'd known enough to know that - a lot of things would have been different." He winced. "Next day it was back. And the next, and the next... that was a *really long* Christmas break. Partly because - did I mention I didn't know about blocking stuff? Yeah. Paul started... seeing things. Stuff out of the corner of his eye, blink and you'd miss it. A shadow running over the roof with two tails. Gates creaking open in the wind, with glowing fingers pulling at the latch. Parents fussing over a baby seat - only for one second, what's in it doesn't look like a baby. It looks like sticks bundled into a doll, with frog eyes, and it *smirks* at him.

"Long story short, turns out that was some kind of weird final warning. *Do it our way, or else.*

"Guess Paul never was good at warnings."

Too curious for his own good, Aariel had growled. While at the same time teaching him the subtlety and stealth you needed to be curious and survive.

"Some say intelligence is half the battle," the Sword had rumbled. *"Fools. But knowledge of your enemies allows you to choose which battles are worth risking your existence for.*

"Pride drives the clash of the battlefield, demon lord against demon lord. You *will not bear such pride. You are a spirit born of*

mortal blood, with mortal weaknesses. If you have any shred of pride left, you will abandon it to serve our lord, or I will crush it from you-!"

Aariel hadn't - quite - crushed him. Hurt him, oh God yes. Torture and pain were what you breathed in Hell, like the air. Aariel had wanted him intact, sane, and - most of the time - unwounded enough to scout on his own and survive. Anything else was up for grabs.

Aariel hadn't crushed him. But parts of him were broken, in ways Aidan didn't want to look at too closely. And maybe that was the real reason he was sticking to Myrrh like a sandspur. She'd been there. She knew what happened to souls in demonic hands.

And if all his cracks finally spread and shattered, she could stop him.

Aidan?

Right. Keep going. "Back at school, hanging out with some buddies, you do the *craziest* things when you're thinking about the last semester of grad school," Aidan shrugged. "Like, say, getting locked in a pizza place with your buddies 'cause you made friends with the night manager. Everybody's having a good time, cleaning out the leftover pizza, helping clean up for the night...." He took a breath. "And then something *growls* outside."

He could hear it even now; all the malice in all the junkyard dogs in the world, distilled and simmered with a mad splash of rabies for kicks.

I'm in a police station. It's over.

Wasn't much help. October in North Carolina wasn't as cold as January, but he could still taste the furnaces going in the air. There was a smell of tomato sauce lingering from somebody's microwaved lunch, and the quiet mutter of cop to listening cop was so close to memories of grad students grumbling about their specialties, it wasn't funny.

Focus. You got the setup. Now - give them the crime.

"Dunno if any of you guys have ever seen a hellhound," Aidan said bleakly. "Kind of hope you haven't. They're... they don't all look alike. Most of them are like dogs; big, *huge* dogs, but wrong somehow. Dogs are our friends. They're help. That's what K-9 units are all about right? Hellhounds aren't help. They're like watching a kid on a trike morph into a meth-dealing Outlaw biker. They're foul, and they know it, and they'll shred you just for kicks." He glanced at Church. "You saw that malursine. That's Hell with a bear. Think Hell with a dog."

Church's throat worked, and she gave a jerky nod. "Got it."

"That bad?" Captain Sherman murmured.

"I'm never going to need horror movies again." Church shuddered, like shedding swamp water. "So then what?"

Aidan closed his eyes a moment, trying to see that night without hearing it, smelling it; tasting the blood where he'd bitten his own tongue not to start screaming. Because somehow he knew, he *knew*, if he got started... he might never stop. "Half the people it looked at shrieked and fell on the ground. Don't know what happened to 'em. Hope they lived. Though if they came out like Halo, maybe that's not a hope...."

Screams. Roaring. Shattering glass. Almost breaking his ankle in a chair, but diving and rolling to get untangled, get *out*-

"Some people made it out the back door, hoping like hell they could get to the donut shop down the street. Cops and donuts, right? Paul was one of them. Only he split off from the crowd and ran the *other* way, 'cause he knew it had his scent. Don't ask me how he knew. He just *knew*. Cats and dogs... yeah, that comes up later, give me a bit.

"There was a lot of running and screaming and it was damn cold. But he went over a graveyard fence, gashed himself up good on the spikes on top of the stone wall - consecrated ground, right? Ought to be safe from something like that. It was warmer. Quiet. Paul thought he'd made it. Tried to catch his breath, slow down, *think*, he didn't have a phone, was he just going to be stuck inside the walls 'til daylight-

"And here's a part you're only going to have my word for," Aidan said quietly. "Wouldn't blame you for not believing it. Heck, for all I know, there could have been some kind of illusion mixed up in the whole mess. But Peter... Peter had ways of getting the goods on people. On *anybody*."

Church nodded once, short and choppy. A few of the detectives shuddered.

"There was a flashlight, a ways away. And a guy unlocked the cemetery gate."

He could still hear the screech of cold metal, see the light glinting off the ice crust on snow. Remember, if faintly, that rush of relief; another human being in the night. *Help.*

Oh God, how wrong he'd been.

"He said his name was Sergeant Mallone, and that he'd already called 911."

Brr, the tension in the air. Tight shoulders. Pale knuckles. Mitchell chewing on his mustache. Yeah. This wasn't going over well at *all.*

But no one was jamming a word in edgewise. They might look sick to their stomach, but they didn't....

Oh God. I think they believe *me.*

"He'd get an ambulance, all... Paul should do was come over here and get out of the wind. Yeah, creepy new crypt and all, but any port in a storm, right?" Aidan swallowed hard. "You guys know Father O'Malley. And Church says he's been pointing you at a few things about magic, and blessings, and how things get around both of them. So maybe you already know where this is going."

"New crypt." Captain Sherman; Church was nodding along with her. "As in, not consecrated."

Coral's veil rustled. "But the graveyard should have been, yes?"

"Should have been," Aidan agreed. "Probably was. But there was ground still broken up over to the crypt. The sergeant was standing right on it. And when... Paul stepped on it...."

One blinding moment of his gut clenching with fear, *I never should have-*

"...then there was black water everywhere, *everywhere,* sweeping Paul off his feet into the crypt and freezing solid. So there was ice under him. Black ice. On top of the snow. On *top* of any consecrated ground." His shoulders shifted a little. "Took me a while to figure that out. But you guys are cops, you know the drill. Can't just drag a guy out of his home without a warrant. But if someone boots 'em out the back door... you got him." A long, shaky breath. "And there was Peter with the unholy water, and the knife, and the coldest damn smile you've ever seen.

"You don't want to know what happened next. Dying *sucks.*

"And it sucks even more when you don't even get to walk into that light and *die*. The knife and the blood and the water - they all opened a hole, and one little spirit had enough fight left in him to spit in Peter's face and dive right through it. Which, by the way, is not what Peter thought was going to happen. I think. You get your news from a demon, you never know what to believe, but seems," he rubbed over his heart, *feeling* the ache, "seems like Peter thought he was going to get his own spirit-battery for sorcery out of the deal.

"That didn't happen. Paul ended up taking the one-way escalator, all the way to Hell. Where, I kid you not, he ended up with someone even less happy to see him than Paul was to even be there. Which would be Dad. His and Peter's *real* Dad, not the judge. Who turned out to be sterile, and whoa, you don't admit *that* in the judge's family. Have to be a man. Have to have a son to carry on the family name. Even if you make a deal with a demon to do it."

Aidan's hands were shaking.

"So Dad - oh, just call him the Lion, did I mention cats and dogs? Yeah. Think of the biggest, meanest man-eater you ever heard of, and he's ticked off, 'cause he's got a problem on his hands. Half-human son up on Earth? No problem, might be useful, who knows? Down in Hell? Half-*human*. He's *never* going to be able to take a demon one on one. He's *weak*. He makes the *Lion* look weak. And you really, really don't want to know what happened after that. Here on Earth, pain has to stop. You take too much, you die. Down there? Believe me. Being able to die is a *gift*."

Myrrh's hand covered his own.

"After a while it got into a pattern. Torment. Show up in court. Torment. Toss Paul at weak little demonlings, tell them to try and kill him. Torment - this time by letting Peter call up big brother in a spirit-circle, tell him all the ways Peter was *comforting* their grieving mother. Rinse, wash, repeat. Went on... think that was maybe a few years. Only variety in it was sometimes Paul got to wander around after the latest try-not-to-get-killed bit. At least 'til he passed out. Not exactly the safest thing to do in Hell... but he was hitting the point he didn't care if he woke up anymore.

"Then one day he woke up in the shadow of some rocks, with brush piled all around him to keep him warm and out of sight. And a cup of water - do you know what it's like just to find a mouthful of water in a fire-demon's court? And a lady all wrapped in shadows, head back against one of the bigger rocks, catching catnaps while she kept watch.

"She cracks an eye open, and looks at him, and... it's not that she's smiling, 'cause if she was, he'd be running. She's just *there*. Like the mountain. Like the stars. And the first thing she says is, *You're fire-born. May I call you Aidan?*"

Aidan leaned back in his creaking chair, skimming a glance over the eight detectives listening. "That's pretty much it. Myrrh kept me sane in Hell. Let me believe... well, that not everybody was a demon waiting to happen." He paused. This was almost as hard to say, even if it was good stuff instead of bad. Maybe *because* it was good; trying to hope again was like walking on a broken leg. It *hurt*. "And then last night - man, was it just last night? - we're running like hell from things trying to eat us, and... then we're in a graveyard. With a bear-demon trying to kill us," he nodded toward Church, "and you, and your partner. And anybody else it can get its claws on."

"Okay, now, that's the part I don't get." Church rubbed her arms, warding off a chill.

"Malursines tend to slaughter anyone in reach, if they're permitted," Myrrh shrugged. "This one was probably in a particularly foul mood. Its materialized skull was still present on Earth, meaning it lacked some of its power in Hell; yet while the skull remained confined, it hadn't been summoned. Meaning part of it still sensed souls about it like a rain of savory morsels, and not a bite could cross its fangs. Like being locked into a cage in a candy store. All these tasty souls surrounding its prison for decades, and it couldn't gnaw off so much as a sliver...." She caught Church's deadpan look, and blinked innocently.

"Demon wants to eat people, I get," the detective said wryly. "You two being there to stop it - *that*, I don't get. Aidan's saying he was...." Words failed her; she shivered. "If we dug up Christophe's grave - I read that autopsy report. There were... pieces missing."

Yeah. Aidan felt like shivering himself.

"If you exhumed that grave, you would find a body," Myrrh said quietly. "My existence on Earth is magic, not miracle. Hell is a realm of the spirit. Any creature that steps from that realm to this must form a body from the matter of this realm. That is what I did; that is what Aidan was able to do, following after me."

Huh. He hoped she was right. Somehow, the idea of being in a made body didn't hurt so much. Heck, it was almost comforting, compared to the idea of getting his soul jammed back into a body where Steven had picked up an obsidian knife and-

Don't think about it.

Aidan tapped his toes against one wheel of his chair. "That's the part you didn't get? I told you about Mallone, and... why do you believe me?"

Detectives glanced at each other. Heath cleared his throat, and eyed his captain.

"Sergeant Eric Mallone," Captain Sherman said grimly. "Sometime I'll show you those casefiles. He died in a suspicious crash fifteen years ago, a few weeks before Personnel Standards was going to slam him with a full sheet of charges. Some of which included stealing drugs from the evidence locker, covering up paperwork around the BNCF derailment, and suspected involvement as an accomplice helping a Hunter kill... well. You."

"The train derailment." Aidan had to swallow hard. It'd still been in the news when he'd met a hellhound face to face; suits and countersuits about who was to blame, who should pay up, how much environmental damage had been done. And that was just the petty stuff. "That killed eighty-six people."

"Over a hundred, last count," Captain Sherman corrected him, grim as death. "Adding in the people who took a few more years to die. Like the ones who got killed by the flu that came through here five years back, because their lungs just couldn't take anymore."

Myrrh winced, and bowed her head. Aidan could see her lips moving, and didn't have to hear it to know it was the Ave Maria. "I am sorry, Captain," the hell-raider said quietly. "I knew, too late, I and others would die that night. I had no idea how many would perish with me."

Silence. Aidan swore he could hear the heat kick on again,

thrumming in the air ducts. "Wait," he managed, voice thin. "That... the BNCF derailment... that killed *you?*"

"And the malursine a man had summoned to deal with me. The irony must have enraged the creature nigh as much as having its skull locked away. Chlorine gas, wasn't it?" Myrrh's smile had a faded sadness in it. "It's a little hard to tell when you're choking to death. Someone had enchanted it to seek out lungs and slay, making it deadly far beyond its norm. And all I could think was, how many others are going to die here because...." She closed her mouth, and shook her head. "My target that night was Nicolai Abramanhoff, called by many Rasputin. I'd uncovered evidence that he was using animal sacrifice to call some of the more malevolent elemental spirits, and was about to gather the nerve for something... darker. I'd located his ritual site, and I meant to stop him." Gray eyes glittered like hoarfrost. "It would appear I was not the first one to find him. Someone knew who Rasputin was, and where he would be, and where I would be. And took steps to kill us both. No matter what the collateral damage."

"I suppose some would say, there's no kill like overkill." Coral toyed with the tips of her black gloves, loosening them to flex fingers as if she'd unsheathe claws. "Area-effect weapons always are a hell-raider's weakness. You're meant to save lives and souls, not kill them indiscriminately."

Which was just... *wrong.* "Coral," Aidan got out. "You're talking about my *brother.*"

"Do you think that makes a difference?" There was a hiss in her voice; she breathed deep, and patted her hair under the thick black lace of her veil. "Young people. There was a time you read the classics, and knew the wrath of the Furies followed those who shed shared blood. If he was willing to sacrifice you, what would he balk at? A hundred strangers' lives would be *nothing.*" She turned her head toward Church. "You wished to know why I was in Nightsong, drinking away my cares? Liquid courage, you might say; I knew the city's aura was becoming ripe for demonic magic, and I knew it had probably killed you. Just as I know who is connected in the shadows to the evil seeping through Intrepid... only I've never had the strength to act. To *stop* him."

She couldn't be serious. Not Steven. His little brother had hated him, sure; had *always* hated him, looked like, for reasons Aidan couldn't quite figure out. But - killing strangers? Steven?

Killing strangers to get at Myrrh. It makes a sick kind of sense.

He just didn't want it to.

"You knew," Church said grimly. "Father O'Malley knew. Is there anybody who *didn't* know? Besides, say, the cops? God!" She flung up her hands. "This is worse than trying to break up the Mafia! Doesn't it ever occur to any of you nightside types to *talk to the cops?*"

"Before or after we are burned at the stake?" Myrrh straightened from her prayer. "There is the problem of *evidence*, Detective Church. Humans, and other creatures, have been refining and altering magic for longer than there have been scrolls to record it. As long, I suspect, as beings have walked upright and played with fire. Can you enter magical evidence into a court of law? Can you even try, without wondering if the magic-users who testify have their own axes to grind? Your last experiment with spectral evidence on these shores led to Salem, and hangings, and a spectacle of justice that shivers souls to this day. Centuries ago the citizens of our country decided magic had no place in the law. If you decide to overturn that now - Coral can tell you the tale of Pandora's Box."

"Except the nightlife's already opened this box," Captain Sherman pointed out. "Savonarola was a big part of that. Say your story's hypothetically true. Wouldn't he be better off sticking to his story of not knowing anything about how his brother died, instead of waving around the Hunter angle? Sooner or later we're going to get some serious magical crime scene techs working cases and looking at old files. Especially cases where the guy who went down for the murder always looked a little off."

Myrrh inclined her head. "But how soon, and how late? The case is closed. It could take years, even decades to draw official attention enough to pry. And I assure you, he doesn't need decades." She tapped her map, patterned yellow strips like a fluorescent zebra spread over the city. "These are the deaths that hint of evil at work... Captain?"

Sherman was rubbing at what looked like an elephant-sized headache. "I can't put out a warrant on *evil at work*, Shafat."

Aidan took a shaky breath. Steven... he wasn't going to think about Steven. "That's what she's been trying to tell you. This stuff - it's not inside the law."

"Everything is inside the law." Church stood straight, a lighthouse against the storm. "We all have to answer to the law. Or else we're not people anymore. Just scared sheep huddling in the dark, hoping the wolves hunt somewhere else. I'm not going to live that way!" She jabbed a finger at Myrrh, daring her to rise to the bait. "And I'm not going to believe you want people to live that way. Because anybody who'd do that - you're not serving God, you're serving a tyrant, and I will march through the damn Pearly Gates and *tell* him that!"

Why you-!

Myrrh's hand twitched; silent warning. *Wait.*

Church swallowed, and forced her hands still. "But I don't think you believe that," the detective got out, voice still shaky. "You have a name. You have a record. *Fugitive recovery agent.* That's licensed, and it's legal, and it lets you skate around the law so long as you're going after a bail-jumper." She brushed at her arms; as if she'd hug herself, if there were just a few less people to be brave around. "So how do we get this guy? Legally. Without another hundred people dying 'cause he tries to take you down by means of train wreck with extreme prejudice."

"Very carefully," Myrrh said dryly. "Though he's given us one key already." She pointed at the silk-wrapped folder. "If he attacks Aidan by legal means, then Aidan is important. The spells Steven will have set up to anchor the Demongate are tied to his blood and aura. A brother loose who wishes to unravel those spells is the last thing he needs... Aidan?"

The room was faded. Far away. "Something's wrong." If he could just figure out what-

It was like the world falling away forever. He was so cold.

Around the room, cell phones shrilled.

"Church-"

"Captain Sherman-"

A host of names, as Coral frowned and moved in to feel his forehead, her hand cool through black gloves. "Whatever it is, I don't recognize it. The effect on his aura almost looks like an effigy burning. But you're an enchantress, I know you have countermeasures for that-"

"I do! And he's been with me." Myrrh was hanging onto him, face pale. "Unless they took blood at the hospital, he's left nothing of himself behind!"

"...Uh-uh," Aidan managed. Not quite nothing. There was one thing they'd had to leave behind. One really, really *important* thing.

"They did *what?*" Church bit out. Swept her gaze across the room, stunned eyes settling on him and Myrrh. "People - the courthouse is on *fire*."

Huh. Imagine that....

"Catch him!"

Chapter Twelve

The courthouse is burning, Myrrh thought, feeling as if she were trying to breathe stormy water. She and Coral had Aidan on the floor, but the man was seizing, trembling as if he'd been dumped naked in a snowbank. *Effigy magic. Aidan's true names are there!*

Thunder from the heavens could not have struck harder. Most sorcerers knew little of name magic, beyond the edge it gave them to pit their wills against summoned creatures. That the sorcerer who'd murdered her friend not only knew it, but could use it-

Aidan's brother. Yaldabaoth's get. And he never denied his darker nature. Of course he'd know!

Think. She had to *think*. Effigy magic could be lethal, even if she could keep his body breathing. The change of name depended on the legal witness, no matter what happened to the documents afterward. But Aidan's essence was fire and shadows; an arcane fire devouring his names could reach through that to burn out the very core of his magic-

And Aidan was *spirit*, not mortal. Spirit made manifest only by demonic power to take form and flesh on Earth. Lose that magic, and he would be gone.

I will find Steven. And I will end him.

Violence later. Soul to save, right now. He'd come back *with* her; she'd never expected this. Not when she could finally answer that flicker of soul-fire in her bosom with the clean pulse of dawn....

Oh.

Myrrh held him, despite the thrashing, the chill of frost and licks of smoke. Held him, and held the pendant behind her phial, bronze and plaited red and part of Aidan's own spirit. Fixed that darkness in her mind; not evil, but the true and holy night, cradling the stars. She carried part of Aidan's spirit, as he carried hers. No demon-bound sorcerer would kill her friend. Not while she had will and breath to stop it.

"Who made the Seven Stars and Orion? Who turns the darkness into dawn, and darkens day into night?"

It was like trying tear down the Temple, blinded. The fire had struck into the core of him; she could hold him, teetering on the edge, but alone she didn't have the strength....

Strong hands landed by hers, as if they meant to pound Aidan's fluttering heart back into rhythm. "Hey! Lindisfarne! Snap out of it!"

Aidan of Lindisfarne prayed, and turned the flames....

For a moment, it seemed as if there were other hands atop Myrrh's. And - possibly - a whisper of old Gaelic.

The heat under her hands died, fading back to a warmth just a bit hotter than human. Amber blinked at her, groggy but aware. "Wha... where'm...?"

We broke the link. "My thanks, Detective," Myrrh said gratefully. "Our time is shorter than I-"

"Shhh!" Church was on her feet, between them and the door. "You don't know the half of it."

All the detectives were between them and the door. Myrrh had a bad feeling about this.

Captain Sherman's voice came from the front of the crowd, pitched to carry. "Since when does Personnel Standards come looking for frauds?"

"Steven knows he's not a fraud," Myrrh breathed. "Burning the wrong name in effigy may hurt, but it won't kill. That magic was meant to kill."

"Magic lesson later," Church muttered, listening hard.

Ah yes. Of course. Myrrh blushed, and gripped Aidan's hand, helping him sit up silently. Once the scholar, always the scholar-

Oh, Joshua's sword of heaven.

The normal human light about two of the Personnel Standards officers was flickering.

Of course. Why on earth would a sorcerer trust one spell to kill his brother? If Steven knew what his heritage was, and it seemed clear he *did*, he'd know how tenaciously half-demons clung to life.

Not to mention, if the lawyer did have a chance to read the paperwork, Savonarola knows I'm back, as well. "I think it's time to go," Myrrh murmured.

"What do you mean, you want Church on administrative leave?" Sherman said loudly.

"Go?" Church hissed. "He can't even stand! The windows are painted shut! And I've never run from a PS goon in my life-"

"We're not running from the PS," Myrrh said patiently. Painted windows, certainly; but a good blow could fix that. The real problem was the drop. Aidan's body could take a four-story fall and walk away without so much as a twisted ankle. Her own was a bit more fragile. "We're running from the demons possessing some of the PS."

Church did a double-take. Squinted, as if she could almost see past the veil of flesh to whatever infernal creature lurked within. "...You've got to be kidding me."

"Last time I checked, the mayor didn't have any jurisdiction over internal police investigations," Sherman went on, crossing her arms with a finality that showed she was not impressed.

"The mayor," Church muttered. "Our philanthropist's good buddy. I take it back, maybe we can bust out a window."

"Why don't you come back tomorrow, when you've had a chance to sleep on it?" Sherman bore onward. "Isn't it past your bedtime-"

Shadows darkened about the possessed officer's form. "We have a warrant."

"For what?" Sherman said incredulously. "Failing to get munched when a bunch of vampires get ticked off? Lieutenant, you couldn't get Hang 'Em High MacRory out of bed to sign a bunk warrant like that, and you know it! Let me see that paper-"

Why could she *never* remember most people couldn't see Hellish auras? "Don't touch-"

For a second, Sherman seemed to freeze.

Oh, angels and ministers of grace. Myrrh could break demonic glamours. She'd done it before. Usually not right after a major healing. Definitely not when she was trying to husband energy for whatever would be waiting at the Demongate's anchors.

Sherman turned toward them, eyes blank. "They have a warrant."

This is going to hurt....

"Excuse me, Lieutenant, Captain." Coral stepped in front of the detectives, an elegant swish of black. "Smile."

The veil lifted, and Myrrh closed her eyes.

Crackle.

Lace rustled again, and Coral sighed. "Why do they always look surprised? I even tell them in my name."

"It would seem classical mythology isn't taught much lately," Myrrh mused. "It's not like the Middle Ages, when everyone knew coral was born of flowers Medusa's blood had turned to stone." She cleared her throat. "You do have a way to restore them, yes?" Given Church was sputtering, and they had a roomful of petrified detectives, and this was going to be one unholy mess.

Literally.

"Oh, I will. But the three of you had better be well away from here, first." Coral glanced at them sidelong from under her veil. "Church. You're my friend, and we've watched bad samurai movies together, and I ordinarily applaud your devotion to the law. It's so much more clean, living in this land and these days, away from the whims of angry Powers on Olympus. But Savonarola just incinerated Intrepid's courthouse. What will that do to every case your force has pending? To the lives of those who should be found guilty - or innocent?"

"I was more thinking that if he's willing to burn down the courthouse, what's he willing to do to the cops?" Church cast a look at Aidan, tottering as he leaned on Myrrh's shoulder. "Can you walk?"

"Let me get back to you on that...." The redhead blinked down at Myrrh. "Why do you have to be so freakin' short?"

"I was born in the third century to parents who thought garlic and fish were only fit for workmen, and olive oil was the height of luxury," Myrrh said dryly, struggling to stay upright as his balance shifted. "And I still hate olives. Let's *go*. Before the demons-"

Shadows pulled free from stone.

"I was afraid of that." Myrrh braced herself, readying a Psalm; saving power for later wouldn't help if they all died *now*-

Thunk.

Splash.

Aidan looked at steaming holy water.

Church looked at his knife.

"...Am I getting arrested?"

"Not by me," Church said decisively, grabbing him from the other side. "Let's go-" She halted mid-stride. "Um. Guys? I know you're having a hard time walking... but I think we'd better skip the elevator."

Hmm. Myrrh traded a glance with Aidan. Four flights of stairs, half-dragging a sick fire mage all the way. Versus a few minutes in a tiny metal box suspended by breakable cables, when they had no idea if they'd neutralized all the demons in the police department.

"I think the word you want is *duh*," Aidan snorted.

Chapter Thirteen

Wooden figures, scattered over a scale map of the city, echoing the more detailed layout on the wide computer screen. Two carved like pools of shadow had just flickered and charred, smoke drifting up in a silken curl toward the ceiling. Another carved weasel with a lantern was moving away from seared paper where the courthouse had been marked. Some distance away, a roughly human form was charred, and not burning; it glowed, like coals waiting to be blown to life.

"Damn. You are tough." A hiss of breath. "And I can't even mark the hell-raider on the maps."

Which seemed counterintuitive in the extreme. She was a source of holy power. From all the sorcery he'd learned, she should glow like a blinding light from the smallest of markers. Halo certainly did.

Yet put a carved figure or a winged icon where he knew she should be, and the spell only drifted, like a leaf in a running stream. It was as if she were no more remarkable than a grain of sand, or stars in the sky.

Except when she draws that sword.

Oh, *then* she blazed, carved wood and computer screens flashing star-bright for one blinding instant-

Then gone. He'd lost two laptops that way already.

Too much power for my little pawns to hold. Far too much for flesh and blood. How can she channel that much magic without battery backup, and still exist?

In a way, he could understand Sword Aariel's fascination with the hell-raider. Hell craved power above all things; and the most intelligent demon lords, like Yaldabaoth, craved subtle power most of all. If there was a way to bind her, *hold* her; chain her powerless, and wring out all her secrets....

No. Others have surely tried that before. Sword Aariel is no match for my sire's power, but he is mightier than most of demonkind. If he hasn't chained her in Hell, then he can't.

Grating on the spirit, but a man - or a demon - had to recognize his limitations. If she was of Alexandria she'd managed to endure more than a millennium of the worst fates humans and demonkind could contrive. And was *still* a thorn in Hell's side.

No. Better to extinguish her utterly.

Steven eyed the other figures scattered over his map, and his computerized list of timetables - railroad and otherwise. Smiled, shifting a barbweasel pawn from the wolf-haunted park where the tangle had brought Feniger down to... *there.*

The demon likely wouldn't survive what came next.

So long as its destruction buys me the hell-raider's death... it won't matter.

My best friend is a medusa. My department just got stoned, for real. The half-fire-demon murder victim is trying not to pass out in my back seat. And the demon-slayer is hanging out my passenger window trying not to blow chunks. Church growled under her breath, and hit her turn signal before bouncing over the curb on a tight corner. *Life sucks.*

"Urgh... Church, eyes on the *road*...." From the glimpse she caught in the rearview mirror, Aidan was rubbing his head. "How did you ever get a license?"

"Hey, I took honors in evasive driving," Church pointed out.

"Probably 'cause you terrified everybody else into ramming their way off the track- *truck!*"

Church rolled her eyes, and yanked the wheel to weave over. They had at least a foot to spare. Wimp.

"Some trucks," Myrrh panted, "carrying gas... remember train...." She choked, and stuck her head out the window again.

Okay, okay, carsick demon-slayer had a point. No more close calls with anything carrying labels like *oxidizer*, or *natural gas*, or *flammable*....

Wheels suddenly lost purchase on asphalt. Church tried to turn into the skid; that was ice, it couldn't be ice on the road in October, but she knew how wheels slid and that was *ice-*

Something black and spiky flickered across a truck's windshield, and brakes screamed.

Oops.

Carrying Myrrh away from a wreck was much, much easier than her trying to heft his sorry ass out of the police department. Though technically it'd been more of a mad bumper cars ride than a wreck, Church's car was *mostly* in one piece and the detective herself was in good enough shape to blister his ears.

Which was good. Because where they'd staggered off the road away from the honking tractor-trailer pileup was supposed to be a city park. Aidan remembered it being a pretty green place, twenty-five years ago; trimmed grass, trees to scramble up, and a set of swings you could push halfway to the sky. Now? There was trash, and a few ominous types hanging around in stray shadows, and enough graffiti to fill a Modern Art museum.

You did this to my home, Steven. To our *home. What the hell is* wrong *with you?*

It couldn't just be being half-demon. He was, after all. And while he could remember some wincingly bad incidents of childhood behavior that had had their mother laying down the law something *fierce*, not to mention dragging him to Father O'Malley on a biweekly basis, he'd never....

God. Maybe I wanted to hurt an idiot or two - but I never wanted anything like this.

"I can walk," Myrrh grumbled.

"Yeah, yeah; probably walk a Marine into the ground," Aidan grumbled back. "Look, you idiot, you're *tiny*. And maybe twenty-five years ago this was a good part of town. But now...." He didn't have a hand free to rub all the hairs standing up on the back of his neck. "This place feels *bad*." Smelled bad, too. In more ways than one.

"It should." Myrrh coughed, and winced. "If Church was reading the map right-"

"Hey!" The detective caught up in a thump of boots, her own eyes glancing surreptitiously toward the same lurkers. Her breath frosted in chill air. "We're on your hotspot, lady-"

Aidan didn't think. Just whirled and pulled her behind him. Dropping Myrrh in the process, but she knew how to bounce, and if he didn't pull this off right they were all *cinders*.

Flattened hands pressed together, he forced his will against the shockwave and flames.

For a moment, all he heard was the blast, and screaming, and *tings* as flung bits of metal trailer tried to make piñatas out of them all.

Then it was past, firelight fading to the spilled gasoline and other liquids flung out of the snarl-up.

Ooo. Pretty... bad fire spirit. Aidan shook himself, and glanced behind him at Church. Who seemed to be patting herself down in disbelief. "You okay?"

"Okay?" she choked out, staring at the trailer cabs. "They're... whoever was in there...."

"So call the Fire Department," Aidan shrugged. "We've got bigger problems."

"Bigger problems than people *burning to death*-"

Growls. Big ones. Not as bone-rattling as Sword Aariel in a bad mood, but impressive enough. Church whirled, gun in hand. "Intrepid PD! Freeze!"

Werewolves. Aidan found himself baring his teeth, ready and willing to try taking apart the oncoming pack with his bare hands. Cats and dogs - and after that night with the hellhound, he'd known he was never, *ever* going to be a dog person.

Don't be an idiot. You've got silver. Use it.

Myrrh was waiting with empty hands, a scary smile on her face as the pack hesitated. "It seems we've interrupted something."

"Oh god." Church sounded like she wanted to be sick, as her gaze caught red drying to brown on thick fur. "Please tell me they just picked off a stray."

"You have the Second Sight, Detective." Myrrh sounded almost sad. "You know human blood when you see it."

Aidan nodded. He should feel sick. He should feel upset. But most of what he felt was *angry.* "I'm guessing one of you is Derek." He tilted his head. "Any of you want to tell me which one?"

"At this point, it doesn't matter." Myrrh's voice was so very, very cold. "Someone has chosen to devour a life on one of the Demongate's anchors." She took a long, slow breath. "Kill them all."

Whoa, wait a minute!

He could almost hear Church's jaw drop. "What - you can't-!"
Howling, the pack descended on them.
We're immune.
Church isn't.
"Aim for the head!" Myrrh called, one hand diving into her sleeve.

Worth trying. Especially since the rawness inside said calling up fire might be a bad idea. So it was knives and dodging claws faster than any wolf had a right to be, even as Church opened up like a volley of thunder-cracks-

Fur started vanishing.

What the hell?

Aidan didn't slow down, aiming for anything Church couldn't move fast enough to target. Myrrh was a white-and-black flicker of motion, hair shining like moonlight as she guarded their left side.

And any werewolf she passed yelped and collapsed, shuddering and shrinking, dark fur snaking back under human skin.

Faster than he could blink, there were no wolves left. Only bleeding, shivering, naked men and women... and a few naked corpses.

Aidan stared at fingers weakly scrabbling at one of his knives, metal stuck deep into what had been a wolf's gold-gleaming eye. Pulled another loose and into his hand, just in case. "What the hell kind of knives are these?"

Myrrh flexed the fingers of one hand, dark iron nails gripped between each finger like improvised brass knuckles. Each tip was wet with blood. "*Mokume game.* Silver layered with steel and titanium, in various interesting alloys. Not that the metal really matters, unless you can't reach the head." She stared down one of the larger men who'd tried to gather himself to stand. "It's old folklore. Forgotten by too many in these times. But for those who know the correct incantations and prayers, to strike a werewolf on the head, with knife or with nail, is sufficient." Gray eyes narrowed. "Do not try to regain the wolf's shape. I will offer mercy only *once.*"

"Incantation, huh?" Church's voice was shaky, but her hands were busy reloading. "You better teach me that one. I'll get a nail-gun." Her gun *snick*ed, as she raised it back to ready and headed for the shadows the pack had boiled out of. "Let's go see if we should call an ambulance... ah, no."

Knife still in hand, Aidan joined her by the half-eaten corpse. Most of the internal organs had been scooped out, and the hands had been chewed to pieces, but there was enough skin and flesh on the skull to guess at a face. Myrrh was right behind them, for which he thanked - heh. Maybe he should just say he was grateful. "You know him?"

"Rajas Feniger." It was half disgust, half frustration. "Damn it, I wanted to talk to him!" Church rounded on shocked, whimpering people. Her glance flicked to the one still pawing at the knife, black creeping outward along the werewolf's veins as it shuddered and finally collapsed. "Who's in charge here?"

"It doesn't matter." That ice was back in Myrrh's voice. *Cannibals.* I've known children who fought the curse to protect their playmates; mothers who embraced a silver knife rather than harm their children! How dare you? You walk among humans and pretend to think yourselves noble? Jackals have more nobility than you! The lamia of the desert, who sup the blood of men, have more courage! Flee! Get ye hence! Get ye *gone!*" She raised her hand, and light flickered about her fingers.

"Crazy bitch!" One of the less injured werewolves broke and ran, flashes of firelight from the highway wreck playing across his goose-bumped skin. Others scrambled to follow....

Except for one. Sixteen, maybe seventeen, Aidan judged, watching him rock on dead grass, scarred down one arm like something had used him for a chew-toy.

Something did. Aidan winced. *He's just a kid.*

Church held her weapon ready, but her finger was outside the trigger. "You're letting them run?"

"Cannibals," Myrrh almost spat. "But those who survived to flee are not this man's murderers."

Church grimaced. "Didn't have enough handcuffs for all of them anyway.... You're sure?"

"She's sure." Aidan drew in a breath of fresh and old blood. Rage trembled inside him, but reached no further, hauled back by an iron chain of evidence. "He was dead before they put any teeth in him. See the jugular? The teeth that snipped it out- way too small and neat to be a wolf. More like a cat, or a weasel...."

Blood and waste and a scent of thorned fur. He knew that scent. He could all but taste it, in a memory of marsh and fire. "Church. Keep your eyes open."

Dark brows rose, as the detective glanced over bodies. "You think they're crazy enough to come back?"

"It's not the werewolves I'm worried about."

Church swore under her breath, eyes searching the shadows. "So here's your *evil at work*, Shafat. What the heck do we do?"

"We find the oldest death we can, and purify it." Myrrh started pacing deeper into the park, hands held out in front of her as if to feel heat from the ground. "That will damage the mystical foundation the sorcerer hopes to use to open the gate to Hell. It will not prevent the Demongate, but it will delay it."

Sitting on cold grass, the teenager went very still.

Aidan sucked in a breath through his teeth. *Bingo. Play this right, we can get him to talk.*

Not that he wanted to *talk*. The teen had broken laws of God and man, and he'd look really good as *charcoal*.

...No. No, that was years in Hell talking, and he was not going to listen. No matter how tempting a thought it was. The kid was with the werewolves; he'd stood by while they ate somebody, dead body or not. He didn't deserve a second chance to do worse-

None of us do.

He knew that. His mother had *raised* him to know that. Like Myrrh had said; everyone born on Earth was a sinner, one way or another. For what they'd done, what they might do - *nobody* deserved a second chance.

Except that we do. All of us. Even the worst of us. Because all of us fail, and all of us fall. But sometimes we pick ourselves up again. And sometimes... sometimes we need somebody to grab our hand and pull.

"Yeah." Aidan pitched his voice to carry, keeping it as low and confident as he could. "Reason the detective's not chasing the rest of your pack is we've got bigger fish to fry. As in somebody who wants every other living thing in this city *dead*. Werewolf, vampire, human - he doesn't care. He's opening a gate to Hell, a doorway for demons to walk on Earth, and everything but him here is going to die." He gave the kid a long look. "You okay with that? You gonna run and hide and hope things don't catch you? Or are you going to get off your ass, beat that wolf back into the cage where it belongs, and act like a man?"

A sob. A stifled sniffle. "...Demons?" The accent was thick, but to Aidan's surprise, that wasn't a problem. "You gotta be kidding me, man. That's stuff the Padre waves around in church, it's not for *real*."

Aidan almost slapped himself in the face. "You turn into a werewolf, there's a vampire club downtown, and you don't think demons are real? When's the last time your mom sat you down in church, you idiot?"

Despite the chill, the young face flushed. "Don't you talk about my mama!"

"Then why don't you prove she didn't raise a moron!" Aidan fired back. "In case you didn't notice, you're the small fry! You want to prove you're more than that? Give us some help!"

Belligerence froze into disbelief. "...Help?"

"I know what they told you." *I know*, Aidan knew, *because I heard it too.* "There's no going back. There's no *I don't want to do this anymore*. There *is* no *out*. You're bitten, and you're a monster, and that's *all you'll ever be*." He bared his teeth. "It's a *lie*."

Olive skin went pale.

"You're bitten. You're a monster," Aidan bit out. "Like it's anything that noble. You're a *junkie*, kid. Just like any crackhead. A junkie with a habit that's going to kill you. Only your drug is human blood and pain." He took a step forward. "But part of you is still human. And humans *fight monsters*. That's what we are. That's what we do. Doesn't matter if the monster's inside you. Beat it! Beat the bastards who did this to you! Get up and *fight!*"

The teen's breath hitched. "How?"

"You're a *werewolf*." And Aidan had learned a little about them in Hell. Even if he hadn't believed it. "What's the oldest death you smell here?"

The teenager got up. Looked at the ladies, and went a little redder, hands going in front of himself.

"Word of advice, from a guy who's been in Hell," Aidan said dryly. "One of those ladies would just as soon arrest you for indecent exposure as look at you, and Myrrh? Trust me. *She doesn't care.*"

"Not quite true." A tattered newspaper sailed out of the night. "It is unbefitting one of God's children to be naked. What is your name?"

"See what I mean?" Aidan muttered, as the teenage werewolf held paper in disbelieving hands.

The boy wrapped paper around his hips, one hand drifting up to touch the bloody scratch across his forehead. "This- the bite is not gone...."

"No." Myrrh stopped on one patch of soil back behind one of the park bathrooms. "But there is a cure, if you will fight for it."

"You... you were right." Haunted eyes flicked at Aidan. "They said... the only way out was...." The teen looked at a knifed body, and shivered.

"Guess what?" Church still had her gun in hand, but it wasn't pointed at the kid anymore. "They lied about *that,* too."

"Whether you choose to aid us or not, go to the Church of Our Lady," Myrrh said steadily. "Confess to one of the Fathers there. Your penance will be *severe.* It will not be repaid lightly. But there is hope."

"...Raphael." He shifted on bare feet, toes curling away from frosty ground.

"The healer. That may help you." Myrrh tilted her head. "Well?"

"Didn't you look on the map?" Church muttered.

"I did." Myrrh kept her gaze on the scarred teen.

Aidan opened his mouth - and closed it again. *Oh.*

Myrrh was going to be sending a *kid werewolf* to O'Malley and Ricci. A kid who, like it or not, had at least been there during a bunch of werewolves having themselves a little cannibal feast. Damn right she wanted a chance to check if he was lying.

From the way Church's glance shifted between Raphael and the various bodies, she'd connected the same dots.

Gaze flicking to the corpses, Raphael gulped. Sniffed the air, and gagged.

"Look on it as a down payment on what you owe God," Myrrh stated. "And what you owe yourself."

He gave her an incredulous look, and started circling.

"We got time for this?" Church muttered.

"It takes a moment to gather the strength for a working this deep," Myrrh said clinically. "We mean to put a crack in the foundations of the sorcerer's magic. A bit of time to muster my resources will make it easier." She drew a breath. "I do know a good Psalm for this. It will help."

"...You're going to *pray* the bad guy's plan to death."

"Don't you, Detective?" Myrrh smiled. "What is an investigation, but a prayer for justice made action?"

"You are *so weird*."

Yeah. Wasn't it cute? "Find something?" Aidan called to Raphael.

"I am no' sure." The teenager was halted several yards away from Myrrh, shifting from foot to chilled foot. "Is not a *smell*, here. Is... jus' cold. And not good."

Church glanced around, as if trying to place the spot; then grimaced. "Vagabond. Died of pneumonia. About five years ago. Coroner ruled it as natural causes."

Aidan looked at the ground, and shuddered. It was faint, and faded, but he'd swear he caught the glitter of black ice. "Pneumonia's one more way to drown. This was Steven."

"But...." Raphael looked at Myrrh, who hadn't moved.

"Even a werewolf's nose has limits," she said practically. "In a spot where only one had died, you might sniff out bone even a century old. Here? Five years is doing well." She eyed the spot he was standing on, and waved her hand to the right. "You may wish to stand back. The effects will be... bracing."

Aidan looked at her, and at their dubious companions, and shook his head. "Better get back farther."

Myrrh clapped her hands together once, and bent her head. "Bless the Lord, oh my soul...."

Quiet spread out around them like a silken sheet. Wind stilled. Leaves stopped rustling. Even the flames seemed faint and far away.

Aidan half-closed his eyes, wondering if he ought to get a bit farther back himself. That still sense of *presence* was scarier than any werewolf; the sense of a Power that could use light as a garment, and stretch the heavens out like a curtain....

"Who walks upon the wings of the wind," Myrrh murmured.

A breeze rose; Aidan gulped.

"Who makes winds your messengers, and fiery flames your servants." Head still down, Myrrh dropped him a wink.

Oh man. Don't drag me in the middle of this!

But he'd promised. He wasn't backing out now; even if he did feel like a teeny-tiny bug under one huge microscope.

"...The waters stood above the mountains," Myrrh declared. "At thy rebuke, they fled; at the sound of thy thunder, they hasted away!"

Holy.... Aidan missed some of her chant, feeling something close around them like unseen armor. *Steven's* water. *And she just... awesome.*

Oh boy. I think he's going to notice this....

"High hills are a refuge for the wild goats," Myrrh murmured, glancing at Church, "the rocks for the conies...."

"Hey!"

"Shh," Aidan warned. "Chanting."

"You appointed the moon to mark the seasons; the sun knows his going down." Myrrh's gaze was on Raphael, unflinching. "You make the darkness, and it is night; the beasts of the forest creep forth."

From the rustling in the grass and trees, they might be doing just that. *Let that be rats,* Aidan prayed swiftly. *Raccoons. Stray dogs. Just, not a bear. I'm not up to a bear right now, thanks, God.*

Or a wolf, for that matter. "You mess her up, kid, and we're going to dance," Aidan muttered.

"She sounds *spooky*," Raphael shivered. "An'... *Madre de Dios!*"

Aidan looked at the light glimmering over the ground, red and green and coruscating like the Northern Lights as it met darkness. "Close."

A third laptop whined and sparked, before the sorcerer could yank the cord from the UPS. Latin curses filled the air as the drive within ground to an ear-piercing halt.

Too much power. I didn't have this problem twenty-six years ago!

Then again, back then one megabyte had still seemed an impossible amount of memory. No one had used computers for spell-chants two decades ago. There wasn't enough *room*. It would be like expecting a steam engine to soar to the moon.

Only a steam engine can be struck by lightning, and still trundle on. He growled under his breath. *Forcing me back to physical simulacra, like a Stone Age witch doctor! I'm going to kill her slowly.*

At least proper planning meant he *had* those backups. A scattering of wooden wolf figures still marred his table map of the southernmost anchor, fleeing the ebony knot of barbweasel carvings. Which seemed... odd. True, he hadn't expected one werewolf pack to be sufficient forces to take down the hell-raider on their own. But with his targeted barbweasel demon throwing electrical spanners in the pileup, and the nets of coincidence and sudden road ice his own magic had put into play, no sane driver should have been able to avoid a crash. Between the flames, the chemicals, and the iron, an enchantress of her power should have been weakened. Easy prey.

Unfortunately, Detective Church was no sane driver. As all too many screaming car chases and citations could attest. The only reason the woman still *had* a license was her unnatural lack of accidents - and that seeming luck had led him to cross her path years ago, throwing out tempting bits of magical lore to hook what had seemed to be an unawakened magic-user into darkness.

Yet all that lore had done was focus the detective's not inconsiderable powers of observation on his underlings; and then, surprisingly, on him. Why, *why* did a soul with Second Sight have to cling to law and the police, instead of taking advantage of all the opportunities the world should have spread before her?

And why had her parents chosen to saddle her with that annoying name? Oh, he'd been able to acquire the text of her full name easily enough. But the woman refused to *give* it to anyone. Meaning the names he used had only a fraction of the power they should have to compel her.

Annoying. But between the fire and the dead bodies, he should shortly have enough hapless mortal foils on the scene that the hell-raider would be forced to surrender. Innocent blood would tie her hands; she wouldn't dare fight her way out, it would be pure and simple murder-

Why was part of the map sparkling?

Behind them, flames flickered, and the first wails of alarms split the air. Yet the darkness around them held the static of a thunderstorm, the sighing boom of waves on a trackless ocean.

Deeper. We must reach deeper. Myrrh took a breath, and pressed onward, spirit digging at the foundations of evil and blood. "You hide your face, they are troubled," she breathed. "If you take away their breath, they perish, and return to their dust...."

No; the anchor was properly shadowed again. False alarm-

"Whatever you're doing, hurry it up!" Church had her arm down by her side, turned so any who came upon them wouldn't see the weapon until it was too late.

"Church!" Aidan hissed.

"Naked guy. Dead guys! There's only so long I can stall anybody, and that's only if PS hasn't woken up and put out a BOLO-"

Shadows sprouted fangs, as living bramble swarmed them with eyes of blood.

"Kid, *down!*"

They leapt from the darkness, lithe shapes of thorns and fury. Their fangs were as long as Saguaro thorns, and sharp as sandspurs; their claws were thick, sharp briar meant to latch on and cling, even as the barbweasel shredded flesh and bone. Aidan knew. They'd savaged him before.

Never let them close!

Fire blazed in his hands-

Pain. Like muscles stretched near tearing.

Bad idea, Aidan thought, eyes watering as magic rebelled. And then there was *real* pain, skin and muscle gouged and ripped by a flow of furry thorns, as the tangle swarmed them. Church was firing again, bless her; though he didn't know what good silver bullets would do against critters that had heartwood instead of blood-

They're not.

She's going to die.

Because he couldn't reach the fire and Myrrh *would not* stop chanting. She was depending on them; he could feel the coiling power about her, deadly as lightning. If she let her attention slip even one moment-

"Power comes from four sources."

"We all have a spark of the divine."

Well, he had a *spark*, anyway. But when it came to fighting off barbweasels, what came to mind was Myrrh having a *really bad day*.

"For a fire has flared in My wrath, and burned to the bottom of Sheol," Aidan snarled, tearing one little demon off his legs, never mind how the blood ran. "Has consumed the earth and its increase, eaten down to the base of the hills! Fanged beasts will I let loose against them, with venomous creepers in the dust!"

The power that moved wasn't like the fire. Fire was a pulse, a heartbeat; blood thrumming in his veins, as necessary as air.

This... was like *singing*.

Church yelped. "Sweet mother of-!"

"Aiyeeee!" Naked flesh was jittering. "Vermin, *Madre de Dios!*"

"Leave 'em alone!" Aidan rasped, blinking to clear his gaze. Sure, seeing the local rats, roaches, and any other stray creepy-crawlies swarm your enemies was kind of freaky, but it beat the alternative. After all, he could feel their wills, their *outrage at the enemy*, flowing with his....

Oh. Right. Church can't.

Barbweasels were striking back at the swarms, thorn-teeth snapping even as bodies of briar were shredded. One black rat squealed, high and choked off. The teenage werewolf flinched.

Guilt. Aidan sucked in a breath, even as he gritted his teeth and summoned the smallest sparks to eat away termite-riddled heartwood. *That hurt him. He thinks he's a hard case; dead people, who cares? But something else dying* for *him....*

He's not all the way lost. The wolf hasn't eaten him. Not yet-

"My meditation of him shall be sweet: I will be glad in the Lord," Myrrh breathed. Her strength was short, but that could not matter. The words were carrying her. The words were light, and she was light; a mere glimmer of the glorious promise of every dawn.... "Let the sinners be consumed out of the earth, and let the wicked be no more!"

There was light.

Aidan caught Myrrh as she wobbled, heart in his throat. For one moment, all the world had been bright as the winter moon; a clear white light that blew like diamond dust through every shadow, scouring it away. He'd feared it would scour him away, too. Humans weren't meant to see that kind of light, and as for half-demons....

But that diamond brilliance had softened as it blew around them, fading to the glint of sun off snow. Still bright. Still too much to look upon. But not *lethal*.

He'd think about it later. He had people depending on him *now*.

Myrrh was still catching her breath. Church was reloading with shaking hands, fingers almost fumbling the bullets. "The hell were those?"

"What got Rajas Feniger," Aidan said clinically, picking up what was left of the fallen rat. "I'm guessing the werewolves were meant to take the fall for this. Not exactly like they could *explain* no, we didn't kill him, we just ate him. But barbweasels can't resist scraps." He cradled the empty shell of flesh and bone, hurting inside. "Thanks, little guy."

White fire blazed in his hands, warm as a summer breeze. Burned away, leaving only pale ashes behind.

Church was staring at him, watching bone ash flow free in the wind. Glanced at Myrrh, whose eyes were red with smoke and tears. And subtly, so subtly he would have missed it if he hadn't been watching, let her gaze brush the werewolf.

Young. Bleeding where the thorns had ripped him. Face lost and stunned, as if the moon had come out at midday.

Yeah. I think we can save this one.

"And that's how you do things *Old Testament* style," Aidan

grinned at the kid. "Still think the Padre's sermons are a waste of time?"

Raphael gulped.

Aidan straightened. "Okay. Let's get going, find a motel that takes cash-"

Myrrh winced, leaning on him heavily. "No. We can't hide. We must attack."

Church, darn it all to heck, was nodding. "Magical backlash. One of his major spells just went kablooey. If we're going to take him in, we need to go *now*."

"Detective." Myrrh focused on the woman, her face sad, but resolute. "We both know I'm not going to take him in."

"Yeah, I know," Church breathed. "But I'm going to try." She swallowed hard. "And if he decides he's not coming in... then that's how it's going to go." She straightened her shoulders. "We need a car." She turned a speculative look on the fourth member of their impromptu wrecking crew. "You know, the uniforms working burglaries said there was a pack down here boosting stuff."

Newspaper wrapped around him, Raphael blinked.

Steven Savonarola stumbled back from that blazing nova, tears dripping from watering eyes. Without decades of practice in shielding away unwanted magic, skirting under the magic of Hunters and demons and the blessings of the Church itself-

Stimson's hand gripped his arm, tiger-strong, the veils of illusion that were his nature rippling to deflect the last stray energies. "I believe we may have a problem, sir."

Ah. British understatement. Sometimes Stimson played his assumed role entirely too well. "What was that?"

"I have never seen anything like it." Stimson's face was blank; unnerving to any who did not know the truth under the human shell. "But the blood I am heir to recalls skyfire in Mughal India, when a bodhisattva prayed for iron from beyond the stars."

First Aariel, now Stimson. This was beginning to become tiresome. "Saint, enlightened soul - it doesn't matter," Steven bit out. "She is mortal, with all a human's weaknesses."

"Yes, sir," Stimson agreed soberly. "If the legends are true, she has all the vulnerabilities of any human magic-worker. And knows them well."

Damn. Myrrh was old. There was no way she wouldn't know about magical backlash.

They'll be coming here. Now.

Steven smiled. A few more days would have been preferable, a few more weeks to be utterly sure... but he'd planned for foes of such caliber before. They would come for him, and they would die.

"Take the secondary kit and cross the boundary into Hera township," Steven directed. That would put his servant outside Intrepid, and away from any of the hell-raider's attempts to scry. "If my brother manages to survive the first few minutes we may have a bit of smoke and water damage to clean up. And it's so finicky to reconsecrate anointing oil."

"Indeed, sir." Stimson bowed, and left.

Steven looked at the shadowed figure in the corner of his workroom, half-lit by the UPS glow, restless and waiting. "Be patient. Church will be here soon enough."

Light. Even sealed beneath the earth, Sword Aariel could feel it. For one brief moment a human soul had implored-

Lips writhed back from a lion's fangs. He'd prefer not to think about *that* any more than he had to.

The day had started out so *well*. The hell-raider was out of his lord's demesnes, which made his life simpler. Aidan was out of Yaldabaoth's grasp, which should have made his life *much* simpler. Like it or not, the cub didn't have the raw strength to force demon soldiers to obey him, and lacked the sly, bloodthirsty cunning to manipulate them into holding his power base for him. He did have the speed and stealth to be an excellent scout... but the cub was stubbornly, defiantly incorruptible.

Like his mother.

Steven had been young, and a certain lack of imagination was only to be expected. But an incorruptible brother would have been a covert sorcerer's best cover. To trade that for the mere monetary gain of an earthly heir's portion - bah.

Though Steven's overall plan had been fiendishly clever, and ruthless enough to gain Yaldabaoth's smiling approval. Drag the corporeal supernatural into the light. Make certain the Hunters were hampered by human laws, so all their time and striving went into the pursuit of the more gory, obvious supernatural crimes, and not into the subtle deaths and degradation that built a Demongate. Make the vampire covens invested in their new freedom to revel in their superiority over humankind, so they would fight to eviscerate any resistance - legally, or otherwise. All paving the way for demonic power to sweep into the vacuum of human despair. The situation had been under control-

Sword Aariel blinked. Extended his claws, very carefully, to brush near the edge of the warded circle. Most sorcerers would have had to douse the floor with blood to raise enough power to seal a demon lord within. They knew no other way; slower means to build up magic tended not to grip well on infernal power, and the Hunters of old had been vicious when it came to hunting down any that promised to work better. But ancient smith-enchanters had learned to capture Hellish lightning in a bottle, and while Hunters might wipe that knowledge from Earth, the libraries of Hell held it fast. Steven had taken Persian alchemists' work to heart, replacing pots of acid, iron and copper with golden wire tied to modern batteries....

Sparks still flew from the demon's touch. But now they were faded purple, not brilliant blue-white.

Coldly, Aariel smiled.

Watch for more ice, the weather said there shouldn't be any but there was, *Savonarola doesn't give a damn what the weather is-!* Church kept her eyes on the road, and tried not to yank the steering wheel any more than she had to. Raphael had already made enough of a mess getting the ignition going, and she had no idea how she was going to explain this to the captain. "I thought you were a fire mage!"

"I *am*." Aidan's voice was taut. "I can't believe that worked."

"And why should it not? Adam gave name to all the beasts of the field and birds of the air." Myrrh's voice wasn't loud, but it caught the detective's ear like firm fingers. "To enchant is the first, the strongest of all magics humans are heir to. Any born of humankind may touch that magic, with will and power enough." A hitch of breath. "And I am a terribly effective example."

That, Church could buy.

"Five blocks from Our Lady's." Church shuddered as she idled the stolen blue SUV to a stop on the side of the street. Before she'd always thought that was a bad joke, a lawyer living in walking distance of the priest that would boot him back out the church door, if he could. Now? "Your brother likes living dangerously."

From the back seat came words just a hair away from a growl. "Yeah. He's good at that."

Which was probably the adrenaline talking, and right now she was all for that. At least Aidan still had a growl in him. The way Myrrh was curled around herself in the passenger seat, one hand clinging to the shoulder strap in pure misery, their demon-slayer didn't have much oomph left.

But we're out of time, Church thought bleakly. She was no expert on magic, but Coral had dropped plenty of hints over the years. *He's not going to get weaker than he is right now. Every minute he gets is another minute to pull off a sacrifice. Or worse, to sic even more than PS on us. Bets he hasn't got people in the FBI? Even Homeland Security?*

Heh. She wouldn't take that bet. Not even on a dare. "Okay." She jabbed a thumb toward her back seat. "You? Out."

Raphael's jaw dropped, even more than it had when a detective had asked him to boost a vehicle for their motley crew, or calmly raided the spare tire compartment for a pair of grimy sweatpants so he had a shred of decency... and more important, stopped shivering so violently his teeth were chattering. "But - you say this man is trying to kill everyone in the city. And you helped me-"

"Clue, Raphael." Church was an adult, not a cranky macho teenage werewolf with a sore ego. She was not going to roll her eyes. "That's what cops do. For everybody. Legal or illegal."

The teen bristled; she could see the hairs rise on the back of his neck. "I have papers!"

"And if I run them, the Social's going to come back some little old lady who died in a church pew praying, right?" Church almost growled. "Werewolves *break the law*. All of them do. That's why the curse bites down so hard." She might not know the twists and turns of magic the way Myrrh did, but she'd seen how the hell-raider and Savonarola leveraged words and laws to set the world on fire.

The malursine couldn't eat me while I had my shield. Laws matter *to magic.*

Couldn't eat her, but it'd been all too happy to go after Tom. Why, damn it? Franklin was one of the good guys. Annabel was worried over nothing. So he got his wife gifts after some of the stakeouts where they came up empty; wasn't that what guys did for their wives when they had to skip out on family time?

...And she was babbling in her own head. Probably because thinking about tackling Savonarola made her want to go gibber in a corner. You could take a sorcerer if you interrupted his spell, sure. But that was only if he was still casting it. Who knew what the bastard had had time to set up on his own turf?

Church pushed fear away with a snarl, and a glare at a suddenly daunted teen. "Werewolves are cursed, and the worst part of it is, they know how to spread it. I swear some pack-leaders can *smell* lawbreakers."

"They can." Myrrh had a little more color in her face; more ghostly white, instead of sickly gray. "Some who fight the curse have even been the Hounds of God."

Okay, creepy idea there. "So drop the *buts*, and get yours to Our Lady's so you can get under cover. Tell one of the Fathers what's going on - O'Malley, Ricci, doesn't matter. They'll believe you. They'll *hide* you." Church met dark eyes in the rearview mirror, chilled colder than October could ever manage. "Kid, if we don't come back, you need to find a deep hole and pull it in after you. When Steven Savonarola's done with his tools, *nobody* else gets to play with them. You get me?"

"You think he will kill you." Disbelief slowly morphed into fear on his face. "You think this *brujo* can kill a cop."

"He's already tried a few times." Church motioned to the sidewalk. "Get going. You don't want to be here when things get set on fire."

The teenager shuddered, and scrambled out the door. Bare feet slapped the pavement as he tore off into the night.

"One down," Church muttered, wishing it made her feel any better as she heard ancient words whispering behind her. "Um. Do I want to know how you're messing with the universe now?"

Surprisingly, Myrrh reddened. "It's not magic, Detective. Just an old prayer. One I started using some time after my first Hell-raid." She glanced at Aidan. "I... haven't had to translate it into English often."

Red brows climbed, curious.

Myrrh's cheeks went redder. *"Oh Lord, I am most heartily sorry,*

"For I will owe you many days of prayer, and nights of contemplation,

"For lo, though we are enjoined to nourish good, and to root out evil with fire and sword and power,

"And while wrath against evil is a righteous fury, and a blessing to strengthen faltering hearts,

"Still I go this night, by your grace, to smite an evil that has brought grievous harm upon my friend,

"And I may enjoy applying a righteous toe to an evil fundament just a little *too much."*

Church picked her jaw off the floor, watching a fire-starter turn almost as red as his hair. "Um... that's...." Aidan tried.

Myrrh glanced away, oddly shy. "I don't have that many friends, Aidan."

"Why not?" the fire-mage burst out. "Why *me?* You're good, you're decent, you snark with the best of them, you kick evil *ass....*"

"Yes. Exactly. Ask the detective." Gray eyes sought blue. "You are a true and honest defender of the law, Church. Because of you, people can sleep safely in their beds, warded from rapists, murderers, and evildoers." She paused, gaze level and unyielding. "How many people want *you* around?"

"Touché." Church checked what was left of her ammo one more time, and let out a slow breath. "Let's do this."

Doors thumped as she got out, Aidan moving forward to grip a white-faced Myrrh by the shoulder.

The wrought-iron gate wasn't locked.

Oh. Joy. "Anybody else thinking trap?" Church asked casually.

"Why no." Myrrh's voice was shaky, but the sarcasm was clear. "Whyever would we think that?"

"Comedians." Church squared her shoulders. "Well, if it's

open, we're not breaking and entering...."

The house was dark and quiet, almost tropical heat curling through the air. Yet outside of the multitude of fish and coral saltwater tanks Myrrh kept drawing sigils on with a marker, the halls stood empty. Church cleared the way through doorway after doorway, nerves drawn to the breaking point-

Aidan put a hand on her shoulder. "Wait." Tilted his head, red hair brushing his shoulder. "That way."

That way sounded like power tools. In horror movies, this was *never* good.

Since when did my life turn into a bad horror movie?

"Why do you keep stopping?" Church kept it to a low mutter, as Aidan's hand landed on her shoulder again.

"Used to be in architecture." Amber eyes were studying yet another doorway off to the side, glaring at the lintel as if daring it to make a false move. "Something about this place is built wrong."

Oh joy. "So, what?" She glanced back at Myrrh. "We're going to have demons coming out of the walls?"

Finishing a flourish like a stylized falcon, Myrrh frowned at the corridor. "Not from the walls...."

The squealing of a power saw stopped.

Stick to the plan, Church told herself, determined not to loosen her coat no matter how hot it got in here. Her sore ribs were enough reminder why not. *We keep him at a distance. If he comes quiet, I keep him at gunpoint while Myrrh goes in there and locks the cuffs on him and Aidan looks scary at anyone else who wants to jump in. If he doesn't come quiet, Aidan and Myrrh hit anything weird. And if it's something human - bullets ruin anybody's day.*

One more breath, and Church whipped through the low doorway. "Freeze! Police!"

"Ah, detective." Half-carved block in hand, the spiral horn of a unicorn sprouting from pale applewood, Steven Savonarola waved a curved knife in her general direction. "How thoughtful of you to join us."

Us?

Big room. Big, somewhat noisy room, despite the sound baffles around the generator currently powering the switched-off circular saw on Steven's bench. Big room with too many odd, half-seen markings on the speckled terrazzo floor, and one very pale cop who should have been lying in bed strapped into a chair in easy reach of the maniac sorcerer with the knife. "Tom!"

"Partner." Tom Franklin couldn't manage even a hint of a smile. "What a night, huh?"

Savonarola looked at her, eyes a smoky, knowing gray. "Won't you come in?"

Like hell. Myrrh had been *very* blunt, in her few bursts of words between here and stealing the car, about sorcerers and hostages as two-for-one sacrifice specials. Church hadn't expected Tom - the guy was supposed to be *home*, what was the world coming to these days? - but a warm body between Savonarola and justice? Yeah. She had. And it didn't change anything. "You know everything else about me, Savonarola, then you know my scores on the range. That knife gets near him, you get dead. Put it down and come out quietly."

"Oh, but I'd much rather you came in here." Steven smiled, and touched something small on his workbench. "In fact... I *insist.*"

A remote? That's not magic. What the heck is that supposed to-?

In the hall behind them, glass shattered.

Myrrh said she was going to block spells on the water-

Above, something exploded.

...Ow.

Choking, Aidan struggled to keep above the flood of icy water. He'd managed to block the blast from making pincushions out of them, but a torrent of black liquid had roared from what had been the weird, boxy lintel of Steven's doorway-

And just when he'd thought he *might* stand up to that, a second flood of seawater had taken his feet out from under him.

Water. *Cold* water, oily in a way no honest liquid should be. Whirling him around and around, until he didn't know which way was up, until he didn't dare breathe in case he'd guessed wrong and swallowed water-

A wave crashed over him, sweeping him into a subtle black circle in the polished pebbles of the floor. Light flared as he hit stone, two concentric circles of blue-violet that writhed with uncanny runes.

...I know those runes.

Like it or not, Aariel had beaten some things about Hell into his head. The outer circle was a binding, meant to grip and hold the blood of Yaldabaoth. The inner circle was a tighter binding....

Son of Yaldabaoth.

Damn it.

Though he was a little less worried about the trapping runes than the tentacles of water trapped in *with* him. It was like trying to fight off an octopus underwater. A really, really determined octopus.

"And here, we end it at last." Steven's gaze was flicking to him and away, keeping track of the coughing detective disarmed and washed up almost at his feet and the body-surfing demon-slayer sweeping light through watery shapes of fanged unicorns and twisted tritons. "You were the heir; for Jeremiah Savonarola, and for Yaldabaoth. Now you'll be nothing."

"Oh, you gotta be kidding me," Aidan snarled, fighting his way to his feet with hands full of steam - and then fire, as the tentacled monster inside the circle squealed and evaporated. "This is all about *Dad liked you best?*"

A cruel smile creased his brother's face. Steven breathed in... and then *out*, long and low, like a wind swooping off the ocean. "Is there any better reason to kill you?"

Three pebbles flared, water pouring from them like someone had opened the Dead Sea.

I wonder if someone told Steven about Jamaica.

It was a fragment of a thought, between beating back the waters and cutting through the entities summoned within those waters. She was a child of Alexandria, of books and the Nile; the raging seas had never been friendly to her. She'd barely had the chance to breathe, *"For the word of God is quick and powerful, and sharper than any two-edged sword-"*

Then Steven's pawns had been on her.

Upward slash; wait, that had cut *wood*, from the swift curl of smoke, not just water....

Literally his pawns. Effigy magic. He was carving allies even as he waited!

Mage-craft, sorcery, and enchantment. No wonder other Hunters had missed Steven's evil. Even with decades to master magic, most magic-users worked with one form alone. Half the time spent on learning arcane ways was deepening your reserves, so you could cast without knocking yourself out.

This is too much power. Even for a half-demon. He must have another source!

There weren't that many ways to store this much infernal power. Determine which one Steven was using, and she could cut the flow. If she could just get a moment to *breathe*....

If she got out of this alive, Church swore, she was heading right to the emergency room for some antibiotics. That water was *nasty*.

"Hey," she croaked, blinking gummed eyes at the detective tied above her as she felt around in the puddles on the floor; the world might be whirling, but at least her fingers knew which way was up. Gun, gun - no gun. Damn. "What's a nice guy like you doing in a place like this?"

"Church, what are you doing?" Tom sounded like he had to get the words past thorns. "You don't have a warrant, you don't have backup; PS's going to have your badge-"

"Better tried by twelve than carried by six." Up. She had to get up. If only the room would stop spinning. "He's going to kill you, Tom."

"What? No!" It was hard to tell with all the water, but she thought Tom was sweating. "Look, he just wants you to stay out of the way. That's all he ever wanted-"

His words choked off. Church couldn't imagine the look on her own face. She'd been protected from a demon by her badge. Tom... hadn't been.

I don't care how hard the floor hit me. I'm getting up. "How long?" Church made it to hands and knees, even with water sucking at her like leeches. *Might really be. Coral said blood and water are tied... oh God, don't look.* "How long have you been working for him?"

"I don't work for him, I just...."

Aidan was caught in a three-part writhing whirlpool, water

twisting tighter every time Steven wriggled his fingers. Myrrh was beating back the waves, but she looked about as bad as Church felt.

Guess it's up to me. "Hey, Savonarola!" Church rose to her knees, one hand scything out of her coat as her thumb flipped off O'Malley's practical little cap. "Eat this!"

Glimmering like moonlight, holy water arced toward him. The sorcerer bared his teeth, both hands slashing down and across-

Midair, light froze, and crashed to the floor as ice.

Oh fudge.

Steven chuckled, and shook a scolding finger at her. "Holy or unholy, water is still water."

"Well." Church got to one knee, blinking the room mostly into focus. "Can't blame a girl for trying...."

Is that an engine?

The wall erupted in bricks and splinters, crashing away from a stolen blue SUV.

Behind the wheel, flung like a ragdoll - no seatbelt, why was she even *surprised* - Church glimpsed naked shoulders, and determined brown eyes.

Raphael, you idiot!

Water splashed away from steel and fiberglass, sluicing away from a windshield over a terrified young werewolf's face. Rumbled, and surged back as a howling tide, as Steven braced hands to put a wall of water between him and the onrushing shrapnel-

Now!

Church staggered one more step, and grabbed the power saw. Yanked the cord from it, whirled the orange cable like a lariat once, twice-

The modern world is full of wonders, Coral had said once, crunching caramel popcorn as Church tried to figure out exactly what had fried in her toaster. *To think, humans without a shred of magic can yet tame the thunderbolts of Zeus.*

-Cast it into the whirlpool, praying. "*Nobody* opens a door to Hell in my town!"

Aidan had been hit by lightning before, in Hell. It still sucked.

Don't want to be here, don't want to be-

The pressure of runes around him gave.

He followed that line of least resistance, eyes shut, pressing himself as small as possible against unyielding walls of magical force. Smaller, smaller-

Flame. Bodiless. Weightless. *Out.*

No! He'll put me out. Got to get back, get solid....

The floor hurt. A lot.

Someone was groaning, and someone was screaming. Oddly enough, he didn't think either one was him.

Flat on his back, Aidan curled himself sideways, glimpsing what was left of the circle-trap. The outer circle was dark, cut by a mud of flying brick dust and a stray piece of fiberglass fender. The inside....

Still glowing. Still active. What the hell?

He'd think about it later. The groaning was Raphael, bleeding from the forehead, staggering out of the wrecked SUV like he'd tied on three martinis. The screaming was Steven.

Lightning hurts Fire and Water, Aidan remembered. *But it hurts Water more.*

Myrrh coughed, splashing her way toward Church. "For the conies are a folk exceeding wise," she got out. "Well done." She straightened her shoulders. "You should tend to your partner."

Church moved toward the guy in the chair. Who didn't exactly look all that happy she was rescuing him. Or maybe he was looking at the way Myrrh was hefting light in the shape of a sword, ready for one final blow.

"I'm not going to look away," Church said quietly, loosening one strap at a time. "I brought you here. Any laws you break are on my head."

He's still my brother, Aidan thought bleakly. *I should... I should do* something. "Steven-"

Hair smoldering, Steven was looking at the floor. At the circle, still glowing through the water behind him. "You were never his." The sorcerer's voice started quiet; soared with disbelief. "He *favored* you, and you were never - *everything in here dies!*"

Cold. Sea-cold. Soul-cold. He could see the unnatural frost crackling away from Steven's laughter; blazing white over everything near the sorcerer, hungry fingers of ice reaching out for undefended humans. He could feel the water inside him freezing, his *eyes* freezing, everything going dark-

In the darkness, dawn glimmered.

And God said, let there be lights in the firmament of heaven... *the greatest fire in the world rises every morning....*

Dawn was between him and the ice, and it would not let death pass.

Aidan blinked, feeling ice slush through his heart as his vision cleared. *No, don't do this, I'm not worth it-!*

We are all sinners, my friend. It was a whisper in the wind; a ripple of all the white and gold of dawn. *Who are you to claim you are not worthy, in the eyes of those who love you?*

Fire punched up through terrazzo like lava, and everything was burning.

Somehow he and Church got three bodies out of there. The cop, the idiot, brave kid... and one small, still form.

She's so cold.

Dropping her coughing partner, Church looked up and paled. "Oh, holy mother of...."

"Don't." Aidan looked up at the fire striding from the flames; lion claws, a flaming sword, and familiar, fiery eyes. "Trust me. You'll just piss him off." He took a breath, trying to coax the frozen flames inside back into a glow of embers. "So what brings you up to this neck of the woods, Sword Aariel? Thought your job was to watch Lord Yaldabaoth's back."

"It is." Aariel inclined his head. "I was temporarily inconvenienced."

His brain had to still be frozen, because it took a few seconds to make sense of that. "...He had you locked up in a seal?"

"It was," Aariel said gravely, "most unwise of him."

No freaking kidding. "So what now?" Aidan flung at him, praying he felt breath against his chest. *Come on, Myrrh. You're tougher than this!* "You're in this world. Demongate ready to pop. You going to use it? Five lives to slaughter, right here."

Raphael was shaking in place, a wolf trapped by a sabertooth tiger. Church made a strangled yelp that sounded like *crazy fire demon.* Aidan was going to ignore it.

"Tempting," Aariel huffed, like a great lion eyeing a herd of prey. "Two are great sinners. A third has broken mortal laws, and was willing to break more. But one will never be in Hell's power, unless she be dragged there in chains. And one... is not mine to slay. His mother won that from me, when she saw through my lies, and realized Yaldabaoth had cheated her husband."

"...What?"

A vast, purring chuckle. "You do not think *Yaldabaoth* would give one of his heirs for another soul to cherish as firstborn son?" Furred with fire, that strong hand rested on his forehead a moment, stirring flickers of warmth within. "Silly cub."

Cub. Aidan tried to think. *Yaldabaoth's blood held me. Yaldabaoth's* son *didn't.* "But... the court says you're his *armsman....*"

"Why should I invite traitor's daggers? My brother's back attracts more than enough." Aariel took a step backward, smoke rising from his footprints. "Never doubt your mother loved you. She was unwise in husbands, and unskilled in magic. But she made herself learn, for she loved the life she held beneath her breast, and would not lose it to Hell. She loved you so much, she managed to cheat me. *Christophe.* The Christ-bearer. The wolf-blooded creature that forsook violence, and bloodshed, and became a servant of He Who Shattered The Gates."

Fire flared, and the night was empty.

"Is he... gone?"

Hell. I didn't think she was still alive, Church thought, staring at the iced-over demon-slayer in Aidan's arms. "Damn it, I'll call an ambulance-"

"For yourselves, yes." The white head bent closer to Aidan's shoulder. "Don't... waste your flames. Aariel... could still force the Demongate. If he decides he wants his son... back."

"Myrrh." Aidan's voice was a whisper. Tears dropped to hiss on ice, leaving dark spots of dead skin.

"Don't look so sad," Myrrh whispered, pale hand touching his cheek. "Hell's never held me before. I'll... be back...."

The breath sighed out of her, and flesh shimmered into light.

...Almost all light, Church realized, as at least a dozen knives and other less legal objects fell through the air. And one ancient bone landed in Aidan's grasp.

There's the skull. There's my evidence.

But that desolation on the fire-mage's face was enough.

I'm through taking tips from Halo.

Chapter Fourteen

"...Cause of the fire may be a gas line ruptured by the SUV that struck Mr. Savonarola's home, although we're told the authorities have not ruled out foul play. Between this and the fire last night at the Biltmore County courthouse, we may have a serial arsonist on our hands. Back to you, Will."

"Thanks, Christina. In our other local news at five-"

Stimson switched off the hotel TV, and sighed. This would make certain things difficult. Maintaining his current form required demonic energy and blood. The second was easy enough to obtain. The first....

Still, he would have enough time. Halloween was only two weeks away.

Chapter Fifteen

"The problem with half-demons," Father O'Malley said thoughtfully, "is that deep down, you're half angel."

Standing in the church cemetery, watching a jade-set skull glimmer in the dark before dawn, Aidan blinked. "Um... huh?" Right. Like that made sense.

"Angels are bright still, though the brightest fell. Shakespeare. Wise man." O'Malley gave him a warm, kind look, that almost broke his heart. "Part of you belongs to another realm, and always will. A simpler realm, in many ways. There is always a deep sense within you that life shouldn't *be* this hard. That all you should need to do is your appointed task; to punish sinners, and cast down those filled with pride." The priest shook his head. "It is so very hard to live in this world. To be flesh and blood, and prone to all its frailties. A part of you rails against those limits. You live, and you breathe, and when you try to rip some sinner's arm off and beat him to death with it, no one around you can see that you were just doing what you were *meant* to do. It isn't *fair.*"

"I- that's not-" Aidan protested weakly. "I wouldn't do that. It's not *right.*"

"And there's the human in you." O'Malley breathed a sigh of relief. "Mind, there were a few months back when you were growing up I wasn't sure which side would win out. You tried so hard, lad. But you still hate idiots, hmm?"

"Yeah." Aidan could feel the tips of his ears burning. "But Steven...."

"Ah, yes." O'Malley looked down. "You might say we all failed him. He was so quiet. You, lad - you were loud and noisy trouble from the first day you tripped and fell on the altar. Your mother and I went after you the moment we knew you were struggling. But he was always the polite lad. The *good* child." He shook his head. "We missed him. And we failed him. But none of us made him pick up that knife, Aidan. First and foremost, your brother failed himself."

Aidan glanced at old bone, thinking of the charred mass of timbers and ashes streets away. "Do you think he's really dead?"

"No way to be sure until the Fire Department clears it out, I fear," O'Malley admitted. "One thing we know is that your bloodline is hard to kill." He patted Aidan's shoulder. "We'll find out, lad. One way or another."

Oh, great. Probably by way of ice water sneaking up on them in the middle of the night....

A familiar low fire seemed to hove into his senses, and Aidan glanced over his shoulder. "Detective."

"Lindisfarne." Church glanced at her watch, not sparing a glance for the hapless teen in sweats and ragged sneakers behind her. "Guess the newspaper's right for once. Still a few minutes before dawn."

"You serious?" Breath misting on the wind, Raphael looked like he wanted to be anywhere else. "Nobody comes back from the dead, man!"

"Myrrh has a few advantages," O'Malley admitted, heading over to the young werewolf like a man on a mission. "But she's far from the first to leave Death hanging with an empty mousetrap. Have you read about Lazarus, young man?"

"Looks like the kid's penance starts early," Church snickered under her breath, as O'Malley steered the teenager away by his shoulder, still talking. "You really think the church can cure him? Could have used that a while back, if they can."

"How many werewolves *want* to be cured?" Aidan said bleakly.

"I don't know," Church said, almost casual. "How many have the guts to come back to fight a sorcerer trying to *literally* raise Hell?"

"Idiot," Aidan grumbled.

The cop waved a tetchy finger. "Hey, I said guts, not brains."

"Point," Aidan smirked. Glanced that way, and sighed. "Father O'Malley gave me a few details. Sounds worse than boot camp, with going cold turkey on top of it. If Raphael doesn't mean it, doesn't accept what he did with the wolf, it's not going to work." He flexed his fingers, feeling the fire in his veins. Twenty-five years, and sometimes he still wished he'd never felt flames answer his call. But they were his, as much a part of him as his heartbeat.

Demon-child. It's what I am. What I've always been. But... not *Yaldabaoth's.*

Flames like a benediction, and the honor to walk away from a fallen enemy. To walk back into Hell, because duty and justice demanded it.

Sword Aariel's son. Aidan breathed in the autumn night, savoring air and Earth. *Yeah. I can live with that.*

Coat rustling, he straightened. "Father thinks Raphael's got a chance. Not a good chance-"

"It's a chance," Church nodded. "That's what justice is supposed to be all about." Her glance flicked toward the east. "Damn. It's cold this early."

Yeah. It was. Not that he cared about the cold. All he cared about was the light, as the horizon turned pale, and then lambent gold....

Caught in that net of light, bone glowed white.

And Myrrh was there, coughing, white skin and hair clad only in shadowy fabric.

He wrapped her up in a hug, as Church stifled a yelp and Raphael started praying. "Got you."

"Told you." Myrrh patted his shoulder, gray eyes still a bit bleary. "You... didn't do anything stupid while I was gone, hmm? I admit, I spent most of the hours hiding. Hell was in quite a turmoil."

"Nothing stupid," Aidan got out. Warm; solid and warm and *alive.*

"Depends on what you mean by stupid." Church tapped her notes. "The captain wanted us all hauled in for questioning. Something about a lot of fires, and dead bodies...." The detective shrugged. "I told her if she held off a few hours, she'd have one more person to question. She bought it." Church's grin had teeth. "Something about the reporters being all over us to track down a certain person of interest who showed up in a vid online. Dusting vamps. Really impressively."

Oh no. "Online?" Aidan asked, dreading the answer.

"Oh, it's *viral* by now." The detective winked at them. "Dusted vampires, homicide investigations, reckless destruction of private property; not to mention a temporary werewolf cure. The media's going to be all over that. Sure you don't want to stay dead?"

Aidan looked at Myrrh. Who arched an eyebrow, and looked right back.

Together, they started laughing.

Author's notes:

It's an Orthodox tradition that people stand for the whole service. There have been lawsuits in the U.S. about bringing in pews to Orthodox churches. The churches have refused, and won.

Edessa was besieged and burned by the Turks in the 1140s. There are historical letters referring to the ruins as the haunt of vampires. So, a vampire hunter bringing an icon out of the ruins would be historically plausible.

"*Mar* Myrrh", in the Eastern tradition, would mean Saint Myrrh.

Some suggested reading:

The Lost History of Christianity: The Thousand-Year Golden Age of the Church in the Middle East, Africa, and Asia--and How It Died, by Philip Jenkins.

The Gnostic Gospels and *The Origin of Satan: How Christians Demonized Jews, Pagans, and Heretics*, by Elain Pagels.

The Bible: Authorized King James Version.

Verses referenced: Psalm 104.

For a thousand years in His sight are as yesterday when it has past, Like a watch in the night. Psalm 90:4.

For I listened, as the whirlwind passed over me; but God was not in the whirlwind. The Lord was in the silence. 1 Kings 19

I look unto the hills, from whence cometh my help. Psalm 121:1

Do not take the name of the Lord in vain, for in his name are done mighty works; both mighty, and perilous. Luke 1:49

Wickedness has blazed forth like fire, devouring thorn and thistle! It kindles the thickets of the wood; they turn to billowing smoke! Isaiah 9:8-10

And if one look to the land, behold darkness and distress. Isaiah 5:30

The watercourses are dried up, and fire hath consumed the pasture of the wilderness. Joel 1:20

He suffered, was crucified, and was buried. He descended into Hell; the third day he rose again from the dead. He ascended into Heaven.... Apostle's Creed.

Turn our captivity, oh Lord, as streams in a dry land. Psalm 126:4

I bring not peace, but a sword. Matthew 10:34

When I behold the heavens, the work of Your fingers, the moon and the stars that You set in place... what is man, that You have been mindful of him.... Psalm 8:3

He shall gather the lambs with his arm, and carry them in his bosom, and shall gently lead those that are with young. Isaiah 40:11

Thy way is in the sea, and thy path is in the great waters, and thy footsteps are not known. Psalm 77:19

For as you have done to the least of these, so you have done unto me. Matthew 25: 45

Solomon, locked gardens and the gate of Bath-rabbim; Song of Solomon 7:4

He is a brother to dragons, a companion to owls... Job 30:29

A voice crying in the wilderness. John 1:23

All streams flow into the sea, yet the sea does not overflow. Ecclesiastes 1:7

Let there be light. Genesis 1:3

Adino the Eznite killed eight hundred men with his sword. 2 Samuel 23:8

Oh grave, where is thy victory? 1 Corinthians 15:55

The wicked flee where no man pursues. Proverbs 28:1

Devote yourself to the cause of justice, and aid the wronged. Isaiah 1:16-17

Who made the Seven Stars and Orion? Who turns the darkness into dawn, and darkens day into night? Amos 5:8

For the word of God is quick and powerful, and sharper than any two-edged sword. Hebrews 4:12

For the conies are a folk exceeding wise. Proverbs 30